Pledge to the Wind

the Legend of Everett Ruess

by Robert Louis DeMayo

11/21/23

D1501648

© 2014 Wayward Publishing.
This edition: 2021.
Robert Louis DeMayo. All rights reserved.
ISBN 978-099118311

Cover Design and Maps:
Andrew Holman and Robert Louis DeMayo

Cover Artwork: Tom Fish

Audiobook: James Tedder

This book can be ordered on: Amazon, Ingram, Audible,
KDP and other retailers.

Available in print, audiobook, and eBook.

Robert Louis DeMayo

Table of Contents

Pledge to the Wind

Robert Louis DeMayo

For my sunrise girl,

Saydrin Scout DeMayo

A special thanks to Brian Ruess for his insights into Everett's story and for helping me understand him better. I also owe my editor, Nina Rehfeld, a heap of gratitude for her assistance in incorporating Everett's writings into his fictional speech. Thanks also to Tom Fish for the cover image, and Drew Holman for helping with the cover design. Sherri O'Neil did an excellent job explaining the Grand Canyon's geography, and Jim Tedder did some outstanding work on the audiobook, and I'd highly recommend checking it out. Thanks also to Dave Egan for proofreading the final draft.

My readers, whose feedback helped inspire me, will always have my gratitude: Lucinda Sylvester, Briana Spence, Mary Johnson, Tim Glover, Rebecca Uphold, Steve & Sally Douglas, Diane Munroe Maragos, Marilee Stemmler, Robert & Jan Soper, Heidi Benson, Bettina Peyton, Harold Hoover, Charlie Haithcock, Cheryl Wasley, Andrea Bordelon, Liz Stevens, Cindy Wilmer, Jill Mandell, Joanne Sheehan, Kurt Conlon, Gayle Pace, Craig Weimer, Bob Brill, Katherine Connors, Clifton Greyeyes, Sheryl Sonan, Steve Donovan, Debra Peth, James Triplett, Gus Scott, Anne Luchtenveld and Chris Fitzpatrick.

And lastly, I wanted to thank those near me who have helped in so many ways: My parents, Pat and Ron, my siblings, David and Kathleen, my lovely wife, Diana, and my daughters: Tavish, Saydrin and Martika.

"My face is set. I go to make my destiny. May many another youth be by me inspired to leave the snug safety of his rut, and follow fortune to other lands."

(Everett Ruess)

A note about this publication
by Brian Ruess

I grew up surrounded by items and memories of Everett Ruess. Most noticeable were the watercolors and block prints in the home, together with a few items he collected in his travels, and a stone placed by our front door on which he had painted, "What time is it? Time to live!" Almost everywhere you looked you could find something related to Everett; my father, Waldo, was Everett's big brother. I never actually knew Everett – he disappeared more than thirty years before I was born – but he was a constant if not daily presence in our lives. I always had the impression that my father spent much of his life living in the shadow of the ghost of his little brother, and that shadow followed him until his death in 2007 at the age of 98.

Everett began to re-emerge from the canyons in about 1980 when a couple of people in Utah took an interest in him, which led to the publication of the first book in thirty years, Everett Ruess, A Vagabond for Beauty. Like On Desert Trails before it, Vagabond was primarily a collection of Everett's writings. Very little extrapolation was made beyond his written word, except to explore a few theories of what may have become of him. Vagabond grew in popularity, and further collections were published, still primarily anthologies of Everett's written work.

About this time, I became the family spokesperson for matters related to Everett. For approximately thirty years, I have tried my best to be sensitive to the people who are interested in Everett while trying to honor his legacy, and, candidly, my privacy. During these thirty years, I have had countless inquiries about Everett, everything from simple "friend" requests on Facebook, to book and movie proposals, to autograph or photo requests. There have been interviews from reporters from small papers in Utah to the New York Times and the Associated Press. I have seen everything from Vagabond Ale to Arts Festivals to gallery showings to movies to bad DNA testing of Navajo bones proffered as Everett's.

I have had the opportunity to meet many types of people, some virtually and some personally. Some added value, like the granddaughter of Dorothea Lange, or the random call from a man who had proven that Everett stayed with the famed architect Charles Greene. Others were contentious, arguing points they, like I, could have no factual basis in knowing, or bragging about possessing items previously stolen from our family.

I have also seen several books, from Into the Wild, which makes only a short comparison between its protagonist and Everett, to two recent though very different books devoted to exploring Everett's life and, most prominently, his disappearance. My brother often reminds me that a good story requires conflict, and for most who speak of Everett that conflict is found in his disappearance. Which is interesting because what makes Everett different is not so much that he disappeared, but that he precociously captured in writing and art what he saw and felt around him; his life is unique, not his death. Both of these recent books arose out of the sudden peak of popularity in the Everett "mystery" when we believed and then did not that Everett's remains had been found. Again, a focus on his disappearance.

What has intrigued me about so many of these Everett fans has been that it was not so much Everett they sought but themselves. Most were interested in Everett, not for whom he was but for how they saw themselves in him. Many of the Everett projects carefully crafted Everett in the creator's own image, all the while boldly making assertions of fact based on their own experience, which had no basis in his actual life, or at least not as far as anyone could know. How else could they make Everett into themselves?

It is in that context that I received an inquiry from Robert Louis DeMayo, proposing yet another book on Everett. But something about this one was different. Rather than using Everett's writing and art as Everett's voice to create a work of self-serving ostensibly non-fiction, Robert has used his own voice to imagine Everett's in a work of fiction. Ironically, for the first time, we get a real picture of who Everett might have been, what motivated him, what he thought of himself. His disappearance drops out of view, not even ending his story. The conflict comes not in what became of Everett but in the internal struggle Everett must have felt between his burning passion for his life on the trail and the daily realities of life.

In this work of fiction, then, I saw Everett for the first time, as he might actually have been. I know there will be Everett fans who will read this book and disagree with it, point out possible errors of fact – for example, what role did Frances really play in Everett's life – and they may not be wrong, but they are missing the point. Robert has given us an Everett we can know, can touch, can relate with on Everett's terms, real or imagined. I encourage readers to accept it as that. I never knew Everett, only his ghost, and Robert has done a superb job of giving life to the specter. Through this book, Robert has given meaning to Everett's admonishment that it is time to live.

Pledge to the Wind
by Everett Ruess

Onward from vast uncharted spaces,
Forward through timeless voids,
Into all of us surges and races
The measureless might of the wind.

Strongly sweeping from open plains,
Keen and pure from mountain heights,
Freshly blowing after rains,
It welds itself into our souls.

In the steep silence of thin blue air,
High on a lonely cliff-ledge,
Where the air has a clear, clean rarity,
I give to the wind...my pledge:

"By the strength of my arm, but the sight of my eye,
By the skill of my fingers, I swear,
As long as life dwells in me, never will I
Follow any way but the sweeping way of the wind.

I will feel the wind's buoyancy until I die;
I will work with the wind's exhilaration:
I will search for its purity; and never will I
Follow any way but the sweeping way of the wind."

Here in the utter stillness,
High on a lonely cliff-ledge,
Where the air is trembling with lightning,
I have given the wind my pledge.

Prologue

Agathla Rock, Arizona
(March 1931)

*T*he wind whistles through the thickening darkness; screeching over worn rocks, slowly wearing them down with its relentless caress as it has for countless eons. To the west, the setting sun has cast the valley afire, but a dark storm is racing across the plain and will soon overtake it.

Swirling currents of air dance around a campsite at the base of a towering black butte that soars up fifteen hundred feet. They lift a tattered green canvas, shake it, then coax a blanket off the ground and quickly snatch it away. Next, they assault the small fire and threaten to carry it off: the flames, the ashes, even the battered kettle sitting on the coals.

The storm eclipses the sun, and suddenly the only light is from the wildly flickering fire.

The air feels charged, electric, like the wind, is celebrating a victory.

A young man stands and peers into the gloom curiously. He's more of a boy — sixteen — with barely a whisker on his chin. His clothes are worn and hang from his hips. He wears a floppy cowboy hat that somehow resists the fierce gusts.

He grins and climbs onto a rock behind the fire, where the blowing embers won't reach him. He takes off his hat and stuffs it into his coat.

From a pocket, he pulls a tattered journal.

He can see a glow on the shoulder of the peak where a blast of sunshine has somehow broken through. For a minute he's tempted to hike up and watch the light fade, but the violent charges of wind around his campsite excite him more.

He holds up the stub of a pencil with a worn-down tip. He produces a pocket knife, opens the blade and sharpens the pencil tip.

His hands are dirty and cracked. They're a boy's hands, but they've seen a man's toil splitting wood and hauling gear. The sun and the wind have battered his skin to a leathery brown. His wrists are crisscrossed with scratches and scrapes, the nails jagged and dirty.

He opens his journal to a fresh page and holds it down with his left hand. The parchment glows in the eerie light. His right hand shakes slightly, but it's not from the sudden chill in the air.

He pauses, hesitating only for a moment, and the pencil scratches across the paper:

"Onward from vast uncharted spaces, forward through timeless voids, into all of us surges and races the measureless might of the wind."

A huge gust tears through the camp and rips away one end of the ragged tarp. In the darkness a donkey brays. The wind crescendos into a howl...

Robert Louis DeMayo

Agathla Peak (or El Capitan), located north of Kayenta, Arizona.

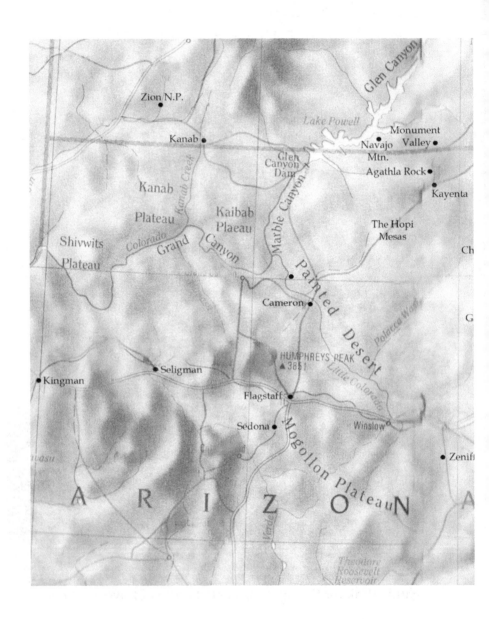

Chapter One

Flagstaff, Arizona
(February 1931)

On the outskirts of Flagstaff, a black Model A Ford pickup pulled over; the cloud of dust it produced was quickly swept away by a strong wind as the passenger door opened and a young man stepped out.

A sign on the right side of the road read: US Route 66 East.

The young man grabbed a small backpack from the seat and shouldered it, then retrieved a sack from the truck bed, swung it up onto his shoulder, and walked around to the driver's side. He enjoyed the movement after the long ride in the truck, and the crunching of gravel under his boots made him want to walk.

Aside from the pickup, there wasn't a car on the road, which was a good thing because the youth barely glanced down the highway when he stepped onto it. Instead, his attention was focused to the northeast, on the San Francisco Peaks, whose snow-covered ridges glistened over the pine tops that lined the motorway.

"Thanks for the lift!" he said and turned to the driver, extending his hand. He nodded at the line of peaks and asked, "Do you know anyone that's ever hiked that range?"

The man smiled and shook his head. His name was Gary. He was in his fifties with sons of his own about the same age as his passenger. He had picked up the boy about eight miles back where he'd seen him walking, his left hand shielding his eyes from the sun directly ahead.

The road they were driving on was in horrible condition, and during the forty-five minutes they'd ridden together, they had covered less than ten miles. And the whole ride this young man had asked him more questions about the area than anyone he'd ever met.

"Would you get wet if you slept under one of those big pines?" he'd asked when they passed one towering ponderosa. The tree soared up over one hundred feet and looked to be at least four feet wide.

"I can't imagine much water makes it down to the base," answered Gary, "although to be honest, I don't ever recall sleeping under one when it rained."

They'd next passed over a dry wash and Everett had asked, "Are there any rivers that flow through here year round?"

Gary scratched his head. "Well, from here, they flow mostly south toward Sedona and the Verde Valley, and I image they're strongest when the snowmelt is heavy, and during the summer monsoons."

He'd noticed Everett still watched him and added, "But I'm not sure if any flow year round."

The questions continued as they crawled along. They amused Gary and made the ride a little less boring. He'd spent his entire life within a hundred miles of Flagstaff, working as a tradesman, but he had never explored many of the remote canyons and peaks.

But just talking to this young man made him want to.

Now, as they both looked down the windswept road, he didn't much like the idea of abandoning him. "You sure I can't bring you into town? Flagstaff is the next exit."

"No thanks. I hope to be in Kayenta by evening."

The man shook his head. "Everett, right?"

Everett nodded.

"Well, Everett, what the heck are you headin' there for? There's nothin' there."

The young man smiled. "Nothing? In Latin, that's *Nemo*."

Gary gave him such a confused, blank look that he started laughing. "I'm sorry, my Latin is a little rusty — I think it means No Man or No One. And, of course, it's also the name of the captain of the *Nautilus*, Captain Nemo."

Robert Louis DeMayo

Gary scratched his head. "I don't quite get you. But I do know that once you hit Monument Valley, you can go through a hundred miles of nothin' before findin´ a town."

Everett's face lit up. "But it's beautiful. I don't care that it's a blank spot on the map—I've been drawn to the area since I first saw a photo of Monument Valley."

He looked across the road at a stand of ponderosa pines, marveling at the powerful limbs and the light red bark crisscrossed with black lines.

Gary asked, "You got enough to eat?"

"I've got some supplies, but I plan to stock up at Kayenta."

He smiled and swung his sack off his shoulder to set it on the ground. It contained a bag of potatoes from a guy in a potato truck who had given him a ride to Oatman two days earlier. The guy had also bought him a big lunch, and then his friend had taken Everett to Kingman.

Everett squinted at the road heading east. He held up his hand to block the sun, which was at about ten o'clock, hovering right over the pothole-ridden pavement.

"You need a hat," said Gary and grabbed a floppy old cowboy hat off the dash. "It's old, take it."

Everett accepted it by the rim and brushed some dust off.

"Thank you! I lost mine a few days ago when I got picked up by a crazy old guy and his dog, Jerry. He had his Buick Eight doing seventy-five with all the windows down, and my hat went flying."

A flicker of movement in the rearview mirror caught the driver's eye. He twisted around and eyed a tired old Chevy coming at them.

"This might be your lucky day," he said to Everett and hopped out. "That's the mail carrier, and I believe he´s headed to the reservation."

"Will he take me?"

"Well, I'm gonna ask him, hold on," he said. He began waving his arms in the air, and the vehicle approached and stopped in the middle of the road.

On the side of the Chevy were the words: US MAIL.

"Hey Andrew," Gary said, and he walked over.

"What's up, Gary?"

"I got a kid here that wants to go up to Kayenta."

Andrew was in his early forties and wore a mustache.

"What the hell for?" he asked. Kayenta was his most remote stop and one he didn't look forward to.

Gary scratched his head. "I don't know — ask him yourself."

Andrew looked over Gary's shoulder at the youth. He'd put on Gary's hat, which appeared at least one size too big, and was looking at the snow-covered peaks to the northeast.

"Hey kid!" he shouted, "You got an invite? Anybody up there know you're comin'?"

Everett turned.

He was young, still baby-faced, but there was a fearlessness in his eyes that both elder men would remember.

"Not yet," he said. "And my name is Everett, not kid."

Andrew suddenly didn't want to bring him along, despite how much he always longed for company on these lonely drives to the reservation. "You're not Injun. They don't want you up there — they barely tolerate me."

Both men laughed nervously.

"Why? I'm human, just like they are," said Everett.

Andrew shook his head. "It don't matter if you're both humans — in their eyes, it ain't your land, and they take notice who wanders around on it."

Everett adjusted his pack more comfortably, picked up his sack and looked down the road. "I intend to be respectful."

The two men stared at him, brows creased. Finally, Everett said, "If you won't take me, I'll just wait for the next car."

Everett threw the sack on his shoulder again, and was about to take his first step east when Andrew sighed and said, "Well, OK kid — I mean, uh, Everett — I just hope I don't end up reading about you in the papers."

Everett climbed into the Chevy, and it slowly crept up to speed; it was drafty inside, and the mail in the crates in the back was fluttering.

He watched the countryside pass.

After a moment he asked, "What's the earliest you ever saw a rattler?"

Andrew shrugged. "I don't recall — maybe April."

On their left, the snow on the San Francisco Peaks glittered, and Everett craned his neck to count the summits of the big mountain.

"You know anyone who's climbed them?" he asked.

"What for?" Andrew replied, and Everett stopped asking questions.

Two nights before, he had slept in a pine forest just outside Kingman, after failing to get another ride; the stars winking at him through the swaying bows, the soft needles beneath him. He had woken early, cold and restless, and begun walking east.

The few vehicles that passed him didn't even slow down, and he had been relieved when two tough-looking characters from New York picked him up with their battered Dodge. He later learned that they'd stopped in Kingman to siphon gas from other people's cars.

They were both in their twenties and flat broke — just trying to get home. The driver had asked him to contribute money for gas and he'd handed over fifty cents. Later they pulled over, and the driver begged two dimes off a stranger.

They made slow progress on the pothole-ridden road. When it got dark, it turned out that the Dodge's lights didn't work. They covered about ten miles by driving in front of another car, and Everett wondered why they didn't just follow the car with the lights.

When it turned off, they had to stop.

They tore up a few fence posts to make a fire, and after the moon rose, they got on the road again. By moonlight, they cruised through Seligman and had just passed Ash Fork when the engine coughed a few times and then died.

The two men planned to walk back to Ash Fork and steal some gas. Everett decided to leave them and was walking east five hours later when Gary picked him up.

Now he was riding through the Painted Desert in Andrew's Chevy. Everett stared at the multicolored mounds and matched colors with those he knew he had in his supplies. It seemed like he wasn't going to have enough vermillion.

The paved sections of the road were pockmarked with potholes and Everett began to prefer the dirt sections.

There was no more pavement when they turned onto Navajo land. The terrain grew desolate. The ponderosa pines had long since disappeared, now replaced with stunted piñon pines.

Andrew watched Everett from the corner of his eye, waiting for it to dawn on the young man that this was no place for casual wandering, but instead, he saw only enthusiasm.

Chapter Two

Kayenta, Arizona
(February 1931)

On the edge of a vast windswept plain sat a small Trading Post and several other adobe buildings; scattered behind them were a half dozen hogans. They looked like oversized bee hives to Everett, and he was curious about the insides of these traditional Navajo dwellings. Tumbleweeds raced across the road, pursued by angry dust devils. The rays from the setting sun were diffused by the dust and lit the area in a soft glow.

Andrew parked in front of the Trading Post. For a moment, they stared at three Navajo men on a porch in front of them: one was older and slept with his hat over his face, another was big with a long face and heavy eyebrows, and the third was Everett's age with a curious expression in his large black eyes as he watched Andrew's Chevy.

The old Navajo and the big one sat on a bench to the right of a closed door. The other stood, leaning back against the building. Everett noticed now that he had a modern haircut — short and trimmed about an inch over his brows — and he wore a short-sleeved button shirt.

A wooden rail ran the length of the porch. On the right end, one ancient horse and a couple of burros were tethered. At the far corner of the porch, a young woman sat with her back to the building. She looked right through the two men and the Chevy as if they didn't exist.

"Not much in the line of accommodations," said Andrew. "You got the Trading Post, the Missionary house or the Tuberculosis Sanatorium."

Everett shook his head. "No, I came here to see the land, not the settlements. I'll be out of here as soon as I get my gear sorted."

Andrew was silent for a moment and looked over Everett. "There sure is something about you that's different—I hope for your sake it's enough to keep you alive."

Everett grinned. "Me too."

"Good luck," said Andrew, and they shook hands.

Everett grabbed his stuff and got out of the Chevy. He was looking at a mesa a few miles away, which was silhouetted by the sun's last rays, and he started to head that way. He had just taken a few steps when one of the Navajos—the big one—shouted at him.

"Hey!"

Everett didn't respond and kept walking.

"Hey you! White man!"

This time he stopped and turned around to face the man. He seemed to be in his mid-thirties. His high forehead was covered mainly by a dull red cloth that was knotted in the back.

"Where you think you're going?" the guy asked.

Everett pointed at the mesa and the man shook his head.

"No. First, you talk to me."

Reluctantly Everett walked back to the Trading Post. When he was a few feet away, he raised his right hand and shouted, "*Ya tooo Haay!*"

The big Navajo laughed and looked at the one standing next to him with raised eyebrows. "What was that?" he asked.

Everett was mad that the man had rejected his attempt to speak Navajo—or Diné as they called themselves and their language.

He looked at the woman at the end of the porch. She appeared to be his age, and he hoped she'd help him, but she only looked away.

The older Navajo who'd been sleeping slid his hat back.

"I want to experience this land and learn about the Indian way of life," said Everett. "Why are you being mean?"

Big One spoke again to Button Shirt in Diné, and they both laughed. Then he addressed Everett. "In our language, we don't have a word for Indian."

"What do you call whites?" asked Everett.

With a sneer, the Big One said, "*Bilagáana*."

Everett looked at the door to the Trading Post, but Button Shirt shook his head. "The Trader isn't in, don't bother."

"This is John Wetherill's Trading Post, isn't it?" asked Everett. "Do you know when he'll be back?"

Big One looked toward the setting sun like he'd never heard the question. Button Shirt met Everett's eyes and shrugged.

The elder Navajo was now awake and watched Everett face the two younger men. The old man's name was Notah, and he'd seen many white men pass through these lands, but none like the young man in front of him.

Notah watched the big Navajo hassle Everett. His name was Jack, and if he stayed clear of the bottle, he could be counted on. But when he got to drinking, his judgment was destroyed by the dark wind.

Today he was sober, only restless and bored.

Jack's eyes beat down on the white kid as Everett waited for permission. The young man defiantly stood his ground, Notah noticed, showing respect even when not given any.

"Can I go now?" Everett finally asked.

Jack took out a pack of cigarettes and lit one. He took a long drag, holding the cigarette between his thumb and first finger.

He exhaled, shook his head and said, "No."

Everett stared at him. "Why not?"

"Because it is our land and we don't want you here," spat Jack. "You'll go out there and die, and then the white authorities will come here and harass us."

Once again, the two Navajos laughed, but they stopped when Notah spoke. He indicated Button Shirt to lean forward so he could whisper into his ear.

Button Shirt nodded and turned to Everett. "The elder wants to know what you have in your pack."

Jack looked away as if he had no further interest in Everett.

Everett stared into the old man's eyes.

He smiled at him and emptied the contents of his sack on the ground, then opened his pack and took out a few things.

In one pile, he placed his clothes and camping supplies. In another, his food which was meager except for the large bag of potatoes, and in a final pile, he placed his painting materials.

Notah indicated the brushes and canvas with a twitch of his lips. Again, he spoke through Button Shirt.

"He wants to see what you paint."

Everett turned up his palms. "I only have some sketches."

The old man nodded and gestured for him to show what he had. Everett handed over his sketchbook, and the elder carefully examined a few pages while Button Shirt looked over his shoulder.

Jack couldn't help stealing a glance and was surprised by the power he sensed coming from the sketches. His hand snaked into his shirt and clutched a small leather pouch that hung by a thong around his neck.

Notah pointed to a drawing of the ocean and a long coastline dotted with twisted, barren trees. He spoke to Everett in Diné as he held up the sketch.

"He wants to know if you have been to this place," translated Button Shirt.

Everett nodded. Last year he had camped overnight on a narrow cliff peninsula that extended into the Pacific, just north of Carmel, California. He had been alone, perched on a shallow crevice into which he'd wedged his sleeping bag.

Far below a foaming sea smashed against the rocks. Over the eons, it had carved out a deep cave at the base of the cliff. When the tide came in, with each wave, a swift blast of air, cold and moist, shot out of a crack in the rock next to Everett's precarious perch, as if coming straight from a bellows.

A dense fog had rolled in, making the lonely cliff feel even more remote. He could see none of the mainland but a rising moon lit distant breakers further out to sea. Below him, the waves pounded the rock with a deafening thunder.

Part of him seemed to be there still. In the image Notah held, he could still feel the power of the ocean.

With a start, he realized that the three Navajos were staring at him.

The young woman at the end of the porch had moved closer and was now only a few feet away. She too leaned forward, examining his art, but when she felt Everett's gaze, she blushed and turned away.

He nodded. "Yes, I have."

Notah kept looking at it. Then, impulsively, Everett gestured for the sketchbook, and when Notah handed it over, he tore out the drawing and gave it to the elder.

Notah smiled, peered at the image a moment longer, and then glanced at the woman. She leaned forward, and he whispered to her, then she disappeared into the Trading Post.

Everett began to repack his gear.

Soon she returned, carrying a small box and a little sack. She gave them to Everett. The box contained raisins and the sack was filled with rice.

"Spotted dog," said Notah in English. "This will keep you alive if your supplies run out."

"That doesn't sound like an Indian meal," said Everett. The elder smiled but said nothing.

Jack continued watching Everett, who was still puzzled.

Finally, he asked Notah. "May I travel on your land?"

Notah whispered to Button Shirt again. He said, "Yeah, but the elder wants you to bring him back a painting."

Everett scratched his head. "Sure. What of?"

Notah's eyes narrowed, and he said in English, "Your spirit."

Everett shouldered his pack and extended his hand to the elder whose grip was weak, but his eyes were strong and focused, and they bore into his as he whispered, "I will see you again."

Everett beamed and sensed things were going his way.

When he walked off, the elder softly called, "*Yá'át'ééh!* Practice, white man!"

25

Everett felt like he'd been welcomed. He walked toward the distant mesa and chanted the words over and over, "*Yá'át'ééh! Yá'át'ééh! Yá'át'ééh!*"

Back on the porch, Notah smiled.

Everett sat in the shadow of a large spire of rock, painting the distant buttes as they glowed in the late afternoon sun. He shivered when he moved to dab his paintbrush and paused when he realized the tip had frozen.

A coyote cried out in the distance.

He moved closer to the cold, sheer rock wall and wrapped himself in a thin blanket. I've got to get better blankets, he thought. He'd spent a few days getting to know the area, but it all seemed barren and inhospitable.

Several hours later he woke in the night and looked up at the sky, glittering powerfully above him.

The night was clear and perfectly still.

He sat up and snapped his fingers and listened to the echo cracking off the rocks behind him.

A shooting star slid across the sky.

Toward early morning it began to hail. Everett painfully stood, and with numb hands, he stuffed his possessions into his rucksack. With the hailstones came a strong wind, flowing off the plains like a tide of air, and he started to shake uncontrollably in the cold.

Behind him, the horizon glowed with the coming sun.

He stomped the life back into his numb feet, and flapped his arms around his body, moving closer to the wall to escape the hail.

The ground lay covered with hard little white pellets.

Twenty minutes later the storm had passed. The sun was higher now, and he followed its warm glow to the edge of the plateau to a point with a view of the town of Kayenta below, about four miles away.

He sat on the edge, with his feet dangling, while he listened to the birds. A raucous jay caught his attention and he turned around in the direction of its cries.

There, a cliff rose about two hundred feet; the morning sun lit up its very top. The jay had been squawking by its base, and when Everett inspected the area, he found a small puddle of water covered with a thin layer of ice.

"Thank you," he said. He used a rock to break the frozen surface.

He took out his canteen and filled it. The day before he'd melted ice, but it had taken forever to thaw down to what turned out to be hardly a handful of water—and it tasted smoky.

He stood back up and was looking at an Indian hogan about fifty feet away, perched by the edge of the mesa. When he walked toward it, he heard the jay swoop in behind him for a drink.

The hogan was made of logs and covered with red clay. He walked inside through a small doorway and looked around. His face was flushed from the constant wind and cold, and it wasn't until he'd entered the shelter that he realized how exhausted he was. He sank to his knees, and he knelt there, controlling his breathing.

The wind outside blew dirt and sand through the many cracks, but it was still warmer than standing in the open.

A square hole in the roof had been designed as a smoke vent, but there was no fire in the pit, so he unrolled his blanket and lay in a patch of warm sunlight that fell in through the hole and watched the clouds float by; they were grey-lined and appeared to be expanding away from him.

Suddenly a raven landed on the edge of the smoke vent and watched him.

"Hello there," said Everett.

The bird cocked its head to the side.

"Please deliver this message to my mother: Send Swedish bread, peanut butter, pop and grape nuts."

The raven appeared to caw agreement and dropped down into the hogan where it did a little dance. Then it hopped outside, through the entrance, and Everett got up and followed it.

When he emerged, he watched the raven hop about twenty feet to the rim of the mesa, and he slowly followed. He glanced at the massive clouds above and then at the plains stretching away to the north. This was what he'd left home for. Since he'd walked away from the Trading Post and began exploring, his thoughts had been filled with poetry and beautiful, joyous colors that were almost overwhelming at times.

The raven fluttered up onto a thick patch of cliff rose and cawed.

Everett smelled the honey and vanilla of the sweet white petals and then addressed the bird again. "Oh yes, also, please tell my brother Waldo that he should quit his job and join me."

The raven cocked his head to the side once more as they continued their conversation.

Behind the hogan, and about twenty feet above it, sat a long shelf of rock. On it, hidden behind bushes, a young Navajo was watching the two. He was Charlie — the same man Everett thought of as Button Shirt. He was twenty, and he also had never seen a white man like Everett — one that talked with ravens and looked at the world like it was magical.

Everett finally went back inside the hogan.

His rucksack was stacked against the wall, and he had unpacked some pots and pans and a little food. I don't have much, he thought, but it's all I need. I've got about enough grub for a month, and if I can grab a few items at the Trading Post, I should be set.

He lay back and began writing a letter, then tired of it and set it aside. Soon he fell asleep.

He woke when he heard singing. At first, he just lay there, listening to the rhythmic chanting, not sure if he was dreaming. I don't know these words, he thought, but I feel the music in my heart — like I've always known the song.

Finally, he sat up and then stepped outside to investigate.

He squinted. The day was awash in hot yellow sunlight that hurt his sleepy eyes, but far across the plain, more dark storms were building.

The singer, Charlie, stood on the edge of the plateau and faced the sun with his eyes closed. Without a break in his singing, the Navajo reached into his shirt and took out his medicine pouch, then he extracted a pinch of yellow powder and released it into the air.

He continued his chanting for a while. Then he stopped, opened his eyes, and noticed Everett standing near the hogan entrance.

He said, "That hogan belongs to my uncle."

"It was empty. I didn't think anyone would mind."

Charlie said, "It is very bad to stay in a hogan without asking permission."

Everett stared off. "Could you ask your uncle if it's okay?"

"He's dead."

A yellow-headed blackbird perched on a nearby tree and they watched it for a moment.

Finally, Everett broke the silence. "Is there a chief I could ask? I want to explore this area, and it would be handy to have an occasional shelter."

Charlie shook his head. "They won't grant it. You're not Indian."

"Could I at least ask?"

The Navajo laughed. "You'd do better to ask the wind."

Thunder rumbled across the valley, and the two turned to the oncoming storm. A bolt of lightning connected with a massive black, volcanic rock tower about seven miles north of them.

Charlie nodded. "That's Agathla Peak. Beyond it is Monument Valley. If you go there, no one will know where you stay."

"Isn't that also Navajo land?" asked Everett.

"There are a few Navajo out there — and you best avoid them."

"Why?"

"They live the old way. You took so much from them that you can't expect much courtesy."

"Me?" asked Everett. "I didn't take anything."

Charlie looked at him. "The white man — that is who you are to them. Stay away from them. They have nothing to share anyway."

Pledge to the Wind

Chapter Three

Wetherill Homestead, Kayenta, Arizona
(February 1931)

A lone structure of stone and adobe lay just outside Kayenta; on the porch stood a goateed man wearing a cowboy hat. His name was John Wetherill, and at sixty, he looked hardened. He also did not seem all that happy to receive company. On a rocking chair behind him sat his son, Ben. Ben was twenty-three but looked older; he wore an eye patch whose strings stretched across a sullen expression.

They watched a young man approach. He was leading a burro that was loaded with gear. A shotgun poked out between several sacks of food, and two thick blankets were strapped to its load, along with a few pans and water jugs.

"You know who that is?" asked Ben.

His father grunted dismissively.

The approaching stranger, Everett, was wearing a backpack, and when he got closer, John made out a small puppy poking out of the top.

It was looking around eagerly.

"Are you Mr. Wetherill?" Everett called over.

The man nodded. "I am."

He gestured to his son behind him with his chin.

"That's my boy, Ben."

Everett nodded at Ben and said to his father, "I was told you were the one to talk to about exploring this area."

The burro stepped forward and nipped Everett's shoulder. Its coat was black, except for a white nose and eyebrows, and the tips of its ears were missing.

"And why should I tell you about it?" asked the old man gruffly.

Everett shrugged. "Well, I did just stock up on supplies at your Trading Post."

"What's that on your wrist?" asked Ben.

Everett held up his hand to display a silver bracelet with three inlaid pieces of turquoise that glittered in the sun.

"You get that at my place?" asked Wetherill.

Everett nodded. "I did. Charlie sold it to me for eight bucks." He knew he had paid too much for it, but the bracelet had all but called out to him when he had first seen it, and he bought it regardless of the cost.

Ben turned away to cover a grin when he heard the price.

Wetherill grunted and assessed Everett's pack animal.

"That burro isn't gonna go far," he said.

Everett kicked the dirt with his boot. He'd purchased the animal from a Navajo who'd been hanging around the Trading Post. He had bartered him down from twelve dollars to six. It was difficult finding a burro this time of year because most were down at lower altitudes with the sheep for the winter; a fact he was pretty certain Mr. Wetherill knew.

At the Trading Post, he'd also purchased two thick Indian blankets, condensed milk and other canned goods, a shotgun and a box of shells, a small axe, and another pot. He'd spent just about every cent he had and couldn't think of anything else he could possibly use—with the exception of some direction.

The old man looked at the shotgun.

"What you aimin' to kill with that? The Indian wars have been over for a long time."

Everett stared north, toward Monument Valley. "I don't know... jackrabbits or prairie dogs."

"Well, anything bigger than that's pretty scarce these days."

He began to direct the boy to an area where there might be game, but Everett interrupted him.

"I didn't come here to hunt…"

He looked up at Wetherill. "Is it true you discovered the Mesa Verde ruins?"

The old man nodded. "I did, with my brothers. I was on the expedition that found Rainbow Bridge as well."

The burro pushed against Everett and he shoved it away. "You guided Theodore Roosevelt through these parts, too, didn't you?"

Slowly the old man nodded again. "Why are you so curious?"

Everett turned away from the house and looked toward the horizon.

He said, "I just want to know everything I can about this place. It suits me nearly to perfection."

Wetherill studied him.

Ben spat off the porch.

Finally, Wetherill looked away. "You look like you should still be in school, or at least with your family."

Everett stared him in the eye. "I think I know my limits."

"You might," said Wetherill, "but this land has no limits. It'll destroy the greatest dreams."

Wetherill glanced at his son's eyepatch. He had been kicked in the head by a horse when he was young. He'd never regained use of the eye, but thankfully his mind hadn't suffered. Still, he wondered what dreams that kick had shattered.

Everett nudged the dusty earth with his boot tip, squinting into the sun.

"Can you suggest any place I might go, Mr. Wetherill?" asked Everett.

The man stared hard into his eyes and said, "Home."

They continued to watch each other, neither one speaking. Finally, Everett turned to leave. The whites out here are just as unhelpful and unfriendly as the Indians, he thought.

Wetherill sighed. "Alright," he said and motioned for Everett to tie off the burro and come up onto the porch."

"I'm particularly interested in ancient Indian ruins," said Everett as he secured the lead to a post.

Wetherill shook his head. "There are some ruins in Tsegi Canyon, Canyon de Chelly, too. And Canyon del Muerto has some areas worth exploring."

"Are there intact dwellings there?" asked Everett. "Most of those I've visited have already been traipsed through."

The old man looked at him sternly and warned, "Be careful where you go, young feller. The Indians don't like anyone entering their ruins—and whatever you do, don't let them see you take anything."

Everett nodded, and the old man grabbed a piece of brown wrapping paper and began to sketch out a map with a pencil.

"Don't know why I'm doin' this."

"I'll be fine," said Everett.

Wetherill handed him the map. "We'll see if you last a month out there. The Navajo reservation is spread over a wilderness of more than twenty-five thousand square miles, and once you set out into it, you're on your own."

They shook hands and Everett unhitched his burro and began walking toward Monument Valley, whose stark rock towers loomed in the distance. On the porch, Ben leaned forward and said something to his father.

He nodded and called to Everett. "Watch out for Bad Jack—he's been drinking lately."

That's got to be the big Indian from the Trading Post, thought Everett. "Okay," he said with a final wave and trudged off, burro in tow.

John Wetherill looked after him for a while, then turned to his son.

"What do you think he hopes to accomplish out there on his own?"

Ben rubbed his patched eye and spat off the porch again.

"Hell, if I know."

In the distance, they could see Everett taking the puppy out of his pack and letting it run by his side, and then just barely heard him say, "Stay close, Curly."

They could see the burro nibbling at a red bandanna that hung out of Everett's back pocket. The boy didn't seem to take notice.

Wetherill shook his head. "I hope I didn't just send that young fella to his death."

Now that he had all his supplies and some direction, Everett would have liked to avoid Kayenta, but it was directly on his way. He just yearned for open land, not civilization.

He skirted the Trading Post, but at the edge of town, a young Navajo girl ran up to him and picked up the puppy.

He smiled at her as she squealed with delight, but then she started to walk off with the pup.

He grabbed her hand, but she yanked it away, and she twisted out of his grasp when he reached for her shoulder.

He got a hold of two strands of beads that she wore around her neck.

The necklace broke; the fine beads littered the powdery red earth. She flashed an angry look at him, but still, she wouldn't release the dog.

"Hey!" he shouted. "This is my dog. Let go!"

He pinched her fingers, and she finally released Curly and ran off crying. He was nervous now and hurried along a path that led north. Every few feet he looked over his shoulder, half expecting an angry Navajo coming after him.

A mile up the trail, he was trudging along, staring at the ground at a set of boot prints that also led north, when he almost walked into a large Navajo standing in his way.

It was Jack—Wetherill had called him Bad Jack. He smelled like alcohol and was angrily glaring at Everett, swaying unsteadily, his eyes sliding over him. He reached for the burro lead, missed it the first time, and then grasped it just as he reeled sideways and fell.

He nearly yanked the animal off its feet.

He grunted and pawed the dust, too drunk to find his balance and get up.

Pledge to the Wind

   Everett snatched back the burro´s rein and led the animal past the drunk man. He ignored Bad Jack´s slurred curses and headed toward Agathla Rock and Monument Valley beyond it.

Chapter Four

Agathla Rock, Arizona
(March 1931)

*T*wo months later Everett was camped at the base of Agathla Rock. About ten feet from his fire, he'd tied a green canvas between the branches of two junipers as a rain shelter. He yearned to go deeper into the wild but found until he was fully prepared with supplies, he still needed to return weekly to the Trading Post.

First and foremost in his mind was the mail. Each week he hiked the seven-odd miles to the Trading Post to send off letters and pick up any that had come in. He'd promised his mother he would write, but he also corresponded with his brother, Waldo, and a few other people who had helped him along the way.

But there were other reasons to go to the Trading Post. He'd had a few setbacks: his Dutch oven didn't work properly, so he'd experimented with other forms of cooking, he needed more rope to load the burro properly, and several tubes of paint had been destroyed when his supplies had slipped off the animal's back, and they had to be replaced.

He had asked his mother to send new paint, and he waited patiently for the tubes to arrive by mail from Hollywood.

Hollywood, he thought. What a strange place to call home. He loved the cinema and had a ready list of favorite actors, but at the same time, he knew it was all illusion. The process of creating those movies —

and the lifestyle of Hollywood actors—held no appeal to him. He thought of their extravagant homes and fancy cars. As broke as he was, he still didn't envy their money.

And he was broke. He had run out of money and now funded himself by doing odd jobs around Kayenta: laboring on stone walls, shoveling ditches, carrying pipes across Laguna Creek. The Wetherills seemed to tolerate him, although he knew they would have preferred a straggler who occasionally paid cash—not just one who only traded.

While moving a pile of large rocks in exchange for his dinner, he'd smashed his index finger pretty good. That night Notah's young assistant had mysteriously shown up and bandaged his hand, and then silently slipped away before he could engage her in conversation.

While he waited for it to mend, he washed dishes for the occasional meal or a place to sleep when he was in town.

He'd even sold one of his watercolors to a rare tourist—a Doctor's wife who paid five dollars for a painting of Monument Valley. The money came in handy for materials to build a set of panniers, or kyacks, as Charlie called them. Charlie was convinced they were essential.

"With kyacks, you don't have to worry about your supplies dropping off unseen," said Charlie. "Just load them evenly."

A kyack consisted of two wooden boxes that were connected by several straps. You could hang them over the burro's back, then place a saddle over them or more gear, depending on your needs.

Whenever he could he stayed in the hogan close to town, but it turned out anything he left there the Navajo would steal. So instead, people got used to seeing him shuffle back and forth with his burro fully loaded and a small puppy in tow.

Agathla Rock was a good base for treks into Monument Valley, and that's why he was camped there now. He sensed a presence in these lands; one that could see straight into his soul, and it was strongest when he camped beneath the lone sentinel.

A sudden gust of wind tore through his camp and ripped free one side of his tarp. He caught the snapping end and retied it.

The wind came at him again, now from the other side, and for some reason, he felt it wanted to communicate with him. It tousled his campsite in an almost playful way, but then it became angry and began throwing gear around and sweeping it away.

He climbed up on a rock to get a better view.

There was a red tinge to the dark night. Somewhere out there, the sun had not completely set.

He took out his journal and began to write.

Lightning flashed, and when the thunder hit, the burro bolted into the darkness. Everett scanned the campsite and couldn't see Curly either.

The burro didn't worry Everett too much. He knew he'd have to search for it in the morning, but that usually only entailed walking in a large circle around his camp until he came across the tracks, and then following them for a mile or so.

The burro´s lazy nature ensured it would never go too far.

But Curly was another matter. The young pup hadn't shown many survival skills, and Everett was unsure how long he would last by himself.

Lightning flickered above in a dark sky that was half-eclipsed by the mighty peak rising behind his camp. For a brief moment, he heard his burro calling from somewhere in the darkness, and then the sound was gone, swallowed by a gust.

The wind threw Everett´s hair about erratically. It seemed to want to lift him off the large rock he was sitting on, clutching his journal.

Everett called out for Curly, but his words were clipped away by a gust.

With difficulty, he found the page where he'd begun writing.

He could barely scribble with the swollen finger, and his letters were blocky and scarcely recognizable. The frayed bandages fluttered as he continued:

"Strongly sweeping from open plains,
Keen and pure from mountain heights,
Freshly blowing after rains…"

He looked up as one gust almost unseated him. The clouds now completely obscured the stars.

He started to write again:

"It welds itself into our souls."

Suddenly a spattering of rain came down, followed by a great burst. He leaned forward to cover his journal. A bolt of lightning hit close by, and he was blinded for a moment. In the darkness that followed all he heard was the mighty wind.

When he could see again he peered into the gloom, hoping to find his camp. His coffee pot lay on its side, half buried in sand, and a layer of red coals glowed angrily from the fire pit.

He looked at the long stretch of rock that led up to Agathla Peak. It would be tough to climb, he thought. The sky above was filled with dark, forbidding clouds and iridescent spider webs of lightning.

He carefully stuck his journal in the inner pocket of his coat, took a deep breath, and began to climb up the rock.

The following day a large raven circled the base of Agathla Rock, zeroing in on an object moving under a small mound of sand. When Everett raised his head, the bird squawked and flew away.

He slowly shook the sand off and sat up. Like peering through a dense fog, his memories of the night before were clouded. He had eventually made it to the summit, although he knew it would take a while to understand what had happened there. The image of himself clinging to the rock, shouting at the wind, hovered in the back of his mind. He'd almost died up there.

When he'd made it down to his camp the wind was still howling, and he had taken shelter under his blanket. It had blown hard for the remainder of the night, and he'd stayed down, knowing he would have no chance of finding Curly or the burro in the storm.

When he finally opened his eyes, he found Curly was sitting in the sand a few feet away, watching, waiting for him.

"Morning, boy!"

The dog leaped forward and began licking his dusty face.

Then it barked and bounded off toward a group of large boulders.

Its barks echoed off the surrounding rocks, and a moment later, the burro appeared about thirty feet away. From his mouth hung Everett's towel — or at least half of it.

"Well, we all made it through that," said Everett. He looked around and smiled, filled with excitement. He began to collect his scattered gear and suddenly felt an overwhelming love for everyone and everything. He wondered if it was from his brush with death on the peak the night before or the gorgeous morning he'd awoken to.

He looked at the dog. "Go find my pack and the food, boy, and you can ride the burro all day."

They reached the Keet Seel Ruins late at night. It had been a week since the windstorm at Agathla Rock, and Everett had replenished the missing supplies. A full moon had risen just after sunset, and in its glow, he led the burro through the quiet canyon that enclosed the forgotten cliff dwelling. He didn't think there was another living person for twenty-five miles.

Crickets sang to the night but fell silent as the man and the burro passed, only to pick up again once they'd moved on. He'd expected to jump a mule deer along the way, but the canyon was suspiciously empty.

His first glimpse of the pueblo made him understand why it had been chosen as a living spot. The wind and rain had worn a giant arch into a massive sandstone wall. It had cut deep into the cliff, and a solid layer of limestone had provided a large shelf upon which adobe houses had been constructed.

Long, black streaks of desert varnish extended like painted strips down the cliff as if pointing to the ruin. John Wetherill had guessed that over one hundred and fifty people had lived in this pueblo, and even from a distance, Everett could see there had to be at least a hundred rooms. They'd first been inhabited around 1250 A.D., but after little more than fifty years, they'd been mysteriously abandoned.

Wetherill had discovered these ruins in Tsegi Canyon along with his brothers in 1895. Everett imagined being the first to come upon a place like this while he wended his way closer.

Everett was impressed with how well the buildings were preserved. The rickety remains of ladders leaned against the walls, and some of the structures still supported second or third stories.

He skirted around the decaying roof of a kiva; the moonlight barely lit the floor twenty feet below.

"Watch it there," he said to the burro, his hand tight on the lead.

Under the powerful glow of the moon, he could see the walls were constructed from sandstone blocks and held together with a mortar made from mud.

He ducked under a low doorway to enter a dwelling. He had no idea of its original use, but it had four walls and still supported a ceiling.

The dark interior spooked him, and he moved to a door on the far wall that led to a common room without a ceiling. Here the moonlight still shone, and he led the burro to a corner, then took off his backpack and grabbed Curly from it.

Suddenly it was dead silent. Even the crickets were mute. He felt truly alone. An eerie feeling came over him, and he stepped back through the dark room to the doorway.

Every sound he made echoed throughout the ruins.

Then, somewhere deep behind him, an owl hooted.

He got a small fire going in a corner of the moonlit common room; on his way through Tsegi Canyon, he had collected some firewood.

He crouched by the fire, feeling some comfort in the crackling flames. When they had gathered strength, he took a club-sized log with one end blazing and walked the perimeter of the room to make sure there were no snakes.

The ground was covered with pottery shards, and he examined a few of them. Miniature corn cob husks also littered the area.

Next, he explored the dark room he'd first passed through. In one corner there was a pile of debris in front of several smashed pots. The mound was about eighteen inches high and seemed composed of yucca fibers, discarded pieces of wood, and lots of pieces of broken pottery.

There was also something that looked like a decayed pelt, but he couldn't imagine that animal skin would last this many years.

After digging about six inches down, he unearthed an ancient black and white bowl. It was only a few inches in diameter but in better condition than anything he'd yet found.

He searched inside and found an ornament inlaid with mother of pearl. He admired it for a moment, then placed both the bowl and the ornament in his pocket.

Excited now, he kept excavating.

And then he unearthed something white and lifted a human jaw bone with several teeth. He eyed it for a moment, then pocketed this as well.

The wind around him began to blow strongly, whistling through the cracks in the ancient dwelling. He returned to his fire, grabbed another burning log, and left the burro to explore more of the ruins.

Pledge to the Wind

44

Chapter Five

Canyon de Chelly, Arizona
(May 1931)

*T*he sandstone wall soared vertically, with barely a crack or divot, and Everett paused, leaning against it, almost one hundred and fifty feet above the canyon floor. Beads of sweat rolled off his face and stained the vermillion rock burgundy where he rested his damp shirt on it.

By wedging his fingers into a long vertical fissure, he had managed to climb, hand over hand, to the ledge he now stood on. It was only a few inches wide — not enough to sit on — but it lay directly under a cliff dwelling, and he hoped this route would provide access into the ruin.

The ruin was only twenty feet above him now. Another fifty feet beyond lay the rim of the canyon, but the muscles of his right thigh were shaking like a sewing machine, and Everett longed for a better resting spot.

He closed his eyes and relaxed his muscles, and controlled his rapid breathing. Then, after a moment, he opened them again.

The sun was beating down on him, but he could see a large cloud that would soon eclipse it. He waited. When the cloud´s shadow slid over him he re-examined the smooth rock above him, searching for a trail.

He was looking for mere notches in the rock, some barely big enough to make a finger or toehold. He knew the trail had to be there, created a thousand years ago by the people who once inhabited this high perch.

The ruin was tucked into an arch-shaped alcove in the rock where a softer layer had been worn—and excavated—away. The arch's left side had caved in, leaving a notch in the canyon rim above it. He could see three rooms extending off to his left, but the only one he had a chance of reaching was directly above him, on the right side of the recess.

Its cool shade looked inviting. He became so fixated on it that he almost missed the trail which led up and to the right.

"There you are," he said.

He inched up to it, belly flat against the rock while he extended his left arm, higher still until finally, his index finger pulled down on a slight bump in the rock. With that leverage, he raised his right foot onto a worn slit in the rock where he stuck the toe of his boot.

In this manner, he ascended the twenty feet, one move at a time, until he scrambled up onto another ledge, this one bigger. He pulled himself up, then flopped onto his back and exhaled.

After a few moments, he stood up and was about to whoop with joy when he saw his mistake. The trail he'd followed had led so far to the right that now he had to traverse back to the left to reach the dwelling. But a large section of the shelf leading to the ruin from here had broken away.

From his vantage point, he discerned that several big chunks of rock had broken free from the mesa rim above and crashed down sometime in the last thousand years. One had broken through the ruin on the far left; another had taken away the old access to the dwelling.

He walked to the edge of the shelf and stopped.

He was no more than ten feet away, but the rounded edge of the alcove blocked his way. He wondered if he could chance a running jump but decided against it, figuring he would bounce off the rock if he were going too fast.

His best bet was to inch closer, jump—and then scramble.

He stood on the end of the ledge. Eight feet to the alcove, another two feet to the door of the first ruin. He looked at the door, which was still mostly sealed with darker blocks of rock than the walls were made of. It looked like no white man had been here yet, and a crazy excitement welled up in him and drove him forward.

His heart raced at the prospect of finding a site that hadn't been looted.

He chanced a look down and immediately wished he hadn't. He knew he wouldn't survive the fall.

He willed the ruin closer and pressed against the rock and leaned over the drop. By gripping small indentations in the rock, he managed to extend a foot closer.

The wind whispered over the rocks with a scattering of dust.

He itched his nose with the back of his left hand, then leaned toward the ruin, shifting his weight until he was committed. He steadied himself, preparing to use a knob of rock by his right foot to launch himself over the void to the shoulder of the alcove.

He put no thought into how he'd get back. He knew he would find a way.

A hawk glided down the canyon and detoured by to check out what he was up to.

Everett smiled at the hawk and then jumped.

He soared over the void and landed with both arms frantically grasping to hold onto the bare, weather-worn rock. His hands searched desperately while his feet scrambled to find purchase.

He slid a little, almost dropped, and caught himself.

With one desperate kick, he flopped into the alcove, right into the door, which crumbled and fell away before him. But he was on his back inside the ruin, catching his breath.

"Yes!" he shouted, and his call echoed throughout the surrounding canyons.

Inside it was dark and he crouched while his eyes adjusted.

He couldn't see much, just dust motes floating through a shaft of light that crept in through the doorway. There was an ancient aroma in the air—one that he sensed he should recognize but didn't.

He waited for his eyes to adjust.

He missed the door on the left wall at first. It had been sealed shut with some type of mortar in the distant past. He poked at it with a finger and it crumbled away.

He could see nothing in the room beyond.

He took a breath, then began pulling away from the barrier between the rooms. His heart raced as he peered into the darkness.

Inside the second room, it was even darker. He sat in the blackness and waited. The air was heavy with a sweet scent that seemed to mask another smell — that of decay.

He felt around with his hands. A fine powder covered the ground, and when he inhaled it, he had to sneeze violently.

His fingers found a clay pot and he slid over to it. He had some difficulty prying off the lid but finally managed. He reached inside and felt dried kernels of corn.

He had read that the Hopi believed they could travel to different dimensions — to other times even. In this gloomy, silent room, he felt indeed that he'd been transported back into the past.

This ruin was most likely Anasazi, not Hopi, although many believed now the Hopi were descended from the Anasazi. A fact the Hopi stated as well.

Could one travel through time? He asked himself in the darkness.

He stood, crouching down so he wouldn't bang his head on the low ceiling, and slowly backed away.

A thin crack in the far wall informed him that there was another sealed door. He crawled closer. Through the narrow break in the mortar, he made out sunlight.

He pushed against it and the door crumbled, flooding the room with light. Now he was squinting, looking into the third room of the dwelling. The ceiling of this one had been destroyed when a large chunk of rock had fallen through it.

He looked back into the room and now saw two figures, placed seated against the far shadowed wall. He held his breath as he approached them and knelt in the gloom.

They were wrapped in dry, brittle leaves that crumbled away when he touched them. His hands rustled against what he guessed was dried yucca leaves — and then they slid over a desiccated human skull.

He didn't dig deeper.

He sat in the dark for a minute, then reached forward again.

The skin was like worn leather, thin and frayed.

Everett sat back and wiped his hands on his pants.

He thought of John Wetherill and his warning not to let others see him take anything, but he felt properly respectful.

He said, "Your ancestors picked a good spot — nobody's bothered you yet."

He stared at them for a long time and finally whispered, "I hope when I go, I can find a quiet place like this."

Everett entered the room after one backward glance at the two mummified bodies, now bathed in the bright light that fell in through the open door. The two skulls stared at him, and Everett shuddered. The dark eye sockets were penetrating even without eyes in them, and the lipless mouths appeared to be grinning.

He smiled back.

When he stood in the roofless third room, he finally had a clear view of the ceiling of the alcove. Through the break in the rock, he saw several pines on the top of the mesa, and a narrow chute that led up to them. He realized that he would be able to scramble up it to the mesa top, and with a bit of luck, he would find a trail back down to the canyon floor.

Everett's camp sat close to a small stream that flowed through the canyon. A pan of water simmered on the coals of a fire. It was May, and flowers dotted the grass under the cottonwoods by the water.

A dead rattlesnake was draped over a low branch of one of the old trees that lined the creek. Everett had stumbled on the snake the day before — at the end of his long trek from the top of the mesa back to his camp — and killed it with a rock. He hoped to make a belt from the skin; he'd lost weight since leaving home, and his pants hung loosely off his hips.

The morning had been hot, even under the dappled shade of the cottonwoods, but the trickle of water had lured him to the creek's edge, and he'd spent several hours watching water beetles and tiny minnows dart around in the water. He marveled at how sunlight passing through bubbles in the water created small stars of light on the bottom of the stream.

Then the high walls of the canyon blanketed his camp in cool shadows. He lay in the soft grass and watched fleecy clouds float by dreamily in a sky of cerulean blue.

The burrow was eating sagebrush in a nearby field.

Curly came up and put his head in Everett's lap, and he patted the dog while reviewing a letter he'd just written.

When he stroked Curly's fur, electric sparks flew off.

He leaned forward and added some gravy mix to the water.

Holding up the letter, he addressed the puppy.

"How does this sound?"

"Dear Mother, Father, and Waldo,

As for my own life, it is working out rather fortunately. These days away from the city have been the happiest of my life. It has all been a beautiful dream, sometimes tranquil, sometimes fantastic, and with enough pain to make the delights possible by contrast."

The puppy was fixated on a nearby gecko, but Everett continued.

"If you were here, you might understand, but too much is incommunicable. You cannot understand what eons and spaces are between us. I feel very different from the boy who left Hollywood two months ago. I have changed."

He looked over his camp and a quote his mother often used came to him, one that she claimed applied to all artists and wanderers.

He added it to the end of the letter.

"Never less alone than when alone."

His mother—Stella Knight Ruess—was the daughter of the noted California pioneer William Henry Knight. She taught drawing in Alhambra and took classes at the University of California. She had encouraged him to paint and write from a young age.

Over the years, she had ingrained their family motto in him.

"Glorify the Hour."

He listened to the water, observed the light reflecting off the ripples, and thought how truly glorious the setting was. He wished his mother could be with him to experience it.

On the other side of the creek, a movement caught his attention, and he looked up to see a Navajo about his age. The young man casually stared at the flowing water as if other business had drawn him there.

"*Yá'át'ééh*," said Everett. *Hello.*

The man looked up and smiled. "*Yá'át'ééh.* You speak Diné?"

Everett shook his head. "Not really, but I'm trying to learn some words. My name is Everett."

The Navajo nodded but didn't offer his name in return.

Everett pointed at his fire.

"I'm making biscuits and gravy. Would you like some?"

The young man walked over and sat down by the fire. He was short, with a barrel chest that made him seem older.

Everett searched through his belongings and took out a mix to make biscuits. He poured some into an empty pan, added water, stirred the contents, then set it aside. Next, he took a flat rock from the fire, cleaned it off, and placed it back on the coals.

The Navajo let his eyes drift over the camp. He watched the puppy for only a moment but lingered on the burro.

"Where did you come from?" he finally asked.

"Kayenta."

The Navajo was silent for a few minutes. Everett was scooping out a few spoons of the biscuit mix and placing them on the hot rock.

"That's about eighty miles away—you walked?"

Everett nodded. "All eighty miles. Wasn't so bad—we cover about twenty miles a day."

The Navajo spotted the dead snake and stood up abruptly.

"What is this?"

"Oh, I had a tangle with him yesterday when I staggered out of that long wash behind us." He chuckled at the image of himself lashing out at the snake while stumbling—and almost falling—because his legs were so shaky from the long walk down off the mesa after climbing up to the ruin.

The Navajo mumbled a short prayer. "Diné believe snakes to be supernatural beings, woven into the very earth. It is very bad to kill them."

Everett shook his head. "Not for me — I hate rattlers."

He pointed at the snake. "You don't have to worry about him — he's gutted. He's not about to bite anyone."

The Navajo looked troubled. "I wasn't afraid of being bitten. And you should still be careful. Things are not the same here as they are in your cities."

Everett shook his head. "I hate cities too."

"What don't you hate?"

Everett shrugged. "Here — I love it here."

The Navajo sat down again, throwing an uneasy glance at the dead snake. The biscuits looked ready, and Everett put one on a plate, covered it with gravy, and then handed it over.

The Navajo took a bite and said, "Someday, I would like to go to a city."

Everett frowned. "I'd sooner walk a whole day behind the burro than spend two hours on a streetcar."

The Navajo took a few bites and asked, "Why don't you like the city?"

"Because those places will wreck you! In the city, it's all about money, and work, and being respectable. I'm done with that stuff — it's depressing."

The Navajo nodded. "I've heard about the depression. The white man is very upset about not having any money. It doesn't bother us here — we never had any money to begin with."

Everett took off another biscuit and handed it over.

The Navajo grunted a thank you.

Curly smelled the food and walked over.

"Who is this?" asked the Navajo and gestured toward the dog with his chin.

"I call him Curly, and the burro is Everett."

"Like you."

Everett gave Curly half a biscuit. "I named the burro Everett to remind me of who I used to be."

"Are you going back to the city?"

Everett gestured west with his head. "No, I'm heading toward the Grand Canyon."

The Navajo glanced west as if he could see the canyon.

"Will be hot," he said.

They both looked at the burro. He was foraging some little ways away in a patch of sun that turned his black coat a deep chocolate brown.

Everett stirred the coals. "We'll see."

Pledge to the Wind

54

Chapter Six

The Hopi Desert, Arizona
(June 1931)

*E*verett led the burro through the high desert, skirting prickly pear cactus and agaves. It was now the middle of summer and the flatness shimmered and rippled with intense heat waves. They walked slowly with heads down, scanning the clumps of snakeweed and rabbit brush for rattlers.

Everett's boots and the burro's hooves scraping along in the sand were the only sounds.

"Keep moving, Everett," he said to the burro.

Then he paused, took off his hat, and scratched his head.

He looked at the burro. "Ya know, I don't think I should have named you Everett—it sounds too much like I'm talking to myself."

They were following a narrow track that veered west through powdery, dull red soil, and with each step, a puff of dust erupted.

Everett said to the burro, "I think I'll call you Pegasus instead."

The dog ambled along beside him at first but then tired and sat down. Everett placed him in the half-empty backpack he wore. All his other gear was piled on the burro, most of it riding securely in the kyacks.

It had been a month since he'd found the ancient skeletons in the ruin at Canyon de Chelly, and in the meantime, he had become competent at traveling across the open plains and deserts. A full moon had come and gone, and they'd traveled with it, moving at night when it was cooler.

Now the moon was only a sliver, and the starlight wasn't enough to allow him to navigate around the thorny ground cover.

They usually traveled about twenty miles a day, starting early, resting through the hottest part of the day, and then continuing through the cool hours around sunset when there was still light.

Above, the sky was filled with magnificent monsoonal clouds that rumbled with rolling thunder. Lightning flickered, and then a spattering of rain came down. He turned his face into it, hoping more would come, and listened to it tapping the dry land around him.

But the downpour didn't happen. Most of the rain was evaporating far above the searing desert. The blinding sun sucked all color from the landscape.

They left the cactus fields behind and entered a land of piñon pines and junipers, crisscrossed by eroded gullies.

Frail curtains of rain tormented him with their promise of moisture.

An hour later the trail rose onto some rocks and he spotted a puddle of rainwater, about two inches deep. The water was clean, and he sat by it and wetted down his face and hair.

"Come get a drink, Curly!" he shouted. "I bet it's gone in an hour."

When he looked up next, he saw a double rainbow stretching across the land. He reveled in the deep colors and the powerful arch of the bigger of the two. Slowly, the colors became more vibrant and finally faded as the rainbow dissolved.

He decided to call it a day soon. In the distance, a ridge of rocks looked like a suitable place to camp. He hoped he might find more water there.

It was early morning and the eastern sky showed the first pale promise of light. Everett crawled out from under the shelter of an overhanging rock. He looked up at the dark sky. The clouds had moved on, and without their protection, he knew it was going to be hot.

A movement caught his eye, and he saw a young mule deer standing about thirty feet away.

He slowly reached for the shotgun, carefully cocked it, and took aim.

He watched the doe through the sights as she swished her tail, unaware of his presence. He thought of his supplies which were almost gone. Maybe one cup of rice left, he thought hungrily.

The doe nibbled on some yellowed grass. Her long, graceful neck and large dark eyes struck him as the work of some great artist.

He lowered the gun.

He stowed the gun on Pegasus and began walking west. The deer lifted its head and watched them walk away.

High above several red-tailed hawks circled, and they followed his progress throughout the morning.

He worked on a poem as he walked. Playing with the words and twisting the verses—in this manner, he took his mind off the day's toil. In the heat, he often counted every footstep he took, but when he drifted off composing a letter or a poem, the miles just melted away.

He said out loud,

"I have been one who loved the wilderness..."

He breathed in deeply and looked around.

"Swaggered and softly crept among the mountain peaks..."

His mind roamed to the cool coast of California, where he'd camped the year before.

"I have listened long to the sea's brave music..."

The wind picked up and he thought of Agathla Rock.

"I have sung my songs above the shriek of desert winds..."

They trudged along. The horizon rippled with heat. He knew they needed to find shelter and rest, but in every direction, all he saw was low brush that offered little cover.

He meandered along, thinking of another line for his poem, and almost stepped on a big rattlesnake stretched out in the shade of a log he stepped over.

He jumped, screaming.

He searched for something to throw at it, yelling at Curly to stay away. He collected several rocks, his eyes on the snake. Then he took aim and killed it.

"That's four since Canyon de Chelly," he said out loud.

Everett and Pegasus passed by Walpi village in the middle of the day. Several faces peered out at him through glassless windows, but nobody spoke. These were Hopi, not Navajo, and he wanted to shout a greeting but realized he didn't know a single word in their language.

The village mainly seemed made from rock and looked like it came from prehistoric times. Yet as he stared at a fence made from modern bedstands, he felt an incongruity in the mix of the modern and ancient.

He stopped to let an old covered wagon pass and again felt like he'd traveled back in time. Pegasus shifted uneasily while eyeing the four horses and two mules that pulled it.

The driver stared through him as if he wasn't there.

He had the strangest feeling that these people knew about him digging through the ruins. Someone began to chant, and he stepped up his pace.

He passed the last home in the village, anxious to be out in the desert again, and then stopped short when a boy hailed him.

"Hey!" said the kid and held up a cup of water.

Everett suspiciously approached him. He was still spooked. He took the water, downed it, and then accepted another.

"Thank you," he said, wiping his lips.

The boy smiled, and Everett finally began to relax.

When he walked off into the heat, the boy shouted after him, "I am Martin!"

The heat had become unbearable, and he took off his hat and wiped his forehead. He scanned the horizon for a place to make camp but didn't see any. The Hopi village was now hours behind him, and he regretted not stopping there.

"We better find some shade soon," he said to Pegasus.

He searched the foreground first, carefully scanning the plateau for a suitable camp. Next, he let his eyes drift over the mid-distance, which looked just as inhospitable. To the east—far across the mesa—the Lukachukai Mountains rose in dramatic slopes of green.

His way ran parallel to shallow arroyos, and when he could, he kept to their bottom, staying out of the direct sunlight.

An hour later he paused at the narrow, slanting entrance to a canyon. The land looked desolate and he didn't want to hike down into it if there was no water. He'd seen several dark storm clouds blessing the land with delicate sheets of rain in the distance but had yet to pass under one.

Above him floated one ominous cloud. It trailed ribbons of virga rain that evaporated long before it hit the ground.

He scanned the area. Out of the shimmering heat, two Indians approached. When they got closer, he saw by their traditional dress that they were a middle-aged Hopi couple.

"Where do you go?" asked the male.

"I'm looking for water."

The man shook his head. "There is no water down there."

The woman handed him a clay jug. "Take this."

Everett thanked them and gulped down a few swallows.

He bent forward, poured some in his cupped hand, and splashed it in his face. This is the second time today someone has given me water, he thought.

When he looked up again, there was nobody there.
He turned around, but the landscape was empty.

The burro plodded along shakily, and Everett wasn't doing much better. He barely lifted each foot before sliding it forward, and his lips were chapped and cracked.

They were moving very slowly. The sun was directly overhead, but there was no shelter in sight. Cicadas cried out in the heat, begging the rains to begin finally.

Ahead, he watched as a small whirlwind picked up several tumbleweeds and tossed them in the air. Round and round, they flew in fantastic spirals, and Everett observed them, fixated, like they were living things, waltzing in the desert.

The wind took them away, still dancing, and he watched the ballet of the tumbleweeds as it spiraled off.

"Did you see that, Curly? Did you see them dancing?"

They continued, almost sleepwalking, following a dry wash. He noticed several damp sections of sand and guessed that in the last twenty-four hours, this area had been blessed with rain.

He stumbled over a loose shoelace and regained his senses. He bent down to tie his laces, and suddenly Pegasus was braying in panic. He ran to him and found the burro up to his knees in quicksand.

He seemed stuck in a clay pit where water had pooled underground and turned the sand into wet cement. The wind had obscured it by blowing sand and debris over the top. He remembered Mr. Wetherill warning him about quicksand.

"Easy boy," he said. He jumped next to the animal to grab his halter and found himself stuck as well. The burro's eyes were wide with fear.

Suddenly Everett found himself trying to get his feet unstuck while dodging the burro's kicks simultaneously. He tucked his head under the burro's stomach and, by brute force, lifted him, getting kneed in the chin at the same time.

The burro shot to his feet, bounded once, and then stumbled straight into a juniper stump and fell over in the sand. He lay there looking at Everett while he extracted his own feet.

After a few minutes Everett managed to get them both out, but he lost a shoe in the process and spent twenty minutes fruitlessly trying to retrieve it.

When they continued Pegasus had a limp.

An owl swooped low over Everett's sleeping form, and the brush of air from its nearly soundless flight woke him. He sat up and looked at a sky that was powdered with stars. The night was dead quiet—even the crickets were still—but every now and then, a strong gust arose and caressed his dry face.

Then the breeze grew, throwing his hair about.

Finally, he turned his face to the wind. "I haven't forgotten you."

He would never forget standing high on the peak of Agathla Rock. The hard black rock had felt sharp and volcanic in the darkness.

On that night the air had trembled with lightning as he moved along a lonely thin edge, feeling his way to the top. There was no trail, only vertical rock fractured by ancient cracks.

The violent winds continued, and the storm crackled above him.

The drop below was certain death. He hadn't dared look down. And the way the plains extended off in every direction added to the feeling of exposure.

There had seemed to be no end to the climb, but he continued. He glanced at the foothills around him and wondered how far the burro had wandered.

He reached higher, and a handhold broke away and he almost fell.

He took a few breaths and steadied himself.

The wind let up when he got closer to the summit. The thin blue air now had a cold, clear rarity to it and his breath was visible.

He reached up again and grabbed hold of a rock just as his foot slipped, and suddenly he was suspended over a drop, clinging precariously.

The wind swirled around him while he scrambled to grab the rock with two hands—he couldn't find footing and pawed with his feet desperately.

Finally, he had a good hold, and he swung his left foot up, caught a knob of rock, and then twisted up onto a narrow shelf.

He shouted at the wind. "Is this what you want? Do you want my life?"

He clenched his teeth and stared into the gusts. "Well, not yet! Heck no! You can wait—I'll finish my pledge when I'm ready."

The sun was beating down on Everett and Pegasus. The sand they were trudging through had a crusty layer to it, and he wished he was light as a lizard, so he could just skip across the surface.

A flash caught his eye, and he jumped to the side just as a huge rattlesnake struck.

He snapped awake instantly. He found a stick, pinned the snake with it, and then cut off its head.

He crouched on the ground and cleaned his knife. When he looked up next, he saw an Indian—a Navajo—moving toward him.

He recognized him in a heartbeat. It was Bad Jack. He was walking with his head down. He had still yet to see Everett.

When he was ten feet away, Everett stood up and held up the dead snake.

"Check out the size of this thing."

Bad Jack jumped back, terrified. The color drained from his face as he fearfully stared at Everett and the serpent.

He grabbed his medicine pouch with his right hand, desperately, and in a tight voice, he hissed, "*Yenaldlooshi!*"

He took a few steps back, then turned and fled into the desert while Everett stared after him.

Chapter Seven

Cameron, Arizona
(July 1931)

An old pickup cruised down the dusty road with two young men inside. Pat and Tad were both twenty and from the Flagstaff area. Tad was driving slowly, skirting potholes.

"Check that out," said Pat and pointed ahead where a young man was leading his burro along the right side of the road. The two were covered with dust and moved very slowly. The kid wore a floppy hat low over his eyes, he had one foot wrapped in a rag, and the other was bare; the burro limped heavily.

The pickup slowly cruised alongside the youth and his burro, but they seemed unaware until Pat spoke.

"You need some water?" he asked.

Everett misunderstood and offered him a near-empty canteen.

"I think there's still a sip."

The men laughed, and Tad pulled off the road ahead of Everett and cut the engine.

"Come sit inside with us," said Tad. "Get out of that sun for a minute."

Everett nodded, not accustomed to talking after the long desert crossing from the Hopi Mesas. He tied Pegasus to the bumper and handed Curly in through the window.

Pat slid over and asked, "So, where did you come from?"

Everett scratched his head. He felt like he was still moving through the desert. He glanced out the window, hoping he might catch a glimpse of the waltzing tumbleweeds that in his daze he'd thought were following him.

Out of the fog, he heard himself answer, "Canyon de Chelly."

His lip cracked, and he winced.

Tad exclaimed, "You walked all that way in this heat?"

Everett grunted. "Winter, summer—it's all the same. You just have to watch your water and travel mostly at night."

Pat had never been on the Hopi lands, and he'd only once driven by Canyon de Chelly. It seemed like this guy had crossed quite some distance.

"Where you heading next?" he asked.

Everett gazes out the window. "Zion—Grand Canyon first—I'm not sure. I think I need to get my supplies stocked up."

Pat said, "You can stay at my place. I can get you work felling aspens if you need money, too."

Everett stared out the window. "I suppose I could stop for a week."

Tad laughed. "At least get some shoes."

They all glanced down at his feet.

"Yikes!" exclaimed Tad. "Those things are nasty."

Everett hoarsely laughed with them.

Behind them, Pegasus bumped into the truck, and they all turned and looked at him.

Tad said, "We really should tend to your burro."

After giving him some water, they coaxed Pegasus onto the back of the pickup. When they were back in the cab, Tad put the truck in gear and began to drive. Everett rode in the middle with Curly on his lap.

"You're gonna like my place," said Pat. "It's on the west side of the San Francisco Peaks."

Tad added, "You might even decide to settle there—heck, Pat's looking for a wife."

Pat reached across Everett to give Tad a jab in the ribs, and they laughed.

Everett was suddenly glad to be around guys his own age.

But then he said, "I don't think I could ever settle down."

"But what about money?" asked Tad, "You need some kind of job."

"Oh, I've got a budget."

Everett counted off his fingers: "Rent... nothing, electricity... nothing, wood for heat and cooking... nothing, ..."

The young men began to laugh, and Everett continued, chuckling: "Magazines and newspapers... nothing, burro insurance... nothing ..."

Pat interrupted him. "Okay, we get the point. But you have to have food."

Everett nodded. "I spend ten to twenty dollars a month on food for myself and oats for the burro, but I can reduce that when I have to."

"And clothing?" asked Tad, looking at Everett's tattered wardrobe.

"Well, I do have another shirt, but it's not in much better shape."

Pat nodded at Everett's feet. "Looks like you should have allowed more for footwear."

Everett wiggled the toes on his bare foot. "You got me there."

The three cruised on in silence.

"You can't travel forever," said Pat eventually. "What'll you do when you get old?"

Everett laughed, and despite his weariness, his laughter was full of youth, happiness, and dreams. The two men would never forget how his gaze — even when peering under eyelashes thick with dust — was still enthusiastic.

He threw his head back and smiled. "Old? What's that? As long as I can move, I'll seek out the open spaces — and as long as there are new lands for me to explore, I'll always be young."

The main building of the Deerwater Ranch had been constructed in the cool shade of some tall aspens, and it had a majestic view of the San

Francisco Peaks in the distance. Everett was trimming the limbs off a big aspen that he'd chopped down, about fifty feet from the cabin.

Pat approached him with a pair of worn boots.

"Here, I thought these might fit you."

Everett set the axe down. He'd soaked his feet the night before, and although they were covered with cuts and popped blisters, they now looked much better.

He pulled the boots onto his naked, blistered feet, and Pat winced. They fit.

"I think we need to get you some socks," said Pat.

Everett stared at the boots and rubbed his chin. "Would you trade the work I've done this morning for the boots?"

Pat shook his head. "Nope, they're a gift."

They lay back in the high grass and listened to the aspen leaves shivering in the wind high above. Down below the breeze whispered over the tall grass, carrying a heavy scent of pines with it.

Everett closed his eyes and sensed a coolness when a cloud slowly drifted in front of the sun. Moments later, the world behind his eyelids became brighter and brighter as the sun returned.

Everett looked at Pat. "I'm not used to having friends. My life of late has been all about exploring the wilderness."

Pat slapped a hand on his shoulder. "Well, you've got one here."

He then nodded at the felled tree and said, "Why don't I help you finish limbing this tree, and you can help me get some grub going?"

"You got a deal!"

Chapter Eight

Sheep Camp north of Flagstaff, Arizona
(August 1931)

*E*verett was splitting two-foot logs with a mallet and wedge. They were about a foot wide, and when he swung hard enough, he cut right through to the chopping block and didn't need the wedge. After several days he didn't use the wedge much.

Behind him, an old Ford pickup with wooden sideboards was just about overflowing with split wood. He placed another log on the block, lined up his shot, and then brought the ax down hard. Two halves flew off the block, away from each other.

Tied to the truck bumper, just out of range of the flying wood, was Pegasus. The burro sniffed a piece of wood by his feet and then looked up at a large pen, about twenty feet away, from which bleating erupted. Everett could see that a group of men — most of them Navajos — were separating sheep, isolating the ewes from their mothers.

Farther back was another corral where a dozen burros ambled about. Several of them had stuck out their heads under the top pole and were eying Pegasus.

An older Navajo observed the men working; he was Frank, the camp foreman.

"Give 'em some water!" he shouted to one of the young men.

He turned and watched Everett split a few more logs. He noticed the burro behind the young man stood awkwardly, favoring his front right leg.

Everett's pile of wood was down to only a few logs. One of them had a large gnarled end, and when Everett placed it on the block, Frank stepped forward.

"You don't want to do that," he said.

He watched Frank tap the metal wedge into place with the flat end of the mall, then step back and hammer it in until the log fell away in two pieces. It took about four strikes with the mall, and although they weren't hard swings, the older man cradled his left wrist after.

Everett collected the split wood and threw it into the truck bed.

Frank set the tool down and flexed his wrist.

He caught Everett watching him and said, "I smashed it a few years back."

Everett nodded and showed him the faint scab on his finger. "I banged mine good in Kayenta."

Frank nodded, then looked over the pile. "Nice job."

He walked to the cab of the truck and grabbed a jug of water.

The Navajo drank deeply and then handed it to Everett.

He swallowed greedily and then poured some water into a wooden bowl by the burro's feet.

"You need more work?" asked Frank.

"Nope, as soon as I get my supplies, I'll be moving on."

Frank looked over Pegasus; there were several wounds on his side and a gouge on his neck from when he'd charged into the stump after falling into the quicksand pit.

"That burro won't make it into the canyon and back out."

Everett gestured with his chin in the direction of the corralled burros. "Could I trade my work for one of them?"

Frank creased his brow. "On top of the supplies you've requested? What else can you trade?"

"I've got some paintings."

Frank watched the men in the corral; one bent over with a handful of wood to start a fire, and another carried several iron brands.

Everett thought about what he could do without. He asked, "How about a shotgun?"

The Navajo looked him in the eye. "Is it a good gun?"

Everett stared down at his boots. "Sure — well, I guess so — I haven't fired it yet. I'm just having a hard time killing animals."

"Let me see it," said Frank. Everett walked over to the other side of the truck, where his gear sat neatly stacked in the shade. On the top of the pile, Curly slept peacefully on a blanket.

He handed the gun over to Frank, who nodded.

"I can work with this."

The next morning, Frank and several other workers stood around Everett as he prepared to depart. Frank held the lead of his new burro.

One of the men handed Everett a pack saddle.

He said, "We took three broken saddles and combined them to make one good one. Your kyacks will ride better under it."

Frank gave him the lead, and the men helped him put on the new pack saddle and strap down some of his gear. The day before, Frank had shown him how to tie a double diamond hitch instead of the squaw hitch he'd been using, and now his supplies would ride more securely.

Frank stroked the warm velvet neck of the burro.

He said, "This burro is older than the one you had, but he has four sound legs and a strong back."

"And he's better looking," added one of the Indians.

They laughed.

Everett walked around the burro, looking into his eyes when he rounded the head, then said, "I think I'll name him Pericles."

The men simply nodded.

He grinned and shook hands. Then, with Curly poking his head out of the backpack, he followed a trail north.

"Let your worries be as few as mine," he said with a smile.

About ten minutes out of camp, he stopped to watch a herd of antelope graze. They gaped at Pericles but didn't move until Curly let out a bark. Then they scampered off.

Everett stood on the south rim of the Grand Canyon talking to a ranger. Ten miles away, far across the Canyon, was the north rim. It seemed a small distance compared to the three hundred miles he'd walked since leaving Chinle, but he knew he'd have to descend over four thousand feet and hike almost twenty-five miles before he would get to the other side.

"So, what exactly are your plans?" asked the ranger.

"Just trying to get a feel for the land."

The ranger gestured at Pegasus. "No, I mean with him. I wouldn't recommend venturing into the Canyon by yourself. I'd think you would need more supplies."

Everett dug into his pocket and produced four pennies. At the sheep camp, he'd spent all but his last dollar on jerky and more rope, but the socks Pat had given him had just about worn through, so in the end, he handed over the dollar to buy new socks and a pair of shoelaces.

"I've only got four cents on me," he said. "But at this point, if I don't have it, I don't need it."

The ranger, Bill, was in his late fifties and looked disapprovingly at the burro tied to a tree with Everett's equipment loaded high on his back.

He scratched his head. "I'd recommend following the park burros down into the hole."

Everett shrugged. "I prefer to go it alone."

Pericles attempted to scratch his chin with his back hoof and got it caught on the lead rope.

He hopped around on three legs and looked pleadingly at the men.

Bill said, "It wouldn't be safe for the two of you alone down there."

Everett met his eyes, but his mind returned to the barren wastes he'd just traversed. One day he had spent an entire day stumbling through a boulder-strewn canyon, only to find the way out dead-ended. Then the next day he was forced to retrace his steps out, and not once in the ordeal had he come upon water.

"What route would you recommend to someone heading for the north rim?" he asked.

"Well," began the ranger, "The Bright Angel Trail would be the safest—it offers the most shade and water."

Everett nodded. This was the third person that had told him this.

He said, "I heard that Indian Gardens campsite is only five miles away, and there's plenty of water there—probably enough to let a tired burro rest for a few days."

Bill furrowed his brows and said, "It does, but the first four miles of that trail are nothin' but switchbacks, and from there, you're only halfway to the Colorado River. After that, you still have to pass through another series of switchbacks next to a drainage, and this time of year, it will be brutally hot."

Everett chanced a small smile, wanting to win over the ranger.

He asked, "But aren't there cottonwoods along the way you could rest under during the hot part of the day?"

Bill watched Everett, certain the young man would enter the canyon with his burro, regardless. "I suppose there are for some of the ways."

On an impulse, he reached into his pocket and pulled out a small compass.

He handed it to Everett and said, "This won't help you too much down there, but I'd feel better if you had it."

"Why won't it help me?" asked Everett.

"If you get lost, chances are you'll get cliffed out and get stuck on a ledge where you can't go down or up. Now, if you're stuck, it don't matter if you know north or not—just stick to the trails."

"Is that the real challenge?" asked Everett. "Losing the trail?"

"Heck no," said Bill as he examined the burro and gear another time. "It's the heat. Stay out of the sun, and drink and carry as much water as you can."

In the wee hours past midnight, all was quiet on the canyon rim. The tourists had all left, and there was not a soul in sight.

Everett led his mule to the trailhead and began the descent.

There was no moon, but the stars burned overhead and lit the trail.

"Adios, Ranger Bill," he said and swayed through the switchbacks, the gloom hiding the drop, and Pericles barely aware of how exposed he was as they slowly descended.

He rested the burro for a few days at the Indian Gardens campsite, lying idly in the shade of an ancient cottonwood and every so often writing a few letters. The heat made even Curly sluggish, and he spent the afternoons curled in a ball against Everett's leg.

Finally, he set out early for the Bright Angel campsite by the Colorado River, the sky still dark and the air cool. But when the sun broke over the canyon rim, the heat rose quickly and was soon relentless.

It was less than five miles down to the campsite, and he thought he set out early enough, but when he crossed a barren section of sand the heat radiated up at him.

For the entire morning, Curly had been sleeping in the backpack and never once poked his head out.

Everett trudged through the sand doggedly, nearly stifled by the heat beating down from above and searing up from below. The tug of the burro's lead pulled him through. He remembered Ranger Bill warning him about the heat, pulled his hat down, and leaned forward, determined to muscle his way through.

Suddenly, he heard rattling and realized he was about to step on a big rattlesnake. He went after it with a rock.

"Whoa!" he shouted.

The snake was a feisty one—and pink!

Pericles bucked off when the battle began, and the kyacks slid to one side and forced him to stop about ten feet away.

The pink rattler put up quite a fight. Squinting in the heat, Everett was almost bitten twice before he killed it.

The sweat poured off Everett, and the exertion and adrenaline left him winded. He adjusted the burro's load and then staggered on. He somehow lost the trail in his delirium and couldn't find the bridge across the Colorado when he finally got there.

The river roared past fiercely, as if challenging him. He searched unsuccessfully for a suitable place to cross. Pericles didn't like the water, and Everett would have just swum across if it hadn't been for him.

"Cut it out!" he yelled at the burro, who had set his four legs firmly in the sand and refused to budge. He'd been told the river was low before the summer rains began, but it was still formidable.

He yelled at the burro and forced him forward with a shoulder into his rump, stoking his own courage at the same time. He didn't want Curly to be washed away, so he tied shut the backpack and cinched it up higher on his shoulders.

The cold water made his heart race and took his breath away. Pericles showed the whites in his eyes, terrified. Soon the current swept them off their feet and he struggled to stay afloat on the burro's side, stabilizing the kyacks while swimming frantically to the other side.

He could feel Curly scrambling inside the backpack and feared he would drown if he didn't get out of the water soon.

The water swept them about a mile downstream, and they were lucky and made it to the other side before hitting a major rapid.

Curly emerged soaking wet, looking half his size. Luckily, Everett's painting supplies were on the top of the load, bundled in canvas, and nothing got ruined. He decided to stop for a few days by the river, to rest and dry his gear.

In the afternoon he lay in the shade, watching blue and yellow damselflies dancing over the water's surface. Once a shadow passed by, and when he looked up, a yellow-headed heron flew by gracefully.

He failed to catch anything in the river and ate only rice and raisins for the next two days.

After one brilliant red sunset, he started up the long trail that led to the northern rim of the Grand Canyon. He followed it for fourteen miles, through a narrow canyon and a long valley, and finally up the steep passage that led up to 8000 feet above sea level.

They walked in the dead of night and ascended slowly, traveling at first by moonlight, and later starlight, alone with only the echo of their footsteps under the blue night sky.

The rocks were still warm to the touch, and they cracked as they breathed back the July heat which they had soaked up during the day into the night. The burro had cautiously picked his way over the barely discernible trail while Curly bounced along behind them.

Higher up, a cool wind rushed down into the canyon, singing through the piñon pines. Their scent made him giddy, and the whisper of the wind passing through the pine needles rang like poetry in his mind.

Chapter Nine

Zion Canyon, Utah
(September 1931)

*E*verett stood before Zion Canyon's great White Throne and felt small and powerless. The monolith rose majestically from the floor of Zion Canyon, and the white sandstone reflected the late afternoon light like a halo.

It had been named in 1916 by a Methodist Minister, but Everett thought the Mormons who came across it in the 1800s, before it was named, must surely have felt the presence of God when staring at it.

Near the top, the rains of the summer's storm season had carved vertical grooves into the stone that looked like scars, as if a giant had clawed at it, struggling in vain to reach the top.

He took out a sketch pad and began to draw.

Pericles stood tied to a small tree with just enough lead to get a drink from the Virgin River's north fork, which slowly trickled by.

Curly snapped at a leaf flowing past.

The burro had been terrified of the long tunnel on the Zion-Mount Carmel Highway. He'd dragged his feet and bellowed with fear, and had to be prodded or dragged the entire mile-long passage. When they made camp, he planned on treating him to some of his rice pudding.

The light faded on the White Throne from bright white to yellow, and then pink. He repacked his sketch pad, untied Pericles, and followed the river upstream until he reached a large, natural amphitheater called the Temple of Sinawava.

Sinawava was the Coyote spirit of the Paiute Indians, and Everett thought he'd get along well with him. Coyotes tended to be thieves, so he had to watch his things when they were around, but they were also good company and only seemed to complain when they were lonely.

The amphitheater had vertical walls that rose two thousand feet; they were stained with long dark streaks of desert varnish in a few sections. Old cottonwoods growing abundantly in the open area were dwarfed by the towering sandstone walls.

Everett slowly spun in a circle, taking it all in.

At the far end of the Temple, there was a break in the high precipices. Here the river flowed out, seemingly coming right out of the stone, and high cliffs continued back on either side of it. The walls pressed together, and Everett and Pericles could only proceed by walking through the knee-deep water of the river.

These were the Narrows, the deepest section of Zion Canyon, that extended so far into the heart of the mesa that the lofty canyon walls almost touched.

The river widened, and Everett prepared to wade across it. He put Curly in his backpack; the dog wiggled around in a circle until he settled down.

He was about to enter the water when he noticed a ranger coming at him. "I wouldn't go in there this late in the day," he said.

Everett shrugged. "I was only scoping it out."

The ranger nodded. He walked around Pericles, examining how he was loaded.

"Nice kyacks," he said and brushed over the boxes.

Everett was looking beyond the ranger into the darkness of the Narrows. It had a pull on him, and he barely heard the ranger's next question.

"Looks like you've got just about everything," he said.

"Huh?" Everett replied. He tore his gaze from the Narrows and let it fall on the ranger's name tag: Don.

Don looked about fifty. He fought the urge to have a cigarette; he was quitting, limiting himself to one a day.

"You been doing this for a while?" he asked.

Everett nodded. "About eight months."

The ranger smiled and extended his hand.

"My name's Don," he said.

"Everett."

"You alone?"

Again, Everett nodded.

Don walked around the burro once more.

"Someone teach you how to do this? Your grandfather?"

Everett chuckled. "Nope, I'm just winging it."

He gathered that the ranger wasn't set on hassling and added, "Desert rats have taught me a few secrets, but I've gleaned some on my own as well. When I'm in a tight spot, something always turns up."

"We get some bad weather in these parts," Don said. "You ready for it?"

Everett smiled, "When it rains, I get wet. When the sun shines, I dry off."

Don frowned and swatted at a mosquito.

He said, "I'm not talking about discomfort—I'm asking about dangerous situations. Heck, I'm not supposed to let anyone go up the Narrows this time a year, let alone with a burro.

Everett watched him, waiting wearily to be told what he couldn't do.

Don reached for his pack of cigarettes in his shirt pocket, then stopped himself. He said, "The rains aren't quite over, so it could be dangerous—you gotta watch for flash floods and hypothermia."

He nodded at the burro. "You might scramble out of a flash flood, but your burro and all your gear wouldn't."

They stood in silence for a moment, then Don asked, "Where did you come from?"

"From the south rim of the Grand Canyon."

"Must have been hot," said Don.

"We traveled half the day and retired during the warm hours." He felt the journey in his legs as he retold it and side-stepped to a smooth, water-worn log to sit on it.

"The first few days away from the north rim were in the Kaibab Forest, among aspens, firs, and pines, with squirrels and white-tailed deer. I didn't take the main road but followed a trail that hadn't been used for so long that it was almost obscured."

Don nodded. "I know that area. You must have passed through Kanab."

"Yeah, I bought some supplies there. After that, I was in the real deserts again, camping in sandy hollows with the crescent moon low in the sky."

Don sat down beside him, and they watched the river flow by. It was getting dark, the shadows thickening.

Everett still wanted to disappear into the Narrows, although he had no particular reason to camp there. He'd expected the warning, the threat of flash floods very real, but he thought: I can do this!

"Where do you usually camp?" asked Don.

Everett said, "I make camp in all manner of places. I've slept under cedars, aspens, oaks, cottonwoods, piñons and ponderosas, poplars, maples and under the sky, clouded or starry."

Don laughed. "I get the point, but there's not much fodder in Zion Canyon — and there's barely anything in the Narrows — just water and rock. Your burro is going to have a hard time."

He shook his head. "He eats grass and bushes for the most part. I can find food for him anywhere. That's why I use burros — they can keep fit when a horse wouldn't."

The ranger scratched his head.

"Listen, about a half-mile below Zion Canyon, there's a nice spot by the Mukuntuweap River. It's beside a field of alfalfa, too. You could camp there and make day trips into the Narrows. They go back fifteen or maybe even twenty miles, so you don't want to rush into it."

Everett smiled and nodded. He liked Don, and his suggestion seemed practical.

"You're gonna have alfalfa for dinner tonight," he said, rubbing the fur between Pericles' ears.

Everett camped under several maple trees in an idyllic setting; the walls of Zion Canyon rose to the north, and the setting sun painted them in soft pastels. He had a coffee pot and a pan of rice simmering on the coals of a fire, and Curly was snuggled against his leg while he worked on a letter.

About twenty feet away, Pericles was happily munching on alfalfa.

"Don't get spoiled on that stuff!" Everett called to the burro.

He dished himself out some rice and added a handful of raisins to it. "Spotted dog for dinner tonight, Perry."

When Everett looked up again, he noticed that the burro had gotten his lead tangled in a thicket of bushes. He fought to free him, but the rope was looped around the very branches the burro stood on.

When he finally got him free, he looked up and, to his horror, discovered he was standing neck-deep in poison ivy.

"Oh, heck!"

Two days later Everett's face was so swollen he could barely open his eyes. He suffered stoically, waiting for the swelling to subside, but it seemed only to get worse.

Insects swarmed around him, and he waved at them lazily, unsuccessful in driving them away.

He took out his journal and wrote:

> *"A cloud has passed athwart the sun, my camp*
> *is in shadow. My face is on fire."*

He lay back and squinted at the shreds of juniper bark on a nearby tree as they dangled in the breeze.

Everett lay on the ground. His eyes had been swollen shut for a few days now, and he writhed and twisted in the heat. His arms and back were also inflamed, and the poison oozed from open sores. Before he'd lost his sight completely, he had heated water and made a large pot of rice, and now he crawled to it, felt his way to the pot, and grabbed a handful.

Flies buzzed around the food, which he'd forgotten to cover.

The stream was only a few feet away from his camp, and he crawled to it and soaked his face in the cool water.

He drank and then flopped on his side and fell asleep.

He heard gravel crunching and turned his head in the direction of the footsteps. "Who's there?" he said in a shaky voice. His words were barely discernible; he had trouble parting his swollen lips.

"It's me, Ranger Don. It looks like you're in rough shape. You need help."

"I just need an antitoxin. I get attacks like this every year—it'll clear up in time. I'll be fine."

Don leaned closer, inspecting Everett's swollen, crusted face.

"No, you won't. I'm taking you to the hospital."

Everett felt around his legs and found a rock by his side. He raised his arm and looked in the direction of Don's voice. "I'm not leaving."

Don took a step back. "Okay, okay, settle down. I'm just here to help."

Everett shook his head slightly. "Listen, my parents are worried enough—if they hear about me in this condition, they'll make me come home."

Don crouched beside him and said, "Well, you're only seventeen—they can do that."

"Not if I can help it. Can't you just bring some tomatoes? I've heard they'll cure it—or gasoline?"

Everett forced himself to sit up. He no longer held the rock.

"You want to help me? Just get me something that will take down the swelling. If I die, it's on me."

Don raised his brows, shook his head. "I'm not gonna let you die—I'll be back tomorrow to check on you."

Everett listened to him depart.

A hundred feet away, Don leaned against a tree and smoked a cigarette. He watched Everett lay back down, wondering if he should call the authorities or the boy's parents. He thought, what kind of kid would rather douse his body with gasoline rather than go to a hospital?

Everett's mind drifted back to that night on Agathla Peak, when the wind had seemed alive. He had been standing solidly on a chunk of rock that loomed over Monument Valley. The wind howling all around.

His chest heaved. He focused his mind and shook his exhaustion. He stared defiantly into the night and shouted.

"By the strength of my arm, by the sight of my eye, by the skill of my fingers, I swear, as long as life dwells in me, never will I follow any way but the sweeping way of the wind!"

Lightning struck, and thunder crashed loudly, close, but he didn't flinch. He yelled even louder,

"I will feel the wind's buoyancy until I die! I will work with the wind's exhilaration! I will search for its purity – and never will I follow any way but the sweeping way of the wind."

Ranger Don was standing over an unconscious Everett with a deeply worried expression. Swarms of ants and flies were crawling on the boy; his breathing was shallow. Carefully, Don picked him up and carried him along the trail to the Ranger Station.

"Don't you worry," he mumbled, "we'll keep this between us."

Ten days later Everett stood by his camp near the river. It was late September, and the first hint of fall floated on the wind. His face was better but still puffy. The time in the hospital had been a nightmare; the friendly nurses couldn't make up for the sterile environment, which was about as far from the wild as he could imagine.

Don had assured him nobody would contact his parents, but he had still worried that they would find out.

Now he was returning to the outdoors. Pericles was foraging in the alfalfa where he'd left him, a light breeze shook the maples, and the stream gurgled peacefully.

Don stood by his side. "I told you he was fine."

They watched two squirrels scurry around, chasing each other.

"Thanks for not telling my parents. They would have worried."

Don smiled.

He asked, "Where you gonna go now?"

Everett smiled. "Everywhere—I'm gonna see it all."

It was late in the day, and Zion Canyon was silent. The burro's clopping steps echoed off the walls of the Temple of Sinawava as Everett led him towards the Narrows. Ghostly cottonwoods reached skyward, their branches already bare of leaves. The Great White Throne loomed behind them, lit up by a bloated white moon that had risen late in the evening.

"It's moon time," Everett said to Pericles. "And that's a good time to be exploring."

Soon they crossed the Virgin River. The sheer walls of the Narrows rose thousands of feet. The moon was high in the sky, and the curve of the narrowing canyon determined whether they walked in a blue shade or a magical, moonlit glow.

The trail ran alongside the river as they plodded along peacefully, up into the Narrows, toward the source of the canyon. Wading through cold, knee-deep water, Everett grinned at the numbing shock of it. The luminescent world before their eyes lured them deeper into the canyon.

Soon the walls crept in closer, the shadows deepened. Seventy feet between the cliffs… then fifty… and soon, the canyon was a mere thirty feet wide. The sandstone cliffs were rising far above, vertically, their very tips awash in moonlight.

Here and there, a glimmer of moonlight made the water sparkle silver. They continued through the mystical shadows, moving upstream through the ever shallower water. In a bend, the moon was suddenly above them, and Everett felt instead it was the great White Throne, leaning forward to watch them depart.

82

They'd covered about four miles when he began looking for a place to camp.

They paused in a moonlit opening. Ahead the walls got even closer. The canyon floor was a shallow rivulet, ankle-deep. It was flowing toward them, slowly, in glowing ripples that echoed musically off the sandstone walls.

Everett smiled at the serenity of this world. A deep love for the natural world — the entire world — overcame him.

"I love you!" he yelled, overjoyed, and a gust of wind swirled down from above and caressed his face.

He raised his arms in the air and moaned with happiness.

A flurry of wind swirled around him, circled him, growing stronger. He let go of the burro's lead, and Pericles nervously sidestepped and backed away from him.

Everett laughed, and he whirled with the rising wind, spinning and twisting and intertwining with the mystical breeze.

He became a dancing tumbleweed.

He closed his eyes and felt the wind lift him, his body slowly spinning, afloat over the frigid water.

He reveled in the wind's embrace, for in it, he felt loved.

Then he opened his eyes. In the silver glow, he glimpsed a form coming at him. He felt no fear, only a great curiosity.

The form came closer, and he gasped when he recognized - himself.

He looked older and worn out, but it was clearly him. The other smiled back and reached out, through the glow, to touch his hand.

When their fingers connected, Everett suddenly found himself standing in cold, ankle-deep water. The moon was gone behind the canyon cliffs, and there was no more trace of the wind.

Looking down at the water, he noticed his silver bracelet.

"How did you get there?" he asked, bending to pick it up.

He called to Pericles. The burro lowered its head and came sloshing through the shallow water. There was a glow from above, and in amazement, Everett realized that the sun had risen.

"Let's make camp somewhere dry and have breakfast."

They turned around and trudged downstream.

Pledge to the Wind

Chapter Ten

Gallup, New Mexico
(August 1932)

Nearly a year had passed when Everett approached an old Navajo sitting in the narrow shade of a telephone pole. The man didn't have much use for white people, but the one in front of him had his curiosity up. He looked young, and a part of him was aged; he obviously wasn't from the area. Something about him fit in. He appeared confident and well-organized but carried a note of desperation.

So many contradictions, he thought, and watched Everett approach and dump his kyacks in a pile. Then the young man returned over the rise he had come from, and a moment later, he came back carrying a worn saddle.

"You have many things," said the Navajo.

Everett nodded and returned for yet another load, this time of art supplies. A horse or a burro would have made this easier, he thought sadly. When he finally had all his items in a pile, he sat in the slender shadow and faced the old man.

It had seemed an eternity had passed since the poison ivy attack last September and the strange experience in the Narrows.

From Zion, he had crisscrossed the desert, traveling south at first to escape the coming winter, slowly picking his way through a land of saguaro, cholla and mesquite. For mile after mile, his burros had trudged ahead of Everett as Curly followed by his side, the afternoon sun always on his right, his hat pulled down tightly as he squinted ahead—always vigilant for rattlesnakes.

He had stopped a few times to work, once hoeing a field of corn for a Pima Indian, working side by side with several Pima. In the afternoon a fine-looking girl had walked to the men and handed them lunch. She offered him some, and he smiled at her. The men had nodded at him and smirked, and then motioned for him to crouch with them while they ate.

The old Navajo examined Everett's gear. He held up a halter and said, "You have enough here for two animals."

For the last year, he had used horses instead of burros, but when he glanced down at his battered saddle, he thought of the tired old horse that had ridden under it and the packhorse he kept the kyacks on.

He turned his mind away from it.

The Navajo lifted a collar and asked, "You have a dog?"

Everett's mind drifted back to a dry canyon he had stumbled through, played out, and almost out of water. Curly asleep in the backpack. The horse following with its head held low.

And then they stumbled upon an oasis of green. Shadowed water reflecting diamonds off the towering rock walls, moss dripping on the lower rocks: coolness and dappled sunshine.

Everett stood on a ledge, about ten feet above the water, and cradled Curly. "Don't worry, boy. I've got you."

He screamed "Geronimo!" and stepped over the edge, and they dropped and plunged underwater.

A few seconds later, they surfaced, and Curly's barking echoed throughout the canyon.

The dog had always been his steadfast companion.

But then one stormy night, about a day's travel from Chinle, he had stumbled into his camp and found Curly eating the last of his food.

"Get out of there!" he screamed.

The dog ignored him, and he charged forward, scaring it. Curly turned and fled into the dark.

Suddenly a dread came over him. He ran to the edge of camp and shouted, "I'm sorry, Curly, come back!"

But he never saw him again.

He had stayed three more days, searching for tracks, hoping desperately he would find him, but Curly was gone.

"The kyacks for sale too?" asked the Navajo

He lifted one of the boxes and noticed one side was caved in.

Again, Everett simply nodded. He didn't want to recall leading his packhorse, Jonathan, over a precarious trail through a steep-walled canyon where the rocks were decorated with pictographs of painted hands, but the images came anyway.

He could remember every detail of the panel: not just the painted hands on the wall, but other pictographs of deer and antelope, devils and snakes and scorpions and turkeys.

It all seemed frozen in time.

A lightning storm had been battling overhead, and when a bolt hit nearby, the horse had jumped back, side-stepped in panic, and tumbled over the edge.

He had run toward the edge, past red, white, and grey handprints, and discovered the horse below, on his side on a steep hill. In the frozen picture in his mind, he wanted to warn himself not to pull off the pack saddle.

But, of course, he did, and when he removed the saddle, the horse slid down the mountainside, rolling over three times before he could stop himself.

Everett had spent the remainder of the night trying to get the horse to rise to his feet and climb back up the hill. Finally, Jonathan stood, but then his legs buckled under him, and he fell into a thick patch of prickly pear cactus.

For an eternity the horse stared at him, and about an hour before sunrise, he died. Stupid decision to take that steep trail, thought Everett.

The moment was still heavy on him. He had stumbled back to Nuflo, the packhorse, and led him to a grassy place where he started a fire. Then he sat and stared at the coals. He could remember every detail of that morning: the song of crickets, the murmur of water in a nearby stream, the clatter of Nuflo's bell as he munched grass nearby.

But staring back at him from the fire were Jonathan's sad eyes as he looked up from his final resting place in the cactus.

His gear lay in a mound. He lifted the old saddle off the pile and showed it to the Navajo. The old man frowned at a large gouge down the middle.

"That's broken."

"I'm lucky I saved the saddle at all," said Everett.

The very morning that he had walked away from Jonathan, he had been following a trail that ran along a turbulent mountain stream. Nuflo and Everett were hoping to find a way up and out of Canyon del Muerto. When the rain hit, the surge of water spilled over the banks and flooded the trail in mere minutes.

Suddenly the horse stumbled and went down, and the weight of his load pulled him under. The water was about two feet deep but moving fast. Everett jumped after him and somehow found the reins.

The horse was blowing and scrambling in the fast-moving water, and it was hard work to pull him out, but finally, they reached higher ground.

Everett had patiently led the waterlogged animal to land and returned for his gear, but all he'd found was the saddle snagged on a branch.

The old Navajo shook his head. "I won't give you much for this."

Everett nodded. "I just need enough to buy some food and get to the highway." He had returned home once during the long year. His two-month stay in Hollywood had been frustrating, and he couldn't believe he was contemplating doing it again. California didn't feel like home anymore, and his family and friends failed to understand why he preferred wild places to civilized life.

But then his stomach growled, and a wave of tiredness crept over him.

"Where you headed?" asked the Navajo.

Everett looked over the desert. A cold wind blew across the land.

He was hungry and broke and couldn't remember the last time he'd felt warm at night.

"California… home," he answered, and the old man raised an eyebrow.

"I don't want to," said Everett, "not like this — in defeat, but I just can't keep going on without supplies or money."

The Navajo nodded. "I'll give you five dollars for the saddle."

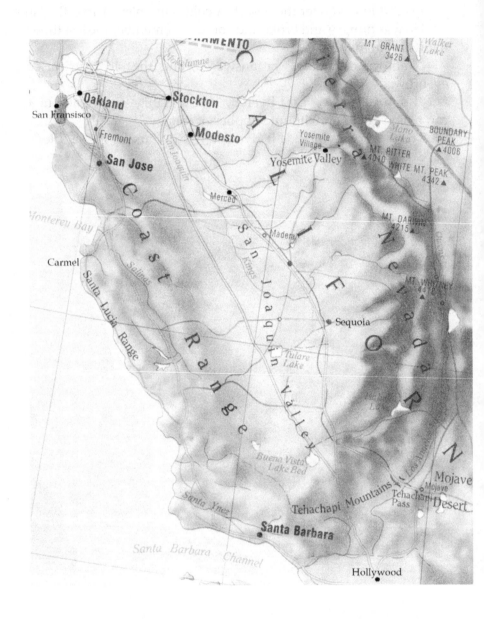

Chapter Eleven

U.C.L.A. classroom, California
(September 1932)

A distinguished older professor in a tweed jacket wrote on a blackboard, the words in perfect cursive letters.

The Road Less Traveled
by Robert Frost

Near the back of the room sat Everett in a wooden chair. He kept shifting his gaze to the window, not wanting to be inside, and even less in school.

He was here because of pressure from his father; now that he was home, living with his parents in Hollywood, he had to keep peace with his family.

His mother's eyes had betrayed concern when she'd first glimpsed his emaciated frame. Stella Ruess believed in giving her son the space to make his own decisions, and the freedom as an artist to follow his bliss, but the skinny child that had stumbled through her door had scared her—and that he was getting rested, and healthy, was all she cared about as he paced through the house.

For this reason, she supported her husband, Christopher, and encouraged Everett to give college a try.

He had fought the idea at first. Instead, he'd hitched over to Red Rock Canyon for a weekend and scrambled through the cliffs until he was exhausted.

When he returned, he had a long talk with his parents. He was the first to admit that he'd made few dollars as an artist, and he wanted to be able to support his dreams. So, with their encouragement, he enrolled for the fall semester at U.C.L.A., taking history, geology, English, philosophy, gym and military drill.

He joked with Waldo, "Maybe with a college degree, I'll be a better-paid vagrant artist."

He'd been attending classes for barely four months, but it felt like an eternity.

There were about twenty other students in the classroom.

Another student, Wes, caught him drifting off in the chair next to him and flicked a small paper ball at him. The projectile barely missed his nose, and he smiled at his friend. Wes was a bit different from the other students, who seemed obsessed with the whole school scene. He liked to hike.

Everett smiled and turned to the blackboard as the professor cleared his throat.

"Perhaps one of the best-known poems in American literature," said the professor. "Can anyone tell me why?"

A tall male student with glasses lifted a hand, and the professor nodded.

The student said, "Because it voices the regrets about directions in life that were not taken?"

The professor made a half nod; a glitter in his eye implied that he knew a more profound truth. "Maybe."

A young woman in the front row raised her hand.

"It illustrates the yearning for that undiscovered path in life."

The professor was about to write one of the lines down when he noticed Everett staring out the window again.

He cleared his throat.

"Mr. Ruess, how do you feel about the piece?"

Everett faced the professor and stared at the blackboard, but he had drifted to Monument Valley in his mind. He saw it clearly, expanding before him with the sun bearing down from overhead. On the horizon, islands of rock shimmered like sentinels, watching him approach.

As always, in his memories or dreams, he was walking.

The trail he followed led directly north. It was a foot wide and bore faded tracks from several burros and one set of boots. To the west lay a distant canyon, and it looked like its shadowed cliffs might be an excellent place to find ruins.

He turned left, creating his own trail over the powdery red earth, his feet breaking the delicate crust with a puff.

With a start, he realized everyone was staring at him.

He returned his thoughts to the poem and said, "I don't like it."

The professor raised his eyebrows.

The class fell silent.

"Mr. Frost is one of the most critically respected poets of our generation! What prompts your judgment?"

Everett glanced out the window for a long moment, collecting his thoughts.

He could still feel the soft crush of the earth beneath his feet. And hear the burro trotting behind him, and sense the breeze that blew at his back, cooling his neck. Now, in the classroom, he felt if he lifted his head, he would spot the first ruin he'd encountered in that canyon, hidden in the afternoon shadows high above.

Finally, he said, "If he's regretting roads he didn't take when he was younger, then I do not pity him. He should have returned and taken the other path."

The professor said, "I believe the poem actually states that he had taken the road less traveled..."

He surveyed the class and recited the last line.

"And that has made all the difference."

Everett said, "From what I know about Mr. Frost, he spent most of his life in New Hampshire on a farm. He later taught in the area, too."

"That is correct," said the professor.

Everett nodded. "That doesn't seem like a road less traveled to me."

The students around him looked intrigued by Everett's words.

The professor said, "Well, maybe his life wasn't unorthodox, but he could certainly capture an idea."

Everett shook his head. He was gaining confidence. "He wrote about something he didn't do himself unless you consider being a poet enough. I don't."

The professor leaned over his desk.

"And what would you have done differently if you were him?"

Everett's eyes darted to the window, but he stopped himself and glanced directly at the professor. "I would've left the farm and explored America — or the world. That's a road less traveled."

The Professor shook his head slightly and muttered, "Well, that's just impractical." Then he began writing the entire poem on the board, slashing violently with the chalk.

Wes leaned over and whispered. "What the hell has gotten into you, Ruess? Don't piss him off."

Everett waved his comment away.

Wes said, "Are you going to the T.S. Eliot lecture in November?"

"I'll be returning from Hollywood that day — I'm gonna be late."

"No problem," said Wes. "Find me in the balcony — I'll save you a seat."

Chapter Twelve

Campus Lecture Hall, California
(November 1932)

*T*he hall was packed, and Everett had to squeeze past dozens of people just to get up the stairs to the balcony. Finally, he spotted Wes and slowly made his way to the free seat by his side.

Below, a man wearing a three-piece suit stood on the stage reciting prose with a soft but intense voice that demanded attention. He was T.S. Eliot, mid-forties, with black-rimmed spectacle glasses, and his hair slicked down and parted to the side.

Wes leaned over and said, "He's in the middle of *The Wasteland.*"

Everett nodded thanks to Wes and leaned forward to listen.

"Here is no water but only rock,
Rock and no water and the sandy road,
The road winding above among the mountains,
Which are mountains of rock without water..."

"It reminds me of Arizona," said Everett.

Wes nodded.

Everett peered down at Eliot. Even from as far away as the balcony, the man's eyes held an intensity, like he'd seen things the average person hadn't, but they seemed weary, and Everett wondered if the man had seen too much.

Eliot continued,

> *"If there were water we should stop and drink,*
> *Amongst the rock one cannot stop or think,*
> *Sweat is dry and feet are in the sand,*
> *If there were only water amongst the rock..."*

Everett licked his lips. He'd run out of water many times and been forced to scrounge water from puddles or chips of dirty ice.

He lowered his head and pictured the crossing he'd made from Canyon de Chelly when he had stumbled out of the desert, shoeless. He would never forget the brutal oppressiveness of the sun weighing down on him, torching him under a cloudless sky. He'd left a single sip of water in his canteen because he felt as long as he retained the willpower not to drink it, he would be strong enough to fend off the buzzards that circled above him.

Those two Flagstaff boys, Pat and Tad, had picked him up, although he never doubted he would have made it to shelter eventually. They had no idea how strong he was. None of them did.

In his heart of hearts, the desert called to him, and it hurt physically to ignore it. He wanted to please his father, who had convinced him that an education would help him become an artist but listening to Eliot's words made the intense heat and brilliant nothingness return.

He closed his eyes and immediately he was back in the southwest, walking, the sun directly overhead. His shadow existed as only a tiny pool that hovered around his feet.

"What am I doing here?" he thought, not realizing he'd asked the question out loud.

"What was that?" asked Wes.

Someone from behind shushed them.

> *"... dry sterile thunder without rain,*
> *There is not even solitude in the mountains,*
> *But red sullen faces sneer and snarl from doors*
> *of mud-cracked houses..."*

Robert Louis DeMayo

That first day he'd arrived in Kayenta felt like only a few months ago, although it was now two years. He recalled Bad Jack glaring at him from the porch of the Trading Post.

Sullen faces and mud-cracked houses, he thought, I've seen my share.

He pictured the old Indian, Notah, watching from under the rim of his hat. On a few other trips into Kayenta he'd seen the old man again, and each time the young woman was with him—always shy, always refusing to meet Everett's stare, there only to help the old one.

Yet, he had been drawn to her. And now, a thousand miles away, he thought of her, sensing a connection despite her aloofness. He'd seen her away from Notah only once, and had he been sitting at an opera, he would have let the music take him as he thought of that encounter.

Instead, Eliot's words drew him back.

He listened to another stanza, but now his breathing had quickened, and he got up and made his way to the exit, and Wes followed. Flashbacks to the desert overwhelmed him, and he stumbled into a man wearing a tuxedo. Wes straightened him up and helped him to an exit.

"Ruess, what's going on with you?" he asked once they were outside.

Everett sucked in the cool night air and let his eyes sweep over the stars. Wes waited patiently by his side.

Finally, he asked, "You okay?"

Everett shook his head. "I never should've gone to college. But, my father talked me into it."

"Is it all that bad?"

They locked eyes. "I have an unconquerable soul," said Everett, "and it doesn't like restraints."

Wes laughed. "Don't be so dramatic. Come on, shake it off—let's get a drink."

Everett looked up at the stars again. He felt like he was going to explode. He hadn't spent one week at home before he'd heard the call again—the wind, whispering through the needles of a pine outside his bedroom window — and it was only the worried sound of his mother's voice that had kept him from heading right back to the southwest.

"I'm serious," said Everett, "I'm not going to let college get a stranglehold on me."

Wes watched his friend warily and saw the panicked look in his eye. It was the only time he'd ever seen any form of fear in the young man. He thought a moment, then turned up his palms.

"We have three weeks off for Christmas — why don't you get out of here for a little while?"

Suddenly Everett began to grin. "That's it! How far away could I get in three weeks?"

He paced in a circle, stopped and said, "I'll go up the coast and camp by Carmel, by the sea."

"Great!" said Wes and clapped a hand on his shoulder. "Now, let's get that drink."

Everett shook his head. "No, I've got to pack. I'll need supplies."

He walked away without another word, and Wes yelled after him.

"When will I see you again?"

Everett didn't look back, just called over his shoulder.

"If you're lucky in three weeks."

Wes shouted back. "And if I'm not lucky?"

Everett whooped and now began to run.

He shouted, "You'll have to come to the desert!"

"The desert?" asked Wes.

Everett laughed, his voice fading. "Or to the mountains! Or up turbulent rivers! Or to forgotten ruins…"

"Are you okay?" shouted Wes.

Everett stopped at the far end of the courtyard, turned and faced his friend.

He waved a final time and yelled, "Never been better!"

Chapter Thirteen

Carmel, California
(December 1932)

Everett was riding a black horse, galloping along the waves with salt water spraying up behind him. Sandpipers skittered along, half an inch ahead of the waves, and he charged at them, laughing as they effortlessly moved out of the horse's way.

Throughout his travels in the southwest, he'd dreamt about the coast of California. He had hitched north from Hollywood once, three years ago when he was barely sixteen, and the memories often surfaced under the hot blue skies of Utah and Arizona.

Now he took it all in: the fresh air laden with salt, the waves pounding on the beach, the sun glinting off the water. He felt alive and full of potential, not restricted, and pinned down like in the classroom.

A man on a dune was leaning over a tripod about a quarter-mile away, and Everett directed the horse toward him. The man, Edward Weston, was one of America's finest photographers. He was in his mid-forties with a receding hairline and black mustache, and Everett considered him one of his few good friends.

They hadn't spent a lot of time together, but Everett sensed an understanding between them. He wasn't intimidated by Weston's photographic clout. He barely thought of his fame. What connected them was the way they both saw nature.

Weston had been setting up a photo but covered the camera with a cloth and stepped away when he saw the rider approaching.

He recognized him and waved.

"Hello, Everett!"

Everett rode up, hopped down, and extended his right hand.

Weston shook it, noticing the silver bracelet on Everett's wrist that jiggled slightly in the handshake. "You were about the last person I expected to see here. I thought you went back in time in Hopi land."

"I did — maybe a part of me is still there," said Everett, looking down and kicking the sand, "I stopped the clock for a while, but…"

Weston waited a moment, then said, "But…?"

Everett continued, "Then I ran out of money and had to come home."

Weston laughed. "The life of an artist is never easy."

Everett held his tongue. His eyes followed a hummingbird that suddenly twittered by, hovering in front of his face for a moment.

Weston chuckled. "This is about as different from the Grand Canyon as you can get."

Everett looked east as if he could see it, could feel the orange-red burn on his crinkled cheeks after a day of hiking in the canyon.

He said, "I miss that glowing furnace."

Suddenly there was great sadness in Everett's eyes. Weston could see it clearly. He sensed a deep longing — whether it was for a specific place or just to travel, he didn't know.

"Are you okay, son?" asked Weston.

Everett smiled and said, "Most times, I feel quite ecstatic, but I slip into more melancholy moods easily."

Weston nodded. "And what else have you been up to?"

"I visited Doc Rice at the hospital downtown and watched him assist in an appendectomy case."

Again, Weston nodded. "Maybe you're meant to be a doctor."

Everett's face lit up in a smirk. He couldn't imagine himself as a doctor — or even just about anyone with a regular nine-to-five job. The thought made him laugh.

"I don't think I could ever settle down. I have known too much of the depths of life already, and I would prefer anything to an anticlimax."

Weston observed the young man.

Everett caught his eye and smiled. "Don't worry, sir, I am in no danger of a nervous breakdown at present."

The horse turned away and tugged on the reins. Everett pulled him back gently and said, "I remember seeing you on this very spot a few years ago—the day we met."

Weston nodded. How bold the young man had been when he'd searched him out and introduced himself as a painter. He had said that he admired both Weston's ability to capture landscapes and close-up forms.

They'd shared their art with each other, and Weston had quickly seen that the young man had talent. Ruess was amongst the most sensitive people he knew, but he lacked training.

"I believe I was photographing kelp that day," he said.

"Yes," agreed the young man, nodding.

He slid off the horse and said, "You introduced me to your sons, and we had great fun swimming. We must have collected at least sixty starfish that day—I can still see their colors in the small pool we housed them in: red, blue, purple, brown, yellow, and vermillion."

"Both Neil and Cole still ask about you whenever we sit down to read *Moby Dick*. Oh, and thank you for your letters—I read them to the boys as well."

Everett nodded, imagining Weston´s deep voice lulling his sons to sleep. After their meeting at the beach, Weston had invited him to their house, and once he saw how well Everett got along with his boys, he'd asked if he wanted to stay the night.

"I can only offer you a cot in the garage," Weston had said, "but it's mostly empty—and it's out of the elements."

Everett had been greatly relieved. That morning, when he had returned to his camp in some dunes by the shore, a bum was sitting there, having just finished a pound jar of peanut butter. The man had shown no guilt about raiding Everett´s food; instead, he'd pried at the last of the peanut butter, staring at Everett as he licked his fingers.

Everett had never told Weston about the bum, and all the older man recollected was Everett bragging about how well he'd gotten along on bread, PB and J sandwiches, and breakfast cereal. He'd stayed a week, and Weston's garage had never been cleaner.

And with this temporary home base, Everett had found some work caddying at the club, gardening for neighbors, and sawing some wood Weston had ordered for the winter.

"So what else have you been up to since the southwest — besides watching surgeries?" Weston now asked.

Everett picked up a stick and dug the end into the sand.

"I did a stint at college."

"So, you're a college student now?"

Uneasily, Everett shook his head. "Well, I don't know for how much longer."

A coyote appeared about fifty feet away, and the two watched it sniff around the dunes.

"Studies can be a challenge," said Weston. "But if you have the right teacher, they can have incredible value."

"It's not that so much. I don't mind the hard work. But I dislike listening to professors who talk about things they've had no real-life experience with."

Weston laughed. "You're an unusual young man, Everett. Most folks twice your age haven't subjected themselves to the environments that you have."

Everett shook his head as he thought of his professors. Then, he asked, "How can you grow as a person or honestly express yourself without tasting the waters of life?"

"The artist's dilemma," said Weston. "Most artists struggle to express what they haven't lived — but not you, you're out there chasing life." He saw the furrowed brow of his young friend and added, "Don't let other people's opinions of your future bother you, just follow your dreams. I've seen your art — you have a clear vision."

Everett scanned the dunes, looking for the coyote but didn't see it. The Navajo called them the Coyote People. He wondered if the Coyote People were watching him now.

After a moment, Weston asked, "So, what's next?"

Everett shrugged. "Well, I'll stay on for the remainder of the semester—I'm no quitter. But I do hate being locked in a classroom, and the longer I'm there, the more I resent my teachers. It probably wouldn't surprise you to hear I'm getting mostly Ds. I did do well in geology, and I somehow pulled a B in English."

Weston watched Everett turn to reassure the horse. All the time spent with the burros had given Everett a remarkable ability to soothe animals, and he couldn't picture him in a stuffy classroom.

He said, "Don't ever tell your parents I said it, but school isn't for everyone. Formal training is a good thing, but you might find it elsewhere."

Everett sighed. "It seemed a good idea at the time."

Weston nodded and let it drop, then asked, "And after the semester is over?" Everett turned and caressed the horse's muzzle again.

"I thought I'd hit the road again and continue with my art."

Weston grinned. "Back to the Southwest?"

He gave Weston a serious look. "Eventually, but first, I wanted to explore the Sierras. I want to traverse them from Sequoia to Yosemite."

"Good!" Weston called and clapped a hand on Everett's shoulder. "How I wish I were your age again, with the freedom just to take off and explore. Do you plan to paint much?"

"Yes," he replied. "Although I don't think I'll need to bring as much vermilion." Weston laughed. "No, it'll be greens and blues—with a lot of white this time of year until the snow melts."

The horse looked restless now, and Everett also felt ready to move on. Weston looked at him, feeling a mix of envy and parental protection. He said, "Listen, Everett, you're not walking the same path as everyone else—don't let the fact that others don't always understand you, bother you. Keep painting—you're very talented."

He nodded, "Thanks! That means a lot coming from you. After the Sierras, I might stop in San Francisco for a few months till winter has passed."

Weston nodded. "Well, if you do, look up my friend Mr. Adams. He has a gallery there."

A light rain began, and Weston quickly set about putting away his camera. "Good luck, Everett."

Chapter Fourteen

Sequoia, California
(June 1933)

A car stopped at the park gate. The driver, Waldo, was Everett's older brother. Through the windshield, they surveyed the redwoods that towered around them.

"You're hiking to Yosemite from here? How far is that?"

"I don't travel in a straight line," said Everett, "but I think I'll cover at least a few hundred miles before I'm done."

They stepped out of the car and began piling Everett's supplies by the side of the road. The scent of pines was overpowering, and Everett started to breathe it in like it was a magical elixir.

"Oh, I've missed that smell!"

Waldo examined his brother's provisions, attempting to think of something to say before he left him. "You have everything you need?"

"Yup - rice, oatmeal, books, paper and paint. I'm gonna start looking for burros as soon as you go."

He nodded, not wanting to leave. "Take care, brother. I'll see you in a few weeks?"

They hugged. Everett ignored the question and it weighed heavily in the air. Finally, Waldo said, "Keep the letters coming."

He looked down at his brother, four and a half years younger but in some ways now older. He read his unspoken words.

"You're not coming back to school for the spring semester, are you?"

Everett was busy unloading his equipment. He didn't respond.

Waldo asked, "How long do you think it'll take you to get to Yosemite?"

"I don't know," replied Everett. He didn't like to be pinned down about times and distances before he had completed them. "I told you, I don't travel in a straight line. It's as far as it is, and it'll take as long as it does."

"You sure you don't need anything?"

He smiled. "If I don't have it, I don't need it."

A moment of silence covered the two young men.

"You've grown a lot, Everett. I sometimes wish I could be as cavalier as you."

Everett gave his brother a long look, wanting to tell him to quit his job and come with him, but he didn't. He knew it would end like similar conversations with his friends, who listed inconsequential excuses why they couldn't just drop everything and spoke of some day in the future when they might join him.

He didn't want to hear those words from his brother. So instead, he just hugged him, smiling, knowing words could never communicate what was in his heart.

"I'm proud of you, Everett," said Waldo and ducked back into the vehicle. Everett smiled and waved as he drove off.

Everett led two burros, one black and the other gray, through the park campground to his allotted site. A stream behind the campsite gurgled happily and he gave the burros enough lead that they could get a drink.

In the next site over, an old man, Andy, sat by a fire. Andy's camp had a permanent look with lots of stacked wooden boxes under a tarp next to his tent. By his side sat a young boy who was making a slingshot.

"What're you gonna do with those?" asked Andy, nodding at the burros.

"I'm heading into the high country and traversing up to Yosemite."

106

Andy shook his head. "Not for a while, you're not. It'll be a few weeks 'til the snow melts enough to get through."

Everett looked around and noticed that there were quite a few other campers. They were all around him, cooking and stoking fires, shouting and talking over each other. He suddenly felt accosted by all these people. He scowled, and Andy noticed it.

"This place sure used to be a hell of a lot quieter," said Andy.

"Oh yeah," said Everett. "When did you first come here?"

Andy cackled and called out, "Heck, son, I've been here forever!"

Everett smiled. He liked the old man. Andy gestured for him to come to sit on a flat rock by the glowing embers. He poured a cup of coffee for Everett and handed it to him, black, not asking if he wanted cream or sugar. Everett didn't think he had either item anyway.

"I've been in these mountains for fifty years," said Andy. He jutted his chin at the creek. "I was the first to stock trout in the streams here. I also started that copper mine above here, too."

"Really?" asked Everett.

The boy nodded emphatically, and Andy ruffled his hair and said, "You tell 'im, grandson."

Everett sipped his coffee and said, "I suppose in fifty years, you could do a lot."

Andy gave a toothless grin. "I've tried my hand at everything from preaching to bartending."

He studied Everett and saw the young man that was just now emerging. He liked him and caught a glimpse of his own younger self. He thought of the times he had crossed the Sierras, sometimes with burros, other times with mules or horses.

He said, "If I was a young buck like you, I'd camp on the other side of the river. And go upstream a bit where it's quieter and you can catch your dinner and eat in peace."

The boy looked over at the burros. One had stretched his lead to the limit so that she could stand in the creek. "What're their names?"

"The black one is Betsy, and the grey is Grandma."

Andy glanced at them and nodded.

"They look like they'll do," he said.

"I hope so," said Everett. "I just picked them up and haven't had them on a trail yet. Betsy already gave me a little trouble—she ran off into the thickets back there and it took an hour to find her."

Andy hoisted himself to his feet with a moan and ambled over to his crates of gear, where he began rummaging around.

After a few minutes, he returned with several clusters of bells.

"Strap these onto the burros, and you'll be able to hear them when they take off."

Everett shook the bells, liking the gentle tinkling.

"Thank you," he said and pocketed them.

Everett's new camp was tucked in a small grove of cedars. Through a break, he could see only a few tourists' sites on the other side of the river, but they couldn't see him.

He cut a branch off one of the cedars, trimmed it down to a four-foot stick, and tied on some fishing line with a barbed hook on it. On its end, he impaled a grasshopper.

"Time to catch us one of Andy's trout," he said to the burros.

They watched him, and he displayed his handiwork to them.

"What d'ya think, Grandma? This ought to do the trick, eh?"

She lowered her head and shook her neck to chase away some insects; the bells jingled pleasantly, and she gave Everett an odd look.

Everett savored the way the ring of the bells mingled with the gurgle of the water.

He dropped a line in a deep pool, and almost immediately, it disappeared. He tugged at it and felt the fish was hooked.

He launched the trout out of the water with a swinging motion, but too strongly, and the fish went flying into the bushes behind him. He went searching for it, and the mosquitoes besieged him.

He slapped at them, griping, careful not to break the fishing line while he traced it and eventually located the fish.

He continued to fish to pass the time, slapping at the mosquitoes. Soon his arms and neck were dotted with red welts. He smoldered some wet bark in his fire but found the smoke only kept the insects at bay when he all but enveloped himself in it, and before long, his eyes were red-rimmed and sore.

The burros were watching, twitching their fur to scare off the bugs, each swish of their tails now accompanied by a musical note.

"You guys look bored," said Everett, scratching at a mosquito bite on his neck. He wiped a dusty plate clean with his shirtsleeve. "I hope that pass opens up soon—I'm sick of getting bitten."

He then put his frying pan on the fire. Eighteen small trout covered in cornmeal sizzled in bacon grease.

"I think after this trip, I'll have to take a break on fish."

"Keep moving, Grandma!" shouted Everett and pushed the burro to force her way through the snow. He had lost sight of the trail some time ago, and now they simply attempted to follow the ridgeline.

It was tough going. The snow was several feet deep and buried underneath lay logs and stunted trees that tripped them repeatedly.

Betsy trudged along behind them, tethered to Grandma by a rope that Everett grabbed at times, sometimes for support, other times to encourage Betsy to get in line.

They were high above the Marble Fork of the Kaweah River, surrounded by aspens that were waiting for the spring sun; their branches were dotted with green buds, ready to burst open.

A snowstorm two days before had blanketed the land, choking the passes. It had begun just as he'd started, but he was sick of the campground and the waiting and the mosquitoes and continued, regardless.

Now, Everett felt a glorious, irrepressible joy as his eyes skimmed the landscape. Towering pines below them straddled a rushing river peppered with monstrous glacial boulders, and soft blue hills flecked with snow lined the horizon. Fleecy white clouds above moved through a porcelain-blue sky.

It had only been a month since he'd left school, but it seemed ages ago. Since he had escaped the congested campground and headed into the mountains, a dreamy intoxication had overtaken his mind. As he passed through the Sierras in perfect solitude, he sensed his soul floating out in song.

At first, it was the tingle of the bells blending with the gurgle of the water, but soon that merged with the gentle breeze to create a sweet symphony around him.

He recalled the music of Brahms and Beethoven in his head and let it fuse with the nature around him, shouting out with elation at the music in his head.

They continued to scrape through deep snow, hoping to recover a sign of the trail before they had to descend off the ridge.

Then the land sloped down gently, and the burros plowed ahead, their momentum helping them break the trail.

When the sun broke through the clouds and reflected off the snow, the vista became blinding, but Everett was humming a symphony by Cesar Franck in his head. The music was so magnificent he was almost surprised the burros couldn't hear it.

He swung his arms wildly as if he was conducting an orchestra.

And then, just as the music was hitting a crescendo, he spotted a narrow shelf below them.

It was free of snow, and a small stream flowed along one side.

"That's our spot, girls!" he shouted. "Get me there, and you each get extra oats tonight!"

When they reached it, he walked to the edge and saw the Kaweah River twisting below them.

The sun was shining warmly on the last few steps to the summit. The snow had melted recently, and the ground was muddy and slippery.

Alongside the trail snowmelt rushed by, cascading down the mountain, resting only occasionally in green pools that shone lucidly in the bright sunshine.

They passed a sign that read: ALTA PEAK - 11,204 feet.

In the far distance, the Sierras extended to the north, but directly in front of them another prominent peak rose. He pulled out a crude map of the area and mumbled, "That's got to be Mount Whitney."

The alpine ridge that led to it was clear of snow.

"Looks like the pass is open. Time to hit the road again," he said out loud.

They had stopped for a week at the ledge above the Kaweah River. During that time, Everett made two trips to a nearby store, and on one of them, the shopkeeper had traded some store credit for a painting of cypress trees near Carmel.

He had encountered two rangers that patrolled the trails running through the Sierras, and several of the young men who worked at a reforestation camp.

The young men offered him to stay and work on the reforestation project, and although they weren't a bad lot and liked the work they were doing, he felt he couldn't bear to be tied down.

He descended back to the treeline, where there was still plenty of snow. Here the trail dropped away in two directions. The burros were there, loaded and waiting on the pass. The trees were thick around them, and the swaying branches had them restless.

Everett checked their ropes and had just finished tightening the straps on their kyacks when he heard the shouting of several packers directing a pack train coming from the north. Soon their footsteps echoed through the cold air, and then he spotted a ranger below him, leading a string of mules.

He watched them prepare to ascend the final rise. The mules were twice the size of Everett's burros and carried impressive loads. Their fur was thick and shaggy.

Slowly, they trudged up the last uphill section of the trail before descending the other side of the pass. The mules were huffing through flared nostrils, and Betsy and Grandma eyed them fearfully as they approached.

The ranger carefully picked his way through the snow; he held the lead in his hand and kept tension on it. At the back of the train, another ranger yelled at the last mule, who had apparently decided he'd had enough.

"Hold on a minute, Freddy!" he shouted from below.

Freddy stopped beside Everett. The mules behind him looked tired as they paused to catch their breath.

"How's the trail?" he asked.

"Slick," said the ranger. He grabbed a tree branch for support.

"Where you heading?" Everett asked. He examined the pack train and paid particular attention to how the ranger had tied down the loads. He was carrying more gear using the kyacks than before, but next to the loads which the mules bore, his gear was meager.

"Down to Sequoia — to Giant Forest."

"Would you mind mailing a letter for me?" asked Everett, hopefully.

"Sure, I'll be there late this afternoon."

Everett reached into his jacket and grabbed the letter he had written to his parents.

"I have been feeling so happy and filled to overflowing with the beauty of life. It is all a golden dream, with mysterious, high, rushing winds leaning down to caress me, and warm and perfect colors flowing before my eyes. Time and the need for time have ceased entirely. A gentle, dreamy haze fills my soul, the rustling of the aspens lulls my senses, and the surpassing beauty and perfection of everything fills me with a quiet joy and a deep pervading love for my world."

He handed the letter over, and the ranger disappeared down the trail.

Everett trudged up the last few steps to the summit of Mount Whitney. He'd left the burros below and felt weirdly weightless without the tension on their leads.

The mountains extended all around him. The snow was gone now above the treeline, and the spring smells floated heavily in the air.

A ranger sat at the top, collecting his breath.

"Well, you made it to the top of the highest peak in the continental United States. Air's a little thin at 14,505 feet, isn't it? How do you feel?"

Everett smiled. "Like I'm just getting started."

Everett was riding on Betsy; Grandma trailed behind with the gear swaying in the kyacks. Quiet alpine meadows and glades lined the trail, far above the shadowy woods.

"No more mosquitoes!" he shouted.

There were no firs or sugar pines at this elevation, only narrow lodge-pole pine and quaking aspen. They passed a mountain stream that was running strong with snowmelt.

Everett had to urge the burros to ford it.

That afternoon they descended into a quiet valley where the streams had thickened. The snow lay in the shadows along the banks, and Everett spotted a large golden trout in one stream.

"Oh, you're gonna make a tasty dinner."

He stopped just long enough to light a small fire, wanting it burnt down to coals when he returned with a fish.

Then he cut a branch and made another fishing pole. After attaching a line and hook, he walked through the high grass and collected a handful of grasshoppers.

With pole in hand, he cast a dangling grasshopper into the pool where he'd spotted the trout.

The grasshopper twitched through its death throes, but nothing bit. Everett slowly began to take in the line.

Suddenly, there was a strong tug and the grasshopper disappeared.

Everett yanked the pole back and pulled the large trout out of the water in one big sweep.

He whooped with joy — and flung the fish into a thicket. He climbed after it, cursing.

"Again?" he asked.

He was bent over, tangled in the dense thicket of branches, when suddenly a rattlesnake sounded off very close to him, rattling angrily.

Instead of retreating, he scrambled through the brush, thrashing wildly with the stick that a moment before had been a fishing pole.

113

Finally, he glimpsed the snake and snatched madly at its midsection and missed.

"Check it out, Grandma!" he shouted, "My first Sierra rattler!"

The snake struck at him twice, but he finally got a hold of its tail and swung it around until the head hit a tree branch with a thud.

His victory-whoop was cut short by a swarm of bees whose nest he had stirred up. They were coming at him, and he was still tangled deep in the bushes.

He struggled frantically to get clear of the bees and the bushes. When he emerged, tearing at his shirt and grabbing with his numb fingers at bees stuck to his skin, he was in a blind panic. The bees were all over him.

He stumbled forward and plunged into the icy meltwater of the creek and sank to the bottom.

He surfaced slowly and paused a long time by the shore's edge before finally dragging himself onto dry land. The water had quickly numbed his legs, and he couldn't force his mind to work. His chest was dotted with red blisters and a rash had appeared on his neck and arms.

He painfully stood, then knelt and vomited.

He collapsed on his side, and after a long moment took off his shirt, then began to chant Navajo in a weak voice.

A glaring fire was lighting up Everett's swollen face. He watched it with restless eyes, the flickering flame dancing before him. His skin shone under a layer of sweat. Wearing only his jeans, he sat as close to the fire as he could.

How lucky that I already had a fire going, he thought. Without it, I'd be dead now.

He shivered and inched even closer.

His cooking gear was still stowed away on Grandma's pack.

Sleep was sneaking up on him, weaseling past his guard under the cover of crackling embers. He fought it off and forced himself back to consciousness. Sleep, he thought, might mean death.

In a daze, he watched the firelight reflecting off the turquoise on his silver bracelet.

He stared at Grandma for a long time.

Finally, he got to his feet, and with great effort, stumbled toward her, unhooked her saddle hitch, and let everything crash to the ground.

He sank to his knees and searched the pile until he found a bundle that contained his journal, some paper and a pencil.

He crawled back to the fire.

Sluggishly, he lifted the pencil and tried to write, but he was shivering too violently and had to wait.

When he finally stopped shaking, he retrieved a dry shirt and pants. Once dressed, he sat by the fire again and sharpened his pencil. He loved sharing his experiences through his letters, letting others glimpse the magnificence he was witnessing. He liked the idea that his letters were a legacy — or at least a record.

He looked down at his fevered body and thought, that is not the story I want to tell. I'd rather swim in the day's memories than drown in the evening's pain. As he wrote, the pain throughout his limbs faded.

Later, he managed to sit up and read some of the words aloud through cracked lips…

"I have been filled for three days with a dreamy intoxication from the serene beauty and perfect solitude. I swam in a deep pool below one waterfall and above another. The granite sides were so slippery that I could hardly draw myself out when I had frolicked enough."

His eyes wandered to the stream where he had almost drowned an hour ago and continued.

"I strode gallantly up the ridgeline, singing some Dvorak melodies 'till the forest boomed with my rollicking song. I feel so utterly, wildly, tumultuously, effervescently joyful that to me at least, the world is a riot of intense sensual delight."

The burros listened silently, swaying and staring at him.

He shrugged weakly. "No need to worry, mother."

Shortly before dawn, he fell asleep and slept for most of the next day. The fever didn't last long, but for several days he was barely able to see out of his swollen eyes.

Everett led the burros over a mountain pass with a thick blanket of snow obscuring the trail. They had difficulty forcing their way through and had to stop repeatedly. The sun was blinding, and he squinted through eyes that were still puffy from the bee stings. His face and arms were sunburnt.

"Come on, Grandma! You can do it!"

On the southern side of the pass the snow lay in patches and was melting rapidly. The sun was beginning to set, and he stopped to look around. In the green patches, the snow flowers were out, blooming with a profusion of colors. Groves of snakelike aspens rose out of the snow, and the bark of the willow trees had taken on a coppery sheen in the later afternoon sun.

Above him an eagle soared, and he watched it circle to a nest higher up the mountain.

He made camp on a promontory with a windy ledge that faced west. The distant peaks smoldered in the sun's last rays.

Then a panorama of clouds moved in, casting undulating shadows over the forests far below. From the north, this ominous storm changed direction and came right at him. One cloudbank sailed over his camp, dusting them with a flurry of snow.

The burros looked nervous.

"Don't worry," he said to them. "We'll be below the snowline tomorrow."

When the clouds parted, and he could see again, he made out Yosemite Valley shining brilliantly about twenty miles away. In the distance beyond he could see Half Dome, and Tenaya Canyon, and several lakes that flashed bronze as the last rays of sunlight hit them.

When they came off the ridge the following day, they forded a river that was so high that he had to stand on the saddle of a wild-eyed Grandma not to get wet.

On the next ridge he again spotted the granite cliffs of Yosemite in the distance.

He patted Betsy's neck. "Twenty-seven days, not bad."

Pledge to the Wind

Chapter Fifteen

Yosemite, California
(August 1933)

*B*y moonlight Everett rode Betsy, with Grandma in tow. All was quiet in the forest as they followed the trail along a river under pale tunnels of foliage.

He lingered in his saddle, watching the branches sway in the night breeze, listening to the river gurgling. These final miles were in some ways the best because he was no longer worried about supplies lasting. He also carried less, so it was easier on the burros.

He heard an owl coo in the trees above him but never got a glimpse of it. His Navajo friends would have said it was a spirit watching over him.

A Forest Service cabin appeared out of the gloom, and he hopped out of the saddle, tied Betsy's lead to a rail, and knocked on the door.

After a few minutes a ranger answered it.

"Son, do you know what time it is?" he asked gruffly.

Everett smiled. "No idea — for twenty-seven days, I've been free of watches and clocks."

The ranger exhaled. "Don't be a wise guy. It's two in the morning. You need a bed or not?"

Everett nodded and chuckled.

"Sure do," he said and then turned to grab one of his bags off of Grandma's load. "Just because I've succeeded in stopping the clock doesn't mean I couldn't use a bed."

The ranger mumbled something, then turned and went back inside. Everett unloaded the rest of his gear from Grandma, took the saddles off both burros and set them on the ground by his stacked supplies.

There was a hand-cranked pump by the side of the cabin, and he filled a bucket and watered both animals before going inside.

The next day Everett led his burros through a large campground at Yosemite National park. The place was overrun with tourists, and he walked through the entire campground, searching without success to find a quiet spot. His burros were a spectacle, and fascinated tourists took one photo after another.

A crowd of children now followed him. He liked kids, and on another occasion, he would have happily let them pet the burros. But now, he just wanted to be alone.

Across the valley floor, Half Dome rose 4,700 feet. He stopped and marveled at it. Only Zion's great White Throne, he thought, compared to this massive slab of stone. The rock glowed in the last rays of the sun; the campground was already in shadows.

He finally settled on a campsite, lit a fire, and cooked a vegetable stew.

The burros were skittish around all the people, and the automobiles scared them. Even once bedded down, they looked irritable.

He was so used to the grand silence of nature, interrupted only by the wind whistling softly through the pines, birds twittering in the morning, and crickets and cicadas calling out in the afternoon heat, that the noise in the campground grated on his nerves like nails on a chalkboard.

"I don't like it either," he said to the burros and glanced around.

About twenty feet away on his left, a man had a radio blasting the news. None of it interested him: not Max Baer of California knocking out Germany's Max Schmeling in front of a crowd of 56,000; not the bloodless coup that had overthrown the monarchy of Siam, and not even the first test launch of a rocket in Germany with which they wanted to put a man in space.

It all seemed meaningless compared to the breathtaking splendor around him.

To his right a family was arguing about who got which sleeping bag. One of the children had climbed into the car and was happily blaring the horn. Everett lost his appetite.

Even the hissing of their gas lamps annoyed him.

He looked at the burros. "We'll get out of here tomorrow."

The following morning, they moved to another campsite that couldn't be reached by car. This one was quieter, on the shore of an alpine lake with the massive stone cliffs rising beyond the trees. The few other campers here went about their business in a hushed manner.

He sat by his fire that evening, watching the surrounding hills glow orange and then fade from green to deep blue. When his fire had died down to only embers, the pines around him seemed to loom higher. Starlight poured through their branches, straight down to him.

He took out pencil and paper, and as the full moon rose and rolled through the clouds, he wrote another letter home.

He read it to the burros by the pale glow.

> *"My solitude is unbroken.*
> *Above, the white, castellated cliffs glitter*
> *fairy-like against the turquoise sky.*
> *The wild silences have enfolded me unresisting."*

Later, he watched islands of mist float dreamily over the lake, which lay dark and mysterious in the moonlight.

Deep in the night, he finally succumbed to sleep.

When the sun had risen, Everett set the burros up with fodder and water, shouldered a small pack, and started up a trail.

A sign read: HALF DOME TRAIL.

The morning was fresh, and he took in great draughts of the pine-scented air and began to ascend. The forest was still dense around him and the sunlight filtered hesitantly through the green branches.

The trail passed under a grove of giant sequoias and ponderosa pine. He stopped and looked up, stretching his neck to see the highest crowns, some of the sequoias were over two hundred and fifty feet. By comparison, the ponderosa pines looked puny.

He wondered how far he would be able to see from the top of one of the big ones. If he had brought a rope he might have attempted it, but because of the long stretches between limbs, he couldn't see how it could be done now without proper climbing gear.

He moved along, and within an hour he had left the sequoias behind, now above them on the steep mountain slope, hiking through lodgepole pines and red firs. Some of the lodgepole pines were a hundred and fifty feet tall and three feet wide, but the forest was thinning up here and didn't seem as grand. Through breaks in the trees he could glimpse the granite cliffs rising.

The red firs were similar but could be distinguished by red resin blisters that spider-webbed throughout the smooth gray bark.

He stopped to sit down at an overlook and took out his journal.

He wanted to write a letter to his father, Christopher but thought it best to prepare his thoughts first. His father had graduated *summa cum laude* from Harvard's Divinity School, and he yearned to talk with him about some of the philosophical questions that had been buzzing around his head.

He lifted his pencil, paused only briefly, and then wrote...

"Does life have infinite potentialities?"

He imagined his father quoting the Bengal thinker Rabindranath Tagore: "Life is immense." Yes, out here on the smooth, rocky slope of Half Dome, life certainly was immense.

But he was looking for the answers to deeper mysteries. Are all things possible? That was what he wanted to know.

His travels had always been marred by the need for money. He wondered, would he always be broke, dependent on odd jobs and other people's charity?

He looked at the quiet forest around him. A tapping sound broke the silence, and he spotted a white-headed woodpecker rapping on a twisted foxtail pine.

He smiled. "I'll take that as a yes."

He continued up, his journal still in his hand. After a half mile, the trees thinned out even more, and he sensed the treeline wasn't far. Then, ahead he could see where the trail led up onto the granite.

He stopped again to write...

"Can one ask too much of life?"

There were no other hikers and it was quiet. The wind whistled through the tops of the few pines that lived this far up.

Again, he thought of his father. His father believed you had to have faith — faith in God. Everett preferred to call it 'faith in life' because he hadn't made up his mind concerning a conscious God. He saw things as cause and effect, action and reaction. His father had said that the greatest givers also seemed to be the ones that got the most out of life — Jesus, Edison, DaVinci.

His father had skirted an answer to the question about asking too much of life. "The great souls," he'd said, "probably never ask that question."

Everett heard a sound and turned to see a bobcat skirting the area. The cat glanced at him, paused, and then moved on.

"Can one be happy while others are miserable?"

This question made him think of his brother, Waldo. He worked hard and had goals. Everett did not doubt that someday he'd have a great job, a lovely wife and family, and financial security, but he didn't think he was really happy. Maybe he didn't know how to be happy.

Everett wasn't so naive to think everyone could simply leave their life and take to the road. If they did, society would fall apart, and the wilderness would be ruined. But could he be happy tramping through the forests and deserts with his burros when those he loved remained behind, running on a treadmill?

That was the question.

The great ones he'd read about—Socrates or Lincoln—seemed more concerned with high goals, not personal happiness or pleasure.

Over the next few hours he followed the steep trail as it ascended the curve of the dome. The sun was high in the sky when he neared the top.

A group of hikers passed him on their way down.

They kept their silence. His gait was steady, but Everett's mind was elsewhere, and he barely noticed them.

On the summit he walked to the edge. Far across the valley, a high waterfall created long trails of vapor. Billowy, white clouds sailed across the sky above and he lay back to watch them, chewing an apple.

"Do all things follow the attainment of Truth?"

His father had said, "He whose life is completely devoted to only Truth, or only Goodness, or Beauty, is a very fractional man."

Yes, Everett thought, my life is dedicated to the pursuit of beauty. With a pang, he thought: maybe that's why I feel fractionalized. I don't always feel complete, even when surrounded by magnificence.

He walked to the edge and stepped onto a rock extending over the abyss like a diving board.

He looked down, leaning forward.

"Can one make great sacrifices without submerging oneself?"

He eyed the long drop, contemplating death. It pulled at him.

The wind picked up and pushed him forward slightly. More and more, he felt himself drifting away from a normal life—from the lives of his parents, and Waldo, and his few friends. Was this the sacrifice he needed to make if he continued on his path?

Or would he—his life—be the sacrifice?

A group of about twenty hikers arrived on the summit. They slid their packs off their backs, some of them sat down. They were laughing and joking.

One of them spotted Everett. "Hey! Be careful there."

He walked off to a secluded spot and began to chant Navajo. The song brought him back to the Southwest, to his treks through those barren deserts, and he knew he wasn't finished with them yet.

A friendly local named Fred was inspecting Betsy and Grandma while Everett picked from his gear what he could carry. The rest he planned to ship from the town of Merced to San Francisco.

"You're not askin' much for the burros," said Fred.

Everett shrugged. "It's what I paid for them."

Fred nodded. "Fair enough — I'll take 'em. Where you goin'?"

Everett made a quick glance at Half Dome, far above them, then said, "I'm gonna hitch over to San Francisco."

The man suppressed a smirk and glanced at Everett.

"I'd suggest cleaning up first."

Everett looked down at his ragged pants and said, "These are actually my good trousers."

He then walked over to Fred's truck and looked at his reflection in a side mirror. His hair was greasy and matted, and he had a scraggly beard.

"Whoa!" he said, taken aback.

Fred laughed. "If I was you, I'd just hop the freight to Sacramento. That'll get you most of the way, and it runs right through Merced every morning at eleven."

"Thanks," said Everett.

As he turned to go, Fred asked, "What you goin' to the city for?"

Everett paused. He'd been asking himself the same question.

"I want to try my hand at being an artist — maybe get some training."

"Good luck!" hollered Fred. Everett thought he would need it. He had never wanted to spend time in cities, but he felt he was ready to try — just this one time.

Chapter Sixteen

Merced, California
(September 1933)

*I*n the town of Merced, Everett shipped his saddle, kyacks and heavier gear ahead to San Francisco. The tack was too bulky, and he didn't think he could hop a freight car and carry it at the same time.

He was at the station before the sun set, looking for a train heading west. An old bum was lounging in the shadows across from the platform, watching him.

After a minute the man ambled over and approached Everett.

"You gettin' ready to hop one of these gondolas?" he asked.

Everett gave him a blank look. "Gondolas?"

The old man's clothing was dirty and worn and he had long, unkempt hair. Everett guessed he was a train tramp. The bum laughed. "Well, they ain't all gondolas. A gondola is a train car without a roof, the easiest to climb on when the train is runnin' because you don't have to worry none about the door bein' locked."

The bum looked up and down the track, and Everett realized he wasn't searching for a train as much as for railroad employees assigned to keep the train and station clear of tramps.

"Where you headin'?" he asked.

Everett nodded toward the setting sun. "San Francisco."

The older man nodded. "If I was you," he said, "I'd clear out of here 'til 'bout 10:30. At 11:00, the hotshot passes through on the way to Sacramento. That'll get ya started."

The two watched a railroad employee step out of his office and look around.

The bum continued. "If they don't see you lurkin' around now, they won't worry about you bein' here later. Get me? Go lay low for a few hours."

Everett nodded, shouldered the small pack he'd kept with him, and walked around the little town as evening descended and the shadows thickened.

When the stars were shining brightly, he returned and found the bum a short way down the track. He waved to Everett, and when he reached him, said, "Better to get on after they pass a station—even at night, there're eyes."

He sized Everett up and asked, "You ever hopped a train before?"

Everett shook his head and the bum said, "You just follow me—it's easy! Just don't trip and fall under."

Soon a train whistle blew in the distance, and the bum whispered, "That's us!"

They watched as the train pulled into Merced, and men unloaded several hand trucks of boxes from one of the back cars. Ten minutes later it chugged out of the station, roaring as it came at them.

The two men stepped closer to the track and fell into a trot, watching it approach over their shoulders. They were running in a mad grab for the metal ladders bolted to the sides.

The bum got on first, and Everett nervously sprinted alongside the train until he cleared off the ladder. Then Everett grabbed the ladder and jumped onto the lowest rung.

When they were settled on their backs, in the middle of the car, the bum said, "The gondolas are the easiest to board, but we don't want to spend the night in the open. Let's look 'round and see what kind of accommodation this place has got."

The bum glanced at Everett, who was looking up at the stars.

"You did good, kid."

Everett smiled back and extended his hand. "Everett."

The bum gave up his biggest smile, but not his name, and shook hands. "You can ride with me anytime."

Everett was lounging in a freight car filled with cantaloupes with two young men and the older bum. One of the young men was a cowboy named Jimmy, and the other a Canadian, Patrick. Both were around twenty. They were all sprawled on top of the fruit, trying not to smash any.

The bum warned them to watch out for the security patrols that checked the carts every so often, but he didn't think there'd be any before the next town—Stockton.

There was a small light in the car, and under its glow, the bum looked ancient. He smelled horrible, too, but he'd been helpful, and Everett ignored the stench as best he could.

They opened one of the fruits with a knife the cowboy carried and were passing around slices.

Patrick said, "It doesn't get any better than this."

Everett ate a big bite and said, "I'm gonna be sick of cantaloupes by the time we get to Sacramento."

The bum shook his head. "You won't get there if you stay in this car. The freight shunts cars back and forth at every stop, and the back end of this train is goin' south at Modesto."

Jimmy said, "Don't worry, we'll move up before then."

They feasted on several more cantaloupes and traded stories. Patrick had been in the Calgary militia. He claimed he could break down a machine gun and load it, on a horse, in two minutes. He'd been down in Mexico with a pal and lost him down there.

Everett asked, "What do you mean, lost? Did he get thrown in jail or die?"

Patrick remained silent. Either he didn't hear the question over the din of the train, or he didn't want to talk about it.

Everett let it drop.

Soon the rocking motion of the train set Everett to sleep. He drifted, swaying from side to side, all sound obscured by the clickity-clack from the tracks below. He dreamt of the dancing tumbleweeds. They were leaping into the air and spinning in circles, slowly, like they were drunk on life.

And then he was out of the desert, dreaming still, but now of Pat and Tad, who'd picked him up outside of Tuba City. He heard Pat ask, "What'll you do when you get old?"

In the dream he laughed, "Old? What's that? As long as I can move, I'll seek out the open spaces—and as long as there are new lands for me to explore, I'll always be young."

"Everett, wake up!" shouted Jimmy, "We gotta move!"

He grabbed his gear and swung out through the open door. He climbed a ladder up onto the roof of the train.

The bum shouted after them, "Good luck, boys!"

Patrick led the way as they ran along the speeding train, leaping from one car to another. Jimmy whooped with joy every time he made the crazy jump to the next car. The stars shone brilliantly above them, but the night was otherwise dark, and it wasn't always clear where one car ended and the next began.

But Patrick's excitement was contagious, and Everett found himself hooting as well, forgetting his fear, fueled on by the blur of the countryside blazing by and the tracks whizzing by beneath them.

The powerful rattling of the train over the tracks had turned into a symphony of percussions in his head.

When they were a few cars from the engine up front, they sat and watched the countryside pass by. Houses whizzed past, lit only by a few lights this late at night. What humdrum lives might be lived there? Everett thought: if only they knew the crazy life I'm living! If only they could break away and truly feel free and alive like I do!

He whooped again and held both hands over his head, letting the wind whistle through them.

The train slowed as it approached Modesto, and from the top, they watched how several cars in the back swung off to a side track.

They continued until they passed through Stockton, where Jimmy hopped off. The bum had informed him that the train would continue to Roseville, the division line, and then pass by Sacramento and eventually stop at Oakland.

"How long are you staying on?" Everett asked Patrick.

"I'll take anything going north," he answered. "I'm trying to get to Calgary. That old guy said at Roseville I'd find a northbound."

It was now close to dawn, and it was cold up top. Patrick shivered and said, "I'm gonna scout out below and see if I can find an empty cart."

Everett smiled. "What a thrilling ride! I feel like an eagle soaring above the land! How far do you think to Roseville?"

Patrick shrugged. "Maybe an hour yet—around dawn."

"I'm gonna stay here—I'll find you when they start braking."

Patrick nodded and left. Everett watched the houses tick by. He stretched his arms out at his sides and let the wind fill his cupped hands. He let his fingers ripple like they were the tips of feathers. His hair blew about wildly.

They reached Roseville as the eastern sky was beginning to lighten. The crescent moon, which had risen so late in the night, now began to fade, and the stars paled.

The train stopped, and Patrick and Everett both got off.

Another train tramp, an older woman named Patty, nodded at them when they were clear of the train. Everett gestured at the train they had just hopped off and asked, "This still going to Oakland?"

Patty nodded. "I'd say in two hours it will. They gonna add a few cars first."

She also told them there'd be a train heading north about the same time.

About a block away, Everett found a café that was just opening and bought bacon and eggs breakfasts for himself and the Canadian, for twenty cents each.

The northbound came in first, and Everett shook his new friend's hand and then watched him hop the freight and pull away, waving.

The Oakland-bound train was two hours late in departing, but he watched them couple the cars and was ready. While waiting he spotted a few other tramps lurking in the shadows.

He hopped on about a quarter-mile beyond the station. He had just settled down on a gondola when he saw Patty sitting on a hill overlooking the tracks, watching to see who was rolling out of town.

The train clipped along at a good speed until they passed Sacramento, and then it went even faster. They must have gotten up to forty miles per hour in the straight stretches.

They passed salt marshes, and the salt in the air made him look forward to seeing the Bay and the distant ocean. After all his time in the mountains, he now yearned for the sea.

In the late afternoon, the train reached Oakland, and he hopped off just short of the station. It took him the rest of the day to walk the twelve miles to San Francisco along US 80.

When the highway led onto a bridge that spanned the bay, he stopped and smelled the sea. The salty richness of the scent helped dispel the sadness of leaving the mountains.

He stepped up his pace.

But the cars roared by him at an obnoxious pace, and clouds of exhaust and the anxious horn blasts made him question his destination.

He stepped off the Bay Bridge into San Francisco and walked north toward Telegraph Hill, where Ed Weston had suggested staying because of its proximity to many paintable vistas.

The city seemed a riot of faces and noises, which initially intimidated him, but then drew him in. I won't stay here long, he told himself—just enough time to get in some training.

A friendly clerk at a hotel on Broadway Street allowed him to stow his gear in a back room for a few hours, and before midday, he'd found a cheap room.

Chapter Seventeen

Ansel Adams Gallery, San Francisco, California
(October 1933)

The gallery had a special showing of black-and-white images of Yosemite. Everett shuffled from one to the next and studied each, remembering the land as he'd seen it. A few, like one of Half Dome, were shot from unfamiliar angles, and he wondered where Adams had taken the photo from.

He had traded his worn tramping gear for respectable clothes and was carrying his artwork under his arm. He looked down at the clean button-up shirt his mother had sent ahead of him and silently thanked her for her foresight. In the same box had been his record collection, more clothes, and an envelope with some cash towards his first month's rent.

By a small desk stood a pretty young receptionist sporting a short, stylish haircut and a silky dress. She watched him and finally approached. Her name was Frances. The whiff of her sweet perfume left him dizzy and tongue-tied for a moment.

"Hi, can I help you?" she asked.

Everett fidgeted. "Y... yes, I'd like to talk to Mr. Adams."

She smiled patiently. "I'm sure you would, but he's a very busy guy."

Just then a man in his mid-thirties walked through the lobby, carrying a print he'd just signed. He handed it to Frances.

Everett recognized Adams at once, and before Frances could stop him, he said, "Mr. Adams, I'm a big fan of your work."

Ansel Adams stopped and smiled.

"Is that so?" he asked, "Which one do you like?"

Everett nodded at a large, mounted print to their right.

"I particularly like that image of the mysterious lake. Did you take it from the Kaweah Gap?"

Adams looked at Everett and raised an eyebrow, surprised that he knew where the Gap was.

"I did," he answered. "Have you been there?"

"Yes, in July, I traversed the Sierras with several burros. Unfortunately, I didn't paint as much as I hoped I would, but I did complete some nice sketches."

Adams nodded. "I miss those mountains terribly when I'm away from them."

Everett glanced toward the street. "To be honest, I had a hard time leaving them too."

Adams looked at the artwork Everett was holding.

"May I see?"

Everett displayed the sketches and watercolors. Adams nodded approvingly and flipped through them.

He paused at one of Monument Valley, and Everett quickly said, "That's more of a template—I also make block prints."

Adams nodded. "From linoleum?"

Before Everett could answer, Adams said, "These are quite good. What's your name?"

Everett grinned and extended his hand.

"I'm Everett Ruess. A mutual friend of ours, Edward Weston, told me to look you up."

Ansel flipped through the images again.

He then paused and assessed the young man and said, "Well, Edward certainly recognizes talent when he sees it. Would you consider trading some art?"

Everett beamed. "Sure. Any chance you'd display them here?"

Adams laughed. "Can't do that, but I'd be happy to tell you some places that might."

Frances had been watching Everett from the corner of the gallery. With his tanned skin and the light in his eyes that jumped around when he spoke, he seemed like a cat, she thought. Something wild.

He had approached Ansel Adams like they were old friends. Clearly, he didn't know how famous Adams was. Everett made a casual joke and she laughed along with them.

He looked over at her, and she caught his eye and smiled.

Finally, Everett left with one of Adams´ images under his arm. Frances followed him to the door.

She opened it for him and said with a smile, "Thank you for stopping by, Mr. Ruess."

"Please, call me Everett."

She paused for only a moment. "Would you like to have a coffee with me when I get off, Everett?"

Everett was sitting across from Frances at a table in a small coffee shop. He was twiddling a spoon.

"So, you've only recently arrived in San Francisco?" she asked.

He nodded, his confidence returning. "Yes, what a fantastic city! In a way I'd been dreading it, and I was afraid I would hate it here?"

"Hate San Francisco?" she exclaimed, laughing. "That's absurd."

"It feels that way now—there's so much to do here," said Everett. "But for the last four months, I've been surrounded by whispering pines and towering cliffs, and when I first showed up, it was more than a little intimidating."

The waitress set down two cups of black coffee. Frances delicately poured two spoonfuls of sugar into hers, then added cream.

Everett sipped his black. He looked at the window that faced the street and said, "And the wind. I was always surrounded by the wind—not like now, being indoors a lot."

He tapped the glass.

He hoped she'd enquire about the mountains or the wind, but she seemed uninterested. He stirred his coffee with the spoon.

Instead, she asked, "What have you done since you arrived?"

He looked up from his cup, his eyes twinkling. "Everything! When I first got here I went to every gallery I could find, looking for dealers who might display my work, but I've also gone to lectures by Lincoln Steffens and Rockwell Kent."

She raised an eyebrow at the mention of Steffens, who was known for his articles on corruption in American cities, but then shrugged and said, "I've never heard of Kent."

"Oh, he's fantastic," said Everett enthusiastically. "He's traveled all over Greenland and Alaska making wood prints."

Her attention was drawn away by a new convertible Chrysler that parked in the street, right in front of the window. He watched her eyes sweep over the whitewall tires and shiny chrome.

After a moment she returned. "Did you have any luck selling your prints to galleries?"

He smiled proudly. "Paul Elder took a dozen."

She looked up hopefully. "He bought them?"

Everett stirred his coffee again. "Well, no. He took them on consignment."

Frances looked at the clock.

"Do you have much more art to sell?" she asked.

Everett nodded. "Yes, I've been very busy. My apartment is full of sketches and paintings."

She gulped down half of her coffee and got up.

"Why don't we go back to your place so that you can show me?"

Everett's apartment was tiny and almost empty except for a variety of images tacked to the wall. Most were watercolors, but there were also oils and sketches. There was one small mattress in one corner, a chair by an easel against the far wall, a pile of gear including a crate, the saddle and kyacks, and his poncho in the other corner.

A simple table served as his desk and kitchen. It was pinned against the wall beneath the one window that faced the street. A side door led to a bathroom with a toilet and sink.

Frances peeked in and noticed a space along the wall where a tub had once been. She gave him a quizzical look. Everett said, "The landlord said the tub disappeared last month when the place was empty. At least there's a sink with running water, hot and cold."

He nervously added, "I haven't put much time into furnishing the place."

She smiled. "Maybe it needs a woman's touch."

One wall had three of his black and white block prints hung on it, clustered together like windows to the southwest. Frances admired them. She liked them more than what he had shown Ansel Adams at the gallery.

He set his new Ansel Adams print against the wall and then searched through his gear for a nail. When he found one, he stepped outside quickly and returned with a hand-sized rock.

He faced the wall opposite his block prints, deciding where to hang the image. Frances moved next to him.

"So, you know Edward Weston?" she asked. "I think his nude images are moving."

She leaned against him slightly.

He nodded. "Yes. He's taught me a lot."

Everett stepped forward and pounded the nail into the wall with the rock as a hammer. Then he fastened a hanging hook to the back of the print.

He hung it and stepped back.

"Did you hear Ansel Adams waxing poetic over my art today?"

She smiled and touched his hand. "I did."

Frances leaned over and kissed him.

Later, it was dark out, and the two lay side by side on his mattress. A neon light bathed the curtains in a rosy glow. Everett's face glowed, and he looked like he'd just won the lottery.

A sombrero hung from a hook near the bed. She didn't believe him when he said he wore it in public. A rolled bundle of blankets lay on the floor beneath it. She asked, "Do you have a dog?"

"No," he replied, "that's my bedroll. I picked it up when I traveled through the Southwest, and it was of good use in the Sierras, too."

She swallowed and then said, "Well, it does look well-used."

He nodded enthusiastically. "Yes, I shipped everything from Merced, and it just arrived."

She snuggled up against him. "At least you don't need it now, here in the civilized world."

His mother had also sent a set of sheets, so he had no need for the bedroll, but still, he tensed slightly at 'civilized.' He let it drop and smiled. "Not unless it gets cold."

Frances propped herself up on her elbows and looked around the room. "What do you do about meals?"

He shook his head. "Can't cook in here, but I get along fabulously on fruit, sandwiches, and milk."

She threw him a sideways glance and frowned.

"I don't even see a clock here — how do you know what time it is?" she asked.

He smirked. "I never wonder what time it is because, for myself, it is always time to live."

She looked at him. "You are a strange person, Everett."

He nodded. "Maybe I've spent too much time alone — but beauty and peace have been with me, wherever I have gone."

Before she could respond he jumped up and grabbed one of his journals. He flipped through it quickly, found the page he was looking for and read out loud:

"On the lake at night, the crescent moon gleams liquidly in the dark water, mists drift and rise like lifting enchantments, and tall, shadowed peaks stand guard in watchful silence."

"That's lovely," she said.

He exhaled audibly.

"I wish I could share my work with more people, but I rarely find the opportunity."

He flipped through another couple of pages. "This one is about the Colorado river," he said,

138

"I have watched white-maned rapids, shaking their crests in wild abandon, surging, roaring, overwhelming the senses with their white fury, only to froth and foam down the current into lucent green pools, quiet and clear in the mellow sunlight."

"You certainly have a way with words," she said.

He blushed, filled with warmth.

"I'm getting better at expressing what's inside of me. But you should read J. Alfred Prufrock's *Love Song*. Now there's someone who can capture a sentiment!"

Frances snuggled closer to him again. The lights outside blinked steadily, and by their glow, Everett read one more excerpt.

"At night, I have watched pale granite towers in the dim starlight, aspiring to the powdered sky, tremulous and dreamlike, fantastical in the melting darkness."

Chapter Eighteen

The Dixon Home, San Francisco, California
(November 1933)

*E*verett knocked on the door of Maynard Dixon, a prominent painter who'd crisscrossed the southwest capturing landscapes in oil and watercolor. He had wanted to meet the man for a long time, and now that he was in San Francisco, the moment had finally arrived.

After barely a minute, he knocked again, until finally a man in his late fifties, holding a paintbrush, answered the door.

"Can I help you?" the man asked. He looked like a rugged remnant of the Wild West. He was wearing a white, buttoned shirt tucked into his jeans, and his thick mustache and weather-beaten face gave him the appearance of a cowboy from the 1880s.

A cowboy that seemed upset about being drawn away from his work, Everett noticed.

He blurted out, "My name is Everett Ruess. I've always wanted to meet you."

The man scratched his head with the wooden end of the paintbrush.

"Maybe you should have set up an appointment."

Everett gave him his best smile. "I suppose I should've. It's just that you and I have been to a lot of the same places in the Southwest, and I thought it would be interesting to talk."

Dixon looked down at the youth, who seemed too young to be off on his own. "I've seen quite a bit of the Southwest," he said. "What areas have we both been to?"

Everett laughed. "I think, most of them. I've done some watercolors in Canyon de Chelly and Monument Valley, but when I look at yours, I see I'm missing something."

Now Dixon smiled back. He could have come up with some excuse and sent him on his way, but there was something about this young man that made him want to know more. His enthusiasm was contagious, but there was also a look in his eyes that intrigued him. It seemed to remind him of his early days tramping throughout the Southwest.

He asked Everett, "What is it exactly that you see in my paintings?"

Everett closed his eyes and pictured the dozens of Dixon's paintings he'd seen over the years. He thought they all had a depth of emotion embedded in them that transcended paint and water. "You paint the feel of a place," mumbled Everett.

"Why don't you come inside?" said Maynard and motioned for him to follow.

Everett's gaze was immediately drawn to the walls, which were decorated with paintings and photographs. The paintings were of scenes from the southwest, but most of the photographs were portraits of people and didn't look like Dixon's work; they were penetrating and seemed to capture the very essence of the subjects.

Souvenirs from Dixon's travels sat on the window sill: a *katsina* doll from Hopi land, a leather bullwhip from Santa Fe, a collection of arrowheads.

Dixon held up the paintbrush. "Let me put this away," he said and disappeared into a back room.

Everett walked around and examined the images on the wall. He figured that the photographs were by Dixon's wife, Dorothea Lange.

He heard footsteps, and a woman in her late thirties with short, dark hair entered the room. She had a cosmopolitan air, a black scarf thrown loosely over her shoulder, and he assumed correctly that this was Dorothea.

"Hello," she said to Everett. "I didn't know we had company."

Dixon returned from the other room. "Honey, this is Mr. Everett Ruess. He's just stopped by to introduce himself."

There was a twinkle in Dorothea's eyes as she studied Everett.

"How bold of you," she said. "Are you an artist?"

He nodded excitedly. "Yes, ma´am, I am. I came to San Francisco to make my mark on the art world."

Dorothea slowly circled Everett, squinting at his face with an artist's eye.

Everett squirmed a bit under her gaze.

She glanced at her husband and said, "Maynard, look at that face. I must photograph it—such a beguiling mix of innocence and sensuality."

Everett blushed.

She noticed his discomfort and backed off a bit. "And how has San Francisco been treating you? Have you managed to sell much of your work?"

He looked at his shoes. "Not really, but I have traded some for concert tickets. I've been in the mountains and I'm a bit starved for music."

Dorothea looked at Everett again. His face appeared to be one that often smiled, with a glow on his cheeks and slight wrinkles at the corners of his eyes, but it also looked gaunt.

She said, "Young man, *you* look a bit starved. When's the last time you had a hot meal?"

He shrugged. "I eat a lot of fruit and sandwiches, but I've only had a few cooked meals in the last two weeks."

Dorothea glanced at Maynard once again.

"I was just setting out our dinner," she said. "Why don't you join us?"

On the way to the dining room they passed a Victrola.

"Oh, how I missed music in the Sierras," said Everett. "I could replay the orchestra in my head, but there's nothing like going to the opera."

"You like the opera? How wonderful!" exclaimed Dorothea as she pushed in Everett's chair behind him. She made sure he had cutlery and a glass of water before she sat down.

"Yes, I do," said Everett. "I hope to go as soon as I bring in a little ticket money."

She handed him a dish of mashed potatoes and said, "Well, allow me to take you to your first opera in San Francisco. God knows it would take an army to get him to go with me."

Dixon laughed. "You'd be doing me a favor, Everett. I'm no fan of the opera."

Everett swallowed a mouthful of potatoes and said, "My mother sent up my collection of records, but I've no player. I could lend them to you until I get settled — they're quite good."

Dixon laughed again. "For some reason we don't use the Victrola often."

He smiled at Everett. "Tell you what. I've got a storage room that I'd like to turn into a second art studio. If you help me clean it out, I'll let you borrow the Victrola."

Everett grinned like a dog that just scored a steak.

Over the next week, Everett helped Dixon clean out the crowded room, carrying boxes and sweeping up trash. They rolled a fresh coat of paint onto the walls and washed the windows, and soon it was a workable studio.

"You're sure this is okay?" asked Everett as he carried the Victrola down to Dixon's automobile.

"Sure," Dixon said, "no problem at all. I've got more chores if you're willing."

Everett smiled. "Just tell me what you want done."

Chapter Nineteen

Telegraph Hill, San Francisco, California
(December 1933)

*F*rom the tower on Telegraph Hill, Everett and Frances watched the Bay. Far off to the west, beyond the Golden Gate Bridge, the sun set in a puddle of orange. Sailboats cruised through the sparkling water, and the late afternoon rays lighted up several small islands.

They had walked from his room on Polk Street, off-Broadway, about a mile and a half away, and all the hills had Frances a bit winded.

"I wish we'd found a cable car," she said.

Everett looked at her. "I did try to find a place in this neighborhood but had no luck. But I love walking through this city!"

She frowned, and he stopped. He said, "I guess I've been inconsiderate. I walk everywhere and didn't think you would mind. We'll take the trolley back."

They were on the overlook now, and together they gazed out over the water. Everett took a deep breath of the air sweeping in from the Bay. "In the morning, when I take my stroll to the post office, the sunlight is magical. As is the birdsong."

She sighed. "I do love this city, but I find your knack for walking a bit excessive."

He laughed. "I walked seven miles yesterday looking for new vistas to paint, and then another couple when I met Dorothea at the Opera House. We heard Mischa Elman."

Frances sounded casual as she asked, "Who is Dorothea?"

"Oh, that's Maynard Dixon's wife, Dorothea Lange—she's a very talented photographer."

"You like her?" asked Frances innocently.

Everett said, "Yes, of course—she's great."

Frances nodded. A pang of jealousy took hold of her, yet she wasn't sure what she thought of Everett at all. One moment he was the best aspiring artist she'd ever met, and the next, he was little better than a street pauper. She had hoped their date would take place in a nice restaurant, but Everett seemed more intent on showing her the views from the city.

The light was fading.

"Let's go visit my friend Tengel," he said, "his place isn't far."

Tengel was a wiry little man who lived in half of a shack on stilts above a courtyard littered with chickens. Everett led Frances through a small alley where they could already smell the birds.

"Don't worry," said Everett, "after a few minutes, you won't notice the stench."

Frances nodded incredulously. Her eyes were watering from the acrid odor.

There were two shacks side by side. A space of about two feet separated them. The two facing windows were open, so you could see right into the other shack like it was another room in the same house.

Tengel grinned widely when he saw Everett. He was in his forties, sloppily dressed in a hole-riddled shirt and a pair of worn black pants that he held up with suspenders. He was missing his two front teeth, but that didn't prevent his smile from warming Everett's heart.

Everett thought he was one of the most interesting and exciting men he had ever met. Together they talk about music, and books, and traveling the world. The man read very slowly, but he was perceptive and fun to talk with about various writers.

"Come in! Come in!" he shouted and held the door. He stepped to a battered chair and slid it over, so Frances could sit.

Aside from a rickety old twin bed, a few wooden boxes, and a low table, there wasn't much furniture. One corner of the room was a kitchen with little more than a hotplate and a few mismatched dishes.

Frances sat in the only chair, so Everett flopped down on the bed, and Tengel continued to stand.

By the bed stood an old bookcase with about forty well-used books. Tengel caught Frances looking at them and pointed proudly.

He said, "It was reading those that brought Everett and me together."

"Yes," said Everett. "I met him at the library when I went to pick up my card. We've been exchanging books since then."

"So, you two read together?" asked Frances uneasily.

"Yes," said Everett. He picked up a copy of *The Brothers Karamazov* and flipped through it. "One of us finds a good book, and we share it. So far, we have read *South Wind*, *Candide* and *Arabian Nights*, and this one," he said, holding up the heavy book, "we're still trying to get through."

A large man in a sleeveless t-shirt was cutting up some meat in the other shack. He had a big gut and was focused on the blade and the cutting board.

"That's Antonio," said Everett. "He's wanted for murder in Italy, so he fled to America."

"Murder?" asked Frances. "What's he doing now? Is he a butcher?"

"No, he's just making something to eat."

Antonio turned and smiled at the three. He waved with one bloody hand. Then he lifted the knife in the other and touched his forehead like he was saluting.

He shouted, "Heya!"

"How are you, Antonio?" shouted Everett.

The response Antonio shouted back was incomprehensible — half Italian, half English.

Tengel laughed and said, "His English isn't so good."

"He's a good chap," said Everett. "He lets me borrow his bicycle when I need it."

In the shack next door Antonio brought the blade down hard on the chopping board, and Frances jumped in her seat.

Tengel said proudly. "Everett and I have also gone to the opera."

Frances looked at Tengel. "Really?" She put her hands on her hips and said, "It appears everyone but me has gone to the opera with Everett."

Tengel held up his palms. "I didn't have money for a ticket, but Everett showed me the best seats in the house—and they was free."

Frances glanced at Everett and raised an eyebrow.

"Well, we went to see Rimsky-Korsakov's *The Golden Cockerel,* but it was sold out—even the balcony seats—so we snuck in the backdoor and sat in the hallway."

Tengel nodded enthusiastically.

"You didn't have seats?" she asked.

"No, we couldn't even see the stage. But the hallway was perfect. What a show!"

Tengel reached by his bed and produced a bottle of wine. He pulled the cork and poured some in a cup and handed it to Frances. Then he put his hand on Everett's shoulder. "Everett has brought color to my life. He is a good friend."

"I think it's a fair trade," said Everett. "He's been teaching me about jazz."

Tengel took a swig off the bottle and said, "Yesterday, we found some good used records at the corner shop. I think you'll like the Louis Armstrong, and who was the other one?"

Everett said, "Dizzy Gillespie."

Suddenly Tengel began gyrating his arms and bouncing around to a crazy beat in his head. He pounded an imaginary drum in front of him, and Frances was taken aback when he started shouting,

"Dizzzzzeeee!... dum dum dum de de dum!"

Everett chimed in when the verse repeated, jumping to his feet and stepping to the beat.

"Goodness," said Frances.

"I agree, it's not as orderly as the opera," said Everett and settled down, "but just as moving. It makes me want to climb something."

His face was flushed, and Frances noticed the glow in his eyes. She took a sip of her wine and then puckered her mouth at the sour cabernet.

"I think I'll stick with the opera."

Everett shrugged it off. "I still love the opera. If we can each scrape up some cash, we plan to go to the Grand Opera to see *Tristan and Isolde* — for a dollar, you can stand in the balcony."

Frances raised her eyebrows, hoping Everett wouldn't ask her to stand all evening.

Maynard Dixon paused in front of a photograph, holding up a scrap of black paper so that it obscured part of the image. He was with Everett in the studio that Everett had helped clean out, and rain was streaming down the windows that lined one wall.

He said to Everett, "This is a good trick to see what truly is essential in an image. When I move the paper around, can you see how certain elements aren't essential?"

Everett nodded.

Maynard added, "Of course, in photography, you have to accept what appears in the viewfinder of your camera. As painters, we can decide what to include, and just as important, what to leave out."

Everett took the scrap of paper and began moving it in front of other objects in the room. "This is very cool."

"Have you completed any work since you've gotten to San Francisco?" asked Maynard.

Everett looked out the window. He felt like he hadn't been very productive.

"I've done two good watercolors and a couple of black and white crayon sketches."

Maynard nodded. "What are you sketching with?"

"I use a china marking pencil. It gives plenty of gradation without smudging."

A small cough came from behind them, and they turned to see Frances and Dorothea standing in the doorway, watching.

"What kind of trouble are you boys getting into?" asked Dorothea.

"Just an art lesson," said Maynard. He glanced at Frances and added, "We're just finishing here."

"Yes," said Everett, "Frances and I are going to Telegraph Hill so that I can do some work. They hold classes there for fifty cents and I thought I might attend one."

He looked at Frances and said, "I hope I haven't kept you waiting."

She shook her head. "I just got here. It's rather bracing outside — and a fog has rolled in. Are you sure you want to go?"

"Definitely! But I better grab my poncho," said Everett.

Frances said, "Not if you want to be seen in public with me."

Dorothea watched them talk from the doorway, wondering what they had in common and how far this relationship might go. Everett didn't grab his poncho, but she sensed he didn't like Frances telling him what to do.

Later that day, Everett and Frances walked through the Telegraph Hill area. On the way he stopped once for an hour to sketch out an old water tower, and then again later, he painted a eucalyptus tree by the water. For most of the time a sporadic drizzle had pursued them, and they had moved along from one awning to another.

When he paused again to paint some fuchsias in bloom, Frances tugged on his arm.

"This is getting boring — could we go somewhere for a coffee?"

"Sure. Let's just swing by the apartment and drop off my supplies."

In Everett's apartment, they found Tengel sitting in a washbasin in the middle of the room, taking a bath.

"Oh, hello!" he shouted.

Frances averted her eyes.

"Don't mind him," said Everett. "We found this old tub, and my place was closer than his, so we brought it here."

He looked at Tengel. "We'll be out of your hair in a minute."

Tengel smirked. "Not a problem. Been a long time since I had a bath, thank you."

Everett placed his art supplies in the corner and noticed two little glasses he'd purchased at a yard sale.

"Look at these," he said to Frances. They were purple and blue, and when he held them up to the light, they glowed.

"They're like wine for the soul," he said. "Aren't the light and colors stunning?"

Frances held one up to the bare light bulb in the ceiling. "They are quite lovely," she said. "Look how the light passes through them and brings out the color."

She set the glass down. Then, Everett said, "I'm thinking about giving them to Dorothea—you know, she took me to the opera the other night, and afterward, she introduced me to the composer."

Frances studied the glasses again and said, "If you haven't already promised them to Mrs. Dixon, I could use them."

Everett paused for only a moment, then said, "Sure... you can have them."

It rained for most of the following week. Everett went out regardless, wearing his sombrero and poncho when Frances wasn't with him. He stopped in a dozen galleries and got some of them to display his work on consignment.

Dorothea offered to photograph him, and he nervously cleaned his black cowboy hat for the shoot. When he arrived at her house, he called Frances to tell her about the session.

"She is quite talented," said Everett. "I'm very lucky she wants to take my photo."

Frances was quiet on the line, then asked to stop by his place after the shoot.

It poured down heavily that afternoon, and Everett made it back to his place feeling half-drowned. He had been restless during the photography session and was glad to be back in his rented room where he didn't feel so put on the spot. The storm outside was building. The skies darkened, and then lightning flickered.

The windows vibrated with the thunder.

Everett put on the Louis Armstrong record he had purchased with Tengel. The first song was *Ain't Misbehavin*.

Another flash of lightning lit the room and he turned up the volume, so the melodic leaps of the trumpet mixed with the rumble of thunder.

He danced to the melody, and when Armstrong launched into a string of gravely scat, Everett spun in circles.

Armstrong continued with the chorus...

> *"No one to talk with, all by myself*
> *No one to walk with, I'm happy on the shelf babe*
> *Ain't misbehavin', savin' my love for you"*

The storm had passed, and it was dark out. Frances was late. He was troubled by the uncertain signals he got from her but wasn't in the mood to fret. Instead, he focused on the good things he had experienced in San Francisco.

He decided to write a letter home and read the first paragraph out loud.

"Dear Family,
I'm on the crest of the wave again as I hope you are, too. I have finally found myself, and have been busy painting. Yesterday I heard four symphonies, and then spent the evening with Maynard Dixon, his wife Dorothea, and some other artists. I had a grand time, and it was certainly good to be among friends and artists again."

He rose and flipped the Armstrong record to listen to *Black and Blue*. This was a mellower song, and the lyrics suddenly seemed to illustrate the emptiness he was feeling in his heart now that he sensed Frances wasn't coming.

"Cold empty bed, springs hard as lead
Pains in my head, feel like old Ned
What did I do to be so black and blue?"

When Frances finally did show up, she looked unhappy. She sat by the window, looking out over the wet city. Water was pouring out through gutters and running along the street.

Everett showed her an arrowhead from the Grand Canyon and told her how he had found it, but she seemed to be barely listening. He got her a glass of wine and played Beethoven's *Moonlight Sonata* on the Victrola. This wasn't the time for jazz.

It got dark out, and the streetlights reflected off the slick pavement. Everett gazed down at the street and said, "I stayed in a place called Oljeto once. The word means 'moonlight on water.'"

Frances smiled at him but didn't say anything.

He sighed, "My emotions seem to be all over the place. One moment I'm ecstatic, then the next, I'm submerged in an undercurrent of unrest. Maybe San Francisco isn't the place for me — half the time I'm broke or without money for carfare and telephone."

She sipped her wine and watched the rain.

"Do you like me, Everett?" she asked.

He stared at her, surprised she needed to ask. "Of course!"

"Well, do you like San Francisco? You always talk about leaving."

He nodded. "I do like it here — I'm just still drawn to the wilderness. Would you ever consider traveling with me?"

She shook her head. "Not to some dusty canyon."

"How about Europe. I've always wanted to go there."

She frowned. "Why do people go there? It all seems so old. Besides, we live in one of the greatest cities on earth. Why go anywhere?"

A gust of wind splattered the glass with rain.

"I don't know how long I can stay away from the desert. I guess it's just my nature to follow beauty where it leads me."

She nodded. "And you don't think you could change your nature?"

He thought for only a moment. "I doubt it."

Chapter Twenty

Polk Street, San Francisco, California
(January 1934)

*C*andlelight flickered on the walls of Everett's small room. It lit up the prints of the southwest like flashing lightning and created weird shadows on the Adams print.

His saddle and kyacks lay piled in the corner, gathering dust.

On the floor in the other corner, the Victrola played Dizzy Gillespie again, and Everett danced in the yellow glow. His shadows on the wall looked otherworldly as he jumped about, releasing restless energy.

On his small desk lay a half-finished letter.

When the song ended he lifted the needle, then sat up to the desk again. He paused over the letter, pencil suspended. He looked out the window at the dark night, made even more ominous by the scattered showers that had left streaks on the glass.

"Dear Frances,
I've just acquired the most heart-rending symphony you ever heard. You must come to my mean hovel Saturday night to hear it. I have to share it with you."

The record finished, and he replaced it with Frank's *Sierra Symphony*. Finally, he put his head down and finished the final line on a letter to Frances.

"Don't refuse, for I must see you. I have laid in store some Roquefort cheese as a special inducement. I saw two girls on the streets this morning who reminded me of you."

He put the letter in an envelope and danced around his room in the dark. Wanting her to come, needing her. He wished with all of his heart that she could see his world, and maybe if he were patient, she would understand the magnificence that drove him into the wilderness.

All Saturday Everett was a nervous mess. In the morning he had visited Tengel, who'd noticed his anxiety right away and accompanied him back to the small apartment so the two of them could clean it nicely before Frances arrived.

They washed his few dishes, moved the tub into the bathroom, and swept the floor. Then Everett decided to get some flowers. He burned with restless energy and walked a four-mile loop through the city until he came across some lilacs in bloom, which he trimmed and brought home.

The rain began halfway through his walk and when he stepped back into his apartment he was thoroughly soaked.

Later that night, a bottle of wine sat on the table with a plate of Roquefort. The Victrola played a classical melody by Mozart, and Everett danced around the room, anticipating Frances' arrival.

An easel was set up with a nearly completed portrait of Frances.

Everett walked to the window and glanced from the painting down at the street, wondering how late she would be. Should he take offense? Or was this just part of the courting ritual?

A few days earlier he'd purchased a magazine that featured several of Maynard Dixon's paintings. He picked it up off the floor and flipped through it now.

One image caught his attention. It was of a young Indian woman, wrapped in a blanket, looking over the land as the sun rose in the distance.

Instantly, Everett thought of Notah's assistant. He couldn't see the face of the woman in the painting, but he felt it was her.

He glanced at the unfinished painting of Frances but didn't have the heart to work on it. He wondered what time it was. He hated to be under the servitude of clocks again.

Much later, the candle had burned down to a stub. Suddenly he jumped to his feet and began pacing the room. He walked to the window, looked down at the street last time, then grabbed the painting and tossed it across the room.

Angrily, he set up another canvas and began to paint, hacking out an image with thick globs of dark paint.

The image took form. This one wasn't of a person, but a ruin set high in a cliff recess.

The next day Everett walked into the Adams Gallery with the letter in his hand. There was no one out front at the reception desk. He couldn't see Frances anywhere.

He drifted around the gallery, examining the images on the wall, but he wanted to be done with this chapter of his life. He was ready to leave, and his heart said, the sooner, the better.

Ansel Adams entered, noticed Everett, and walked over.

"Everett! What brings you back?"

His eyes drifted down to his feet and he mumbled, "I, uh… I came to say goodbye."

Adams smiled. "So soon?"

Everett scratched his head and met Adams's eyes.

He said, "I've been discovering new moods, new lows, new and disturbing variations in myself and my feelings for individuals and people as a whole. I feel smothered here — and I miss the desert."

Everett glanced at Frances' desk and a photo of her that sat on it. Adams caught the forlorn expression on his face.

"Frances is off today," he said delicately. "Is there a message you'd like me to give her?"

The young man fumbled with the letter in his pocket. Grasping it, then letting it remain.

"No," he uttered. Then in a stronger voice he said, "Well, I just wanted to thank you and say goodbye."

He turned to leave.

"Everett, I don't know what it is you are looking for, but when you find it—and I believe you will—please do me a favor."

Everett looked at him expectantly.

"Yes, sir, of course."

Adams smiled. "Share it with the rest of us."

Everett smiled back. "Don't worry about me. I am irrepressible."

"You should be," said Adams. "You have a talent for articulating the changing moods of nature. Not everyone can express magnitude and color as you can."

Everett looked down at his feet again. He said, "I still haven't been able to find a proper outlet for my feelings. Perhaps there's none, and it's necessary for my feelings to die of weariness and refusal."

"Hang in there. You have talent, and that goes a long way."

Everett shook Adams' hand. "I will."

"And where are you heading now?" asked Adams.

Everett took what felt like his first breath in days.

"Back to the desert."

Robert Louis DeMayo

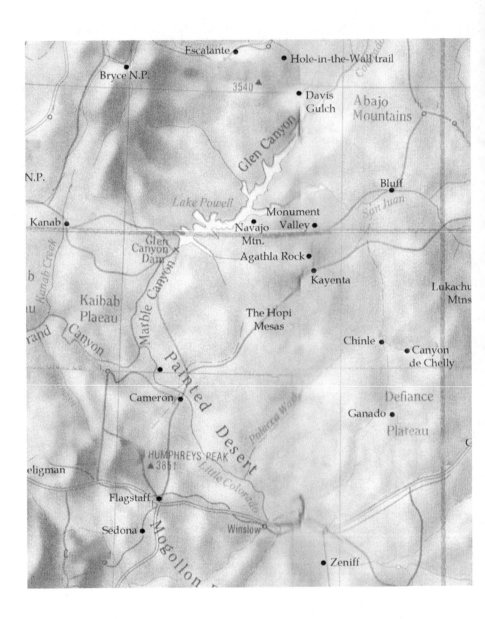

Chapter Twenty-One

Kayenta, Arizona
(April 1934)

*T*he sun had already sunk behind the darkened western hills, but to the north lay Monument Valley whose towers of rock were silhouetted by a sky afire in reds and yellows.

Everett stood beside his brother, Waldo, with all his gear stacked up by his feet. Without the burros to carry the load, it looked like a lot to cart around: two kyacks, a battered saddle, a sack of rice, pots and pans, painting supplies, books, two tarps and several horse blankets.

The Trading Post was about fifty yards away. Everett hadn't wanted to have Waldo drop him off right in front of it.

"Here we are again," he said, ignoring the stares from several Navajos on the porch. He squinted in their direction, determining if he knew any of them.

Waldo glanced at the Navajos uncertainly.

Everett added, "Sure you won't join me, brother? Look at that! Doesn't it just draw you in?"

They turned and beheld the mighty monoliths that lay strewn across the valley. Waldo nodded, ever so slightly, a brief look of regret in his eyes, and Everett felt remorse at having put him on the spot.

"You know I have a life waiting for me back in California," he said, turning from the vista and facing his brother again.

Everett wanted to shout out that that wasn't living. He wanted to confront his brother and ask him how he would ever know what was in his heart and soul if he didn't at least once go off into the wild.

But he didn't. He held his tongue.

After a moment he said, "I do look forward to the time when we'll be going places together on the road. You are surely a good brother to me."

Waldo jingled his keys, restless.

He asked, "Do you have enough reading material?"

Everett lifted a book from the pile. "I'm reading *The Fantastic Traveler*, a book about a boy who creates a dream world more real than his actual world — how appropriate is that?"

He smiled. "And you *are* here with me!"

His arms made a sweeping gesture that took in the entire area.

Everett sighed. "Do you know how difficult this would have been without you?"

Waldo gave his brother a look that said he was exaggerating, but Everett continued. "I could have shipped my kyacks and saddle to Flagstaff, but there are no burros there. Without this ride, I would have had to hitchhike to Tuba City or beyond to buy burros, then drive them on foot all the way back to Flagstaff to get my stuff. And then I would have had to drive them back again to Kayenta."

Waldo laughed. "Too bad you can't hitchhike with the burros."

Everett chuckled with him. "Believe it or not, I've gotten a few rides with them — although only after a lot of time standing in the sun waiting for a truck to come along."

A gust of wind buffeted the car.

Waldo filled the silence with a request.

"Keep writing," he said, "I enjoy your letters immensely."

Everett looked off over the plains with their familiar landmarks.

He sighed. "I'm beginning to feel that they're pointless. Can you convey this beauty to someone who hasn't seen it?"

Waldo looked grief-stricken at the thought of losing that lifeline with his brother. The first time he'd come out west, Waldo thought, Everett had looked like a boy, but he was a man now. Everett was fit and supremely confident in his abilities, and that unsettled his brother.

Deep in his chest, he feared he'd never see him again.

He stammered, "I read your letters and feel like I'm there."

Everett gave him a troubled glance. "Lately, I've been sensing that you can't embrace both beauty and friendship at the same time."

Waldo wished their father had come along. He asked, "And when you say friendship, you also mean family. Don't you?"

Everett smiled sadly and embraced Waldo.

"It's just that I've seen more than I believe I can bear, and I don't want to go back to California. Goodbye, brother."

Everett approached the hogan in which he had stayed two years before. Over the hour it had taken to walk there, he'd thought about his brother. He now had a different swagger about him, and he moved with a sense of confidence, like he belonged here. He stepped inside to see it looked unchanged.

A raven landed in the square hole of the chimney and cawed down at him.

He grinned up. "Yup, I'm back."

He unpacked his gear, creating a kitchen area against one wall, and laying his bedroll against another. The hogan had eight sides, was about twelve feet wide, and even with his supplies spread out, the interior seemed spacious. He reminded himself to collect firewood before it got dark.

Once he had his painting supplies unpacked, he grabbed a small palette and dabbed some paint on it, took a framed canvas in his other hand, and left the hogan with a brush in his teeth.

He walked to the edge of the plateau and looked out at Agathla Rock in the distance. He set the canvas on his knee and held it with his left arm.

He painted quickly, but there was a strong breeze and blowing sand stuck to the wet paint. He worked it into the design.

Then he reached down and grabbed a pinch of the red earth. He smelled it and moved his thumb and forefinger together to get a feel for it, and then lastly mixed it with a glob of vermillion paint and began to apply it to his painting.

The burro slowly ascended the steep path to the shelf where the hogan sat. It was loaded with several saddle blankets, a few water jugs, and a bundle of wood. Everett had been unable to find much that was burnable in the sparse area around the hogan, so he had collected sticks on his way to Kayenta.

Everett led the burro into the hogan as if he were a human guest, and with a note of pride in his voice as he showed him around.

"This is where you'll sleep," he began. "Some people have told me I'm crazy for bringing my burros inside, but I figure if I'm warm, you should be—we're a team after all."

He pointed at his kitchen. "Just don't mess with that stuff. If you get into my food, you'll be sleeping outside."

He picked off a couple of burrs sticking to the burro's side.

"I think I'm gonna call you Cockleburs—not a bad name for a grumpy old fella like you."

The burro cocked his head slightly and stared at him with his ears pointed forward.

"Now, I won't lie to you," said Everett in a new, more serious tone. "I've gone through a few burros in my time, but if you keep your wits and don't go running off, you might make it."

Cockleburs stared at him blankly, and Everett laughed.

"Don't worry about it—you'll be fine."

He reached over and scratched him behind his ears, then hugged him to make the burro feel welcome and loved.

Chapter Twenty-Two

Desert plateau near Kayenta, Arizona
(April 1934)

Several days later, Charlie and Notah were sitting on a ledge above Everett, hidden behind a screen of piñon pines and watching him. Charlie crouched, but the older Navajo sat comfortably on the ground, a thick blanket beneath his folded old legs to help keep the ground's chill at bay.

About twenty feet behind them, Tiba stood with a burro, obediently waiting. She craned her neck to watch Everett also.

Below them, the young white man painted, oblivious. A glowing red sun was just now lifting off the horizon, and he worked fast to capture the soft morning colors before they burned away.

Charlie leaned closer to Notah and whispered, "I've told you about this guy, grandfather. He's friendly, but maybe a bit simple."

Everett turned away from the sunrise and wiped his eyes. Even from a distance, the Navajos could see he'd been crying.

He stuck the brush in an old tin can filled with water and set the canvas on a rock. Then he took a breath, faced the sun, and began to chant Navajo.

Notah smiled inside. When the white man — just a boy then — had first arrived in Kayenta, he had known nothing about Dawn Boy or greeting the sun, but now here he was, blessing the new day, singing loudly in passable Diné.

> *"Let beauty walk before me.*
> *Let beauty walk behind me.*
> *Let beauty walk all around me."*

"Why does he cry when he paints?" asked Charlie.

Notah thought a moment, then asked, "Why do birds sing?"

They listened silently to Everett until he had finished his song.

After a few minutes he collected his canvas and paints and stowed them in the hogan.

"I would meet this man," said Notah.

"He came through about three years ago," said Charlie. "Did you see him then?"

Notah shook his head. "That was a different man."

Everett heard footsteps and turned to watch Charlie and Notah approach. Behind them he could see Tiba, with a burro, following.

Everett stood and waited for them to get closer.

"*Yá'át'ééh!*" he called, and after a pause, Charlie replied back, "*Yá'át'ééh*, Picture Man. Why have you come back?"

Everett smiled at the older Indian.

Notah gave the merest of nods.

"Would you like some coffee?" asked Everett, excited at the prospect of having company.

The old man ignored the question.

"Grandfather, this is Everett Ruess," said Charlie.

Notah looked into Everett's eyes and took in all the changes that had shaped the young man over the last three years. The old Navajo shook his head.

"Everett Ruess is dead. This is another man."

Charlie looked confused, but Everett looked back into Notah's eyes, seeing a mischievous glint to them, and the two exchanged a small smile.

"No, this is him," protested Charlie. "This is the man everyone calls the Picture Man."

Notah made a low whistle, and Tiba approached with the burro in tow. She looked timid and only met Notah's eyes. Everett watched her every move.

Cockleburs stuck his head out of the hogan and brayed when he heard the other burro's clip-clopped footsteps. Notah and Charlie turned and watched him, then observed the two burros until Tiba cleared her throat and straightened up.

"This is my niece," said Notah proudly.

Tiba glanced at Everett, then looked away, but in the fleeting seconds they each recognized a kindred spirit. Notah saw this and silently wondered about the two. He spoke to her in Diné, and she reached into a saddlebag and pulled out a thick Navajo blanket.

Tiba took a step forward and gave it to Everett. Their eyes met again and they both blushed. Over the last few years, he'd seen Tiba a half-dozen times, but only once had it been when they were alone. It had been a fiasco, and since then, she had been downright evasive.

"Thank you. Did you make it?" he asked, hoping to draw her into a conversation.

With panic the young woman looked to her uncle.

Notah said, "My niece cannot speak."

Everett hid a smile and summoned up an encounter with her during his second year near Chinle. At the time he had thought she just didn't want to talk with him.

He turned, ducked into the hogan, and returned with the painting.

He handed it to her. "For you."

She looked down, smiling, then took it and stowed it carefully on top of a saddlebag.

"You decided to stay in my uncle's hogan again?" asked Charlie.

Everett shrugged. "I was going to go into town today and ask permission—not that that gets me anywhere."

Charlie smiled, and under his breath, said, "Let me try."

Then in a louder voice, he addressed Notah and asked, "Grandfather, can Everett stay in the hogan?"

Notah sternly shook his head. "Everett Ruess is dead."

Everett looked surprised, and Notah hid a smile.

He added, "Explain to him that he must find a new name. For now, Picture Man can stay."

The three Indians slowly picked their way off the plateau, following narrow footpaths in the direction of Kayenta. Everett watched for a while and then took out a pen and paper and began to write a letter.

"Dear Frances,
You should see the glorious colors... the golden cliff tops and the grey-blue Piñon-clad slopes..."

He stopped writing and watched Tiba as she led the burro.
He tore up the letter.

Chapter Twenty-Three

Chilchinbeto Trading Post, Arizona
(May 1934)

*E*verett led his burro to the porch of the Chilchinbeto Trading Post, located about twenty-five miles southeast of Kayenta. He'd made the journey in two days, and today alone, he had walked eighteen miles from Church Rock.

He had found some friends in Kayenta, but John Wetherill didn't seem too interested in trading with him. He just wanted to sell him goods for cash, so Everett decided to try his luck trading somewhere else. Chilchinbeto had been the closest option.

Charlie had also warned him that Bad Jack had been stumbling around Kayenta in a foul mood. Everett hadn't run into him yet and thought that with a little luck, he would never see him again.

On the porch of the Trading Post sat two men. One was Hispanic, around fifty, with a friendly smile and a receding hairline; the other looked mid-twenties and familiar. When Everett got closer he realized it was Ben Wetherill, who looked older when he wasn't standing in his father's shadow.

Although his father ran the Kayenta Trading Post, Ben didn't have much to do with it. He had been friendly with Everett since their first meeting.

Ben extended his right arm and they shook hands. He noticed Everett's silver bracelet and said, "You still have that thing?"

"It's my good-luck charm."

Ben squinted at Everett with his one eye and said, "Haven't seen you for a while. Was beginnin' to think you died off in some canyon."

Everett smiled back and said good-naturedly, "It's surprising I haven't."

Ben nodded, "Well, my dad always thought you'd end that way."

Everett laughed. "I've taken quite a few chances and I've always come out on top. I guess I'm lucky."

A gust of wind blew through, and suddenly Everett felt superstitious. So he added, "...have been so far, anyway."

The Hispanic man laughed at this comment, and Ben nodded at him. "This is José García. He runs the Trading Post here."

Everett extended his hand and they shook.

"I knew a Camilo García in Chinle," said Everett. "Any relation?"

José beamed. "That's my brother! He can be a bit sour, but that's because we're both descended from Spanish pioneers."

José looked over the burro.

"You need some supplies, amigo?"

"I do need a second burro," said Everett. "Would you be willing to trade for artwork?"

The man smiled. "I might, but I'd want a lot of artwork for a good burro."

Ben sat up. "You know, there's this big archaeological dig going on here in about a month. I could use someone who knows how to work a burro."

José nodded. "I've got business with the dig, too. I'll give you store credit if you help transfer some supplies."

It all sounded too good to be true, but Everett didn't like committing to other people's plans—especially when they were a month away. He shifted uneasily, trying to decide what to do when Tiba stepped out of the Trading Post.

"I thought you lived with Notah," he said with an unsuccessful attempt to hide his joy about seeing her.

She looked at José, who explained. "When the old one is in Kayenta, she tends to his needs, but often he is in the desert. When he's gone, she stays with me."

Tiba snapped her fingers and looked at José again.

"Oh, that's right," he said, "Notah told me to tell Picture Man that he'd see him soon." He chuckled. "At first I didn't know who he was talking about, but it makes sense now."

Everett scratched his head. "Notah? The elder? Where will he see me?"

José shrugged. "I don't know. In the desert somewhere, I'd guess. Old Notah is a Medicine Man, you know, and who can say why they do anything."

José looked at the burro standing in the hot sun and said, "Why don't you tend to the burro, and then you can show me some of your paintings."

José nodded at Tiba, and she motioned for Everett to follow her.

They walked around the Trading Post to some stables.

"Forgive me for not properly introducing you," said Everett. "This is Cockleburs."

Tiba smiled and patted Cockleburs' neck.

They were almost to the stable door when a large Navajo stepped out of the stables and walked up to Everett. It was Bad Jack, and Everett was startled at seeing him here instead of Kayenta. He thought, if I knew he was here, I might have stayed in Kayenta.

Bad Jack reeked of alcohol. In two steps he was in front of Everett, pushed him to the ground and stood over him.

Suddenly Tiba was there, between them. She produced a rattle made from an animal bladder and began shaking it in Bad Jack's face. He backed away, clutching his medicine pouch, then he disappeared around the corner.

Everett stood up and brushed himself off. He mumbled a thanks to Tiba and then asked, "Has Notah been teaching you magic?"

She gave a coy smile and turned away.

José was flipping through Everett's images on the desk of the Trading Post. He paused at one that was just a sketch. "Where is this? It looks familiar."

"I think it was on a promontory on the north end of Black Mesa," said Everett.

José nodded. "Yes, that's the three fingers — how long before you're finished with it?"

Everett laughed. "I wanted to finish it today. We set out at first light, and as we passed the golden cliff the sun illuminated the top of the rock and the blue-grey pines covering its slopes, and I got lost in the glorious colors. If I didn't have such a long journey ahead of me, I would have stopped and made camp again right there."

José chuckled. "Well, when you finish, come show it to me. For now, I rather like the one of the storm moving across Monument Valley. What do you want for it?"

Everett stared at the floorboards. "I'd like to put some credit towards a burro, but I'm pretty hungry right now. Could you throw in a can of beans?"

José smiled. "Come by for dinner in an hour — my home is right behind the Trading Post. We've got a big table and we can easily squeeze in another chair."

José's home didn't look like much from the outside. Tumbleweeds had piled up against one wall, and the adobe was cracked and covered with red dust, but inside it was cool and clean. The large central room was filled with an assortment of happy Hispanic and Indian children, laughing adults, and women cooking in the kitchen.

There were a lot of people, and upon Everett's arrival, they all moved to a large wooden table and beckoned for him to sit with them. José sat at the head of the table with his Navajo wife by his side.

Everett had been told to sit at the other end of the table. On his left was an old Spaniard who was half asleep — José's father — and on his right side sat Tiba.

These people spoke a mix of Diné, Spanish and English, and everyone seemed to be talking at once. The dinner appeared to be the highlight of everyone's day, and he glowed in the sudden sensation of having a family.

"You've captured the dream," he said to José.

"What do you mean?" asked José.

Everett looked over the faces of those sitting at the table.

He said, "Well, your life seems a perfect mix of your heritage and the Navajo way of life."

José smiled. "I wish I could say I planned it. We have five children, and there are others, like Tiba, who have joined our family."

Everett let out a long sigh. "You know," he said, "I could never really conceive of a happy domestic situation for myself, but this seems lovely."

José shook his head. "Well, domestic bliss has its moments, but it's also not easy to live between cultures — heck, we need three languages just to converse."

Everett cleared his throat and quoted Mark Twain...

"Kindness is the language the blind can see and the deaf can hear."

Then he inwardly cringed, suddenly conscious of Tiba's inability to speak. The smiling faces around the table of those who understood English were hardly a consolation for his blunder.

He said, "The last traders I met were rather difficult people. I'm surprised by the happy atmosphere here."

José laughed uproariously. "Come, now you have to tell me about these traders. I know some are cheap, but what else did they do to offend you?"

Everett took a breath. "Well, the moron at the Lukachukai Trading Post certainly made me feel like hitting him. He's only interested in selling goods and making money. He wouldn't trade with me or even talk with me unless I showed him cash."

José held up his hands, motioning for Everett to slow down. "That is his business — he trades. Traders prefer cash, but this is a poor land, and some Trading Posts go a full year without seeing a single dime pass over their counter."

Everett sighed. "If I were ever to go into business, I'd have only two rules — my guiding mottos."

José cocked his head. "This I have to hear."

"Never count the cost, and never do anything unless you can do it wholeheartedly."

José nodded. "Those are great guidelines to live by, but you might have a tough time making a profit under them."

Everett's expression turned scornful. "I was telling the trader about Canyons de Chelly and del Muerto, and some of the interesting ruins I'd encountered — and he remarked that he had never been to them and never intended to go.'"

José nodded and said, "Just because a man lives in this country doesn't mean he wants to be an explorer."

Everett stared at his plate uncertainly.

He shoveled the last of the food into his mouth, and then he said, "Obviously, his decision was right for him because wherever he might go, he would see nothing beautiful or interesting."

"And what about the Navajos?" asked José. "How have they treated you?"

Everett said. "I think they're a fine people, although most of them aren't very clean. I've ridden with them on their horses, eaten with them, and even taken part in their ceremonies."

Then he broke into a grin. "Of course, when I first came to the Southwest, I didn't understand their ways. I didn't know they would steal anything from a stranger."

José laughed. "That is true, but once you've been introduced as a friend, you don't have to worry about that."

Everett nodded. "I don't think I'll ever forget their weird, wild chanting as they ride the desert. Their cries are magnificent."

José's wife leaned over and whispered into his ear.

He said, "She wants me to point out that we're a mixed family and there are whites, Hispanics, and Indians who disagree with what we're doing."

After a nod from José, Tiba filled Everett's plate again.

"You could always leave," said Everett.

José raised an eyebrow and asked, "Is that an option? To just leave? You can't just give up society."

"I could," said Everett flatly.

José let his eyes drift over the people seated around his dining table, knowing they were something he could never leave. He asked, "You'd live in the wilderness with no need for human company?"

Everett nodded. "Yes, I think I could do it. I like adventure and enjoy taking chances when skill and fortitude play a part."

He paused only slightly, "And if I had a companion, I know I could leave society behind for good. But I doubt many others feel nature as I do."

José shook his head. "People need each other. You'd be lucky if you ever found someone to disappear with... but I don't know how lucky she would be."

Despite all his efforts not to stare directly at Tiba, Everett lifted his head and looked at her. Her eyes held his and said more than words could.

Meanwhile, José continued his point. "How long could you last without help? People need supplies. That's why I'm a trader."

Everett broke his gaze away from Tiba, smiled and said, "I seem to enjoy things more intensely because of the certainty that they will not last."

José asked, "And that's enough for you? You're willing to give up family, security — stability?"

He realized the gravity of José's question and replied with all the honesty he could summon. He said, "Always, I'll be able to scorn the worlds I've known like half-burnt candles when the sun is rising, and sally forth to others now unknown."

José laughed, glad he'd invited the young man to his table.

Everett was in his element. As he surveyed the faces around the table, he enjoyed this familiar setting, but he also knew keenly that he had never regretted the sacrifices he'd made to travel.

He said, "The things I've loved and given up without complaint have returned to me doubled. There's no one in the world I envy."

José smiled. He knew that letting go of the things you loved wasn't that easy. "And what do you love now?" he asked.

Everett's eyes swept over the table, pausing for an eternal second on Tiba, then returning to José.

"I love what you've created here," he said.

Chapter Twenty-Four

Agathla Rock, Arizona
(June 1934)

Agathla Rock lay ahead, about six miles away to the northwest, and Everett rode Cockleburs toward it. Tethered behind was a new burro he'd purchased from José. Everett called him Leopard for his spotted coat. Leopard, loaded with gear, wasn't all that pleased with his situation.

Together they'd slowly become a team, and Everett took some satisfaction seeing the burros following in a line, their loads neatly balanced in the kyacks. In the last week they had covered about a hundred miles on small jaunts around the area, with only a few mishaps, because Leopard, the younger of the two burros, didn't like to be the one on drag, at the back of the line.

It was sometime around noon and the summer heat was dry and merciless. Everett looked hopefully at an ominous cloud front that seemed to be approaching. Blistering heat, or a storm, he thought — either way, I've got a long day ahead of me.

He thought of his friends in Chilchinbeto. A part of him had wanted to stay. He'd spent a day exploring the area with Charlie, riding over rock and sage to visit both Twisted Water and Mexican Water.

Charlie claimed that he knew of a few spots where they could find garnets, but despite several hours of searching, they'd come up empty.

Another friend, Dog Ears Begay, who seemed to know everyone, had accompanied them. Thanks to his introductions, they had lunched at several different hogans on the way, and the many smiling faces made the land seem more hospitable.

A red half-moon was setting to the west, and if he had been staying in the hogan—or any decent shelter—he would have painted it in watercolors.

Instead, he leaned forward into blustering winds that had started up shortly after sunrise. They had stirred up enough dust to obscure the distant buttes and create a ring around the moon. The wind carried the smell of rain and wet sage.

But no rain fell on the trio as they trudged on.

They continued through the morning, slowly approaching the giant tower of rock that had had such an impact on him when he'd first arrived three years before.

The burros each wore a string of bells, but he could barely hear them over the roar of the wind. The storm was brewing in the darkening skies above him, and the strong gusts that swept down quickly obscured his tracks and those of his burros.

His eyes were sore and red-rimmed.

A spattering of rain hit his face, and he looked up again at the rock and the inky sky above it. Part of him didn't care if it rained—the weather didn't bother him, except that there was always the chance that a good soaking might spoil some of his supplies, and paint and canvas weren't easily replaced.

He stared at Agathla Rock and said, "We've had our moment, you and me. I gave you my pledge. Now tell that storm to leave me alone."

A ripple of thunder crept over the clouds.

With his head down, he rode through a sea of purple locoweed. The sand was blowing at him hard now, stinging his face.

He stared up at the dark, volcanic rock. "So that's how it's going to be, eh? Well, I've got nothing more to say to you."

In the late afternoon, Everett stopped in the shadow of the rock and hobbled the burros. He took the supplies off Leopard, but for the

178

moment, left the saddle on Cockleburs and the kyacks on both of them. Then he placed a handful of oats in front of them, which the wind quickly snatched away.

He glanced up at the sky. It was as dark as night and flickering with lightning. He raised his fists and shouted.

"Alone, I shoulder the sky and hurl my defiance!"

A rumble of thunder appeared to answer him.
Adrenaline coursed through him.

"I shout the song of the conqueror to the four winds!
I am not afraid of you!"

A bolt of lightning struck and both burros jumped. Cockleburs slipped right out of the loop that hobbled him, and Leopard somehow hopped away with his front feet still bound. Everett could hear the thumping of the kyacks against the burro's flanks as they both ran off into the dark afternoon.

He stood his ground.

"To the earth, the sea, the sun and the moon,
I shout, I live! I live! I live!"

A gust of wind descended with such vengeance that it drove him to his knees.

"I live!" he screamed hoarsely.

On the ground, he saw the Navajo blanket that Tiba gave him. He wrapped it around his head and hunkered down.

Then the storm hit. Gale-force winds came down with heavy rains. With the blanket as his only protection, Everett wiggled in close to a large stand of cliff rose and covered himself with sand.

When he woke, the morning was fresh and there wasn't a trace of wind. He crawled out from underneath the bush. His blanket was soaked and heavy with dirt. He shook it out and spread it over the brush to dry.

His gear lay in a heap, under a thick layer of sand, and he was glad he'd managed to unload this much before the burros had bolted.

A pair of horned larks sang sweetly from a nearby juniper.

He scanned the horizon, wondering how far the burros had roamed, and then suddenly he heard animals approaching, the tinkling of their bells carrying clearly through the pleasant morning air.

Tiba appeared, leading the two burros towards him.

They seemed to have escaped the storm unscathed.

"Thank you," he said to Tiba as she handed him the leads.

She gave the smallest of smiles and nodded. He tied the burros to a tree. She turned and began walking back toward Kayenta.

"Wait!" he called. "Please have coffee with me before you go."

She looked reluctant but finally sat in the shade of a juniper and watched him while he dug through the supplies. He located a well-wrapped container of coffee and the coffee pot, which he tipped upside down to empty the windblown sand out of it.

He looked at her thoughtfully and said, "I've taken my share of chances out here—trusted my life to crumbling sandstone and steep angles, but it seems to me it isn't a big fall that kills the unlucky folks."

Tiba followed his words even if she only knew some of them.

He walked over to Cockleburs and untied the canteen that was still fastened to his saddle. He lifted it and gave it a shake. It sloshed.

"It's water!" Everett exclaimed.

"I suppose without the burros and the water they carry, I wouldn't last very long out here. And the absence of a morning coffee would be the least of my problems."

He rinsed the kettle with a splash of water, then walked in a circle around the camp, collecting rocks for a fireplace. With a half dozen in his arms, he looked back at her and said, "Guess I should have grabbed one of the water containers when I unloaded the gear last night."

With an amused expression Tiba watched him scoop out a depression in the ground and line it with the rocks.

He smiled. "Should take more care with the burro hobbles, too. Cockleburs slipped his so easily!" He scratched his head. "And I've never seen anything like Leopard hopping off like a giant rabbit."

180

He stood up and brushed off his pant legs, then began collecting sticks. He kept glancing at her and promptly stumbled over a clump of snakeweed.

He straightened up and said, "I'm sorry, I'm not used to having company."

He wondered how she felt about being alone. Before he could stop himself, he continued, "But there's a splendid freedom in solitude — that's why I go to the mountains and deserts."

Tiba watched him, following his eyes and his lips. Everett couldn't read her expression, but he sensed she could understand him, and that made him speak from the heart.

He held his arms out wide. "There are no distractions out here. Nothing stands between me and the wild."

It took him a little while to get the fire going and let the flames die down enough to set the pot on them. They sat facing each other across the fire and listened to the birds around them wake up.

A raven cawed out, then swooped away.

He stirred the coals, losing his thoughts in the glowing embers, until finally, he blurted out, "I don't know how anyone could go back to the world of cities and important occupations after living out here. I've tried it, believe me. All you find are frustrated people struggling to feel alive."

She watched him with that unreadable expression, and he wanted to ask her so many questions but instead fell back into silence.

A flock of red-winged blackbirds descended into the cliff rose where his blanket lay spread out. They chatted noisily, avoiding the blanket as they hopped deeper into the bush to take advantage of the cool shade it created.

Finally, after Everett had handed Tiba a cup of black coffee with some sugar, he asked, "How did you know I needed help?"

She stared at him over the rim of her cup, then looked away.

Everett stood up, grinned, and pointed at her.

He said, "You had to know. How?"

She smiled, and then her expression became stern. She suddenly looked older somehow.

Everett raised his eyebrows. "Notah told you?"

She nodded.

Everett scratched his head and asked, "Well, how did he know?"

Tiba shrugged and they both laughed.

They sipped their coffees in silence.

Then she scanned the horizon, made a circle in the air with her finger, and then looked at him questioningly.

He thought a moment. "You want to know where I'm going?"

She nodded.

Everett pointed to the west, where a deep canyon faded into the landscape. "I'm going to explore some of the ruins over there."

She frowned, then put two fingers on top of her head, like antennas. She shook her head.

"You don't think I should go there?"

Her eyes bored into him.

He said, "I'll be fine, don't worry about me."

She rose to her feet, and he knew it was time for her to leave.

He waved his arms in a circle and said, "Thank you for sharing this altar of beauty with me."

She surprised him by smiling and nodding.

He watched her walk off until her form melted into the shimmering horizon.

High above a dried-out canyon, two buzzards circled, and their shadows slid gently across the cliff wall. Below, in the dark shade by the base of the cliff, Everett had set up his camp.

The burros were cropping the grass nearby, and birds sang out from the bushes around him. He lay back with his head on the Navajo blanket.

This isn't bad at all, he thought. I don't know what Tiba was worried about.

A snort drew his attention and he turned to see a large, black bull eyeing him from about twenty feet away. He hadn't seen any cattle in the canyon, but here was a bull. He looked at his long, sharp horns and, in his mind, saw Tiba's gesture with her two fingers pointed above her head.

"Hi there," he said, using the same voice he addressed his burros with. "I don't mean you any trouble — I've even got oats, look!"

He moved to his pile of supplies but only got a few steps before the bull began pawing the ground.

"Easy," he said, but it did no good. The bull charged straight at him.

Everett scurried out of its way, terrified of the pointed horns. He scrambled up a steep wash with the bull in pursuit, only the steepness of the hill saving him.

His screams echoed throughout the canyon.

He climbed to the safety of a ledge, flopped onto it, and was about to relax when a rattle sounded by his side.

He sprang to his feet and narrowly averted a rattlesnake strike.

He grabbed a big rock and killed the snake.

The burros watched the entire show. For some reason the bull wasn't interested in them.

"That's rattler number five!" he shouted to Cockleburs. "And he almost got the jump on me."

The burros just stared up at him, and Everett took it as admonishment. He said, "Okay, I should have listened to her."

The bull was pacing below the ledge, at the bottom of the scree, searching for a way up.

Everett started taunting the bull. "Okay, I'm game. Do you want to put me to the test? Well, let me warn you, I've passed my own rigorous test, and I know I can take it. And I'm lucky too! Have been so far, anyway."

The bull bellowed and attempted to ascend the scree again.

"Settle down," said Everett. "You won't be the first hostile stranger that I've turned into a staunch friend. It's just you and me — and the burros over there — and no one else cares whether we live or die."

The bull turned back, and Everett already thought the battle was over, but then the bull charged up the hill and almost made it to his ledge. It was close enough that Everett fled further up the hill.

An hour later Everett lay by his fire, but his eyes kept scanning the surrounding brush, which was thick with shadows, and he jumped at the slightest sound. A growing moon hovered above and shone dimly through racing clouds.

Kangaroo rats were hopping around the canyon floor, searching for food in the moonlight. Suddenly a burrowing owl glided by silently and picked off one of the rats.

He built up the fire, stared at it bleary-eyed, and when it died down he added more fuel.

Later, he jumped to his feet to the pounding of hooves as the bull charged at him out of the darkness.

He scrambled to safety again and spent the remainder of the night on the rock shelf looking down at his camp.

They left Bull Canyon the next morning and slowly trudged through another gorge further south. Its flanks were lined with firs and tall pines, and a sad, dry wind roared through them.

Everett was relieved not to see a single cow track.

He noticed some desert varnish on a cliff and approached it, but there was no water at its base. He opened his canteen to pour the last few drops onto his dry tongue.

Halfway up one side of the canyon he spotted a ruin. He hobbled the burros and climbed towards it with his brushes and paint.

The dwelling had only one room and didn't interest him as much as the rock art panel next to it. Hundreds of pictographs covered the rocks, and many petroglyphs had been etched into the sandstone. He studied them, fascinated.

The songs of the birds filled the canyon around him, and then the cry of a lonely whippoorwill sounded out. Everett took his brushes and colors and began painting a sequence of three notes set on a bar in the key of C onto the rocks.

He whistled the three notes and then sang them: "Whip poor will..."

Chapter Twenty-Five

Navajo Mountain, Utah
(June 1934)

*T*he last slanting rays of the sun lit the topmost rim of the red sandstone cliff as Everett left the canyon behind. He had waited patiently before setting out, preferring to travel in the cooler evenings.

He was traveling in the direction of Navajo Mountain, but his destination wasn't set. He listened to the shrill song of cicadas, watched the wildflowers slowly close, and plodded along, following the burros up onto a windswept plain, letting the geography determine his way.

The early evening swayed peacefully around him, and he marveled at its splendor. He had seen so much loveliness over the last few months — and was experiencing more right now! He let his eyes drift over the canyon and the plain ahead, and words flowed through his mind like music, but he couldn't connect them. He felt tortured at his inability to capture this stunning setting in words.

He patted Leopard's rump. "At least we've seen it, eh? And felt it! And heard it! Haven't we, boy?"

The burro quick-stepped ahead of him, and Everett laughed and shouted to the wind. "It doesn't matter!"

The thought got his mind churning, so he sat on a rock and took out his journal while the burros slowly plodded on.

Another whippoorwill sounded with the call he had painted on the rock art panel the day before. This one whistled continuously, maybe searching for a mate, another bird to share the mellow evening with.

He wrote:

"How could I give some tangible suggestion of what has burned inside of me? Try as I may, I feel I have yet to succeed in conveying more than a glimpse of my visions. I am condemned to feel the withering fire of beauty pouring into me, but staying only there — never shared."

He got up and stretched his legs and was about to move on when he had another thought and opened the journal again.

"I am torn by the knowledge that what I have felt cannot be given to another. I cannot bear to contain these rending flames, and I am helpless to let them out. So I wonder, how I can go on living and being casual as one must?"

He heard Cockleburs bray and hurried to catch up with the burros who had stumbled into an area thick with prickly pear cactus. He stowed his journal in a saddlebag, tethered Leopard to Cockleburs and grabbed the lead, and led them away from the thorns and back onto the narrow foot trail they'd been following.

It was difficult to see in the dim moonlight, and after another hour, Everett searched for a way down from the lonely plateau. He'd just about shredded the leg of his jeans after stumbling through some thorny bushes, and another encounter with a prickly pear cactus had left a couple of dozen tiny cactus thorns in his leg and they irritated him as he walked.

The burros were edgy and tough to keep in line. They had covered barely ten miles, but Everett was ready to stop.

Instead, they descended into another canyon, dropping off the cool plain before the sun arrived.

Once they were in the bowels of the canyon, Everett finally stopped to make camp. As the first order of business, he took the kyacks off the burros, then pulled the thorns out of his legs and attended to those the burros had picked up. By the time he finished and got his camp organized, the sun was hovering just below the horizon.

The next evening a blood-red moon shone over Everett as he rode through the pines on a steep trail that ascended out of the canyon and into higher elevation.

The track was narrow with a sharp drop-off on their right. It didn't look like anyone had been on this trail in a long time. Several sections had washed out and there was a lot of debris.

He paused to water the burros and checked to make sure their loads were secure. While they rested, he walked ahead and dragged a few large branches out of the way.

A butte rose on the other side of the canyon.

"That's No Man's Mesa," he explained to the burros when he returned. A strange name the Navajo had chosen for the place, he thought to himself. "No man." He recalled that *No Man* was "nemo" in Latin.

He thought about it and decided he liked it as a name—Nemo.

The burros stepped nervously, and Everett sensed they knew a challenging trail lay ahead. Finally, he set them forward. He walked a few steps behind, keeping them—especially Leopard—away from the edge. Leopard's kyacks held all their supplies, and under the heavy load, he wobbled slightly.

They were heading up out of the canyon, and the drop-off on their right was looming ever deeper. Everett grabbed a tree by a smooth rock shelf for support and leaned over to peek over the edge. The bottom of the canyon was now hundreds of feet below them.

Thankfully, right before them, the rim trail turned away from the cliff. But the track was frighteningly steep as it led upwards onto the plateau. Every few steps the hooves of the burros dislodged a rock and sent it tumbling down at him.

He scrambled ahead of the burros, but this made them stop. No matter how hard he pulled on their leads, they only looked at him and refused to move.

Finally, he got behind them again and got them moving once more by hollering and smacking their rumps.

Over the last stretch the trail became crumbly, and the burros were struggling for footing. Cockleburs was in the lead and barely made it, but Leopard had all the weight and was having trouble. He attempted to claw his way up through the scree and lost his balance.

He slumped back, wild-eyed, and flipped over backward and rolled down the hill. He kicked and brayed in panic but seemed unable to arrest his movement.

At the bottom of the scree, he burst through a patch of scrub oak and came to a stop at the very spot where Everett had looked down at the canyon floor.

"Don't move!" shouted Everett as he hurried down to him.

Leopard lay on his side with his back to the cliff, which dropped off two feet behind him. The stone shelf he lay on was smooth and tilted toward the abyss. Everett was afraid if the burro moved even a little, he would slide into the yawning gulf behind him.

"Easy boy," he whispered.

The kyacks had been smashed badly. Everett grabbed a length of rope from the broken kyack and tied it to Leopard's halter, then secured the other end to a tree.

It took almost an hour of coaxing and pleading to get the burro to his feet.

Everett kept tightening the rope, and eventually, he managed to pull him back to the trail. The burro's legs were shaking, and he looked ready to collapse, and he wheezed when he limped forward.

They waited there for an hour. Everett checked the burro's wounds in the last light of the moon. He didn't appear to have any broken bones or deep cuts, but Everett was afraid of internal injuries. The wheezing was becoming more labored.

The steep final section loomed above them. Everett unloaded what was left in the damaged kyacks and carried most of it to the top where Cockleburs waited.

It took him the remainder of the night to get Leopard to the top. Everett would loop the rope around a tree ahead, and then slowly take in the slack whenever he could get Leopard to take a step forward.

The burro looked dazed and trembled as he slowly inched uphill.

They summited with the day's first light. Leopard took a few unstable steps, then sank to the ground. Everett cradled the burro's head and began to chant Navajo.

In the shadows of a twisted pine, Notah stood watching, unseen.

Slowly, Leopard seemed to relax. With the rising sun, he finally struggled onto his belly with his legs underneath. He appeared disoriented and shook his head and looked around.

When Everett returned down the trail to retrieve the last of his gear Notah quietly slipped away.

An hour later Leopard stood up on shaky legs, and it seemed he could walk. Everett had repaired the kyacks as best he could and put them on Cockleburs. He let Leopard carry only the blankets and a bag of oats.

When they set out again, Everett walked behind them. He watched Leopard limp along and wondered if the burro would make it back to the Trading Post.

He ended their march early that day, deciding to rest Leopard and resume travel in the evening.

In the distance Everett could barely make out a fire burning at the base of a lonely butte, and he headed for it. They had been traveling for about five hours, crossing another plain under a waning moon that slowly arced across the sky.

While they were walking along, the fire had winked on and off, making him wonder at times if he'd imagined it.

He slowed down when he got closer.

A family of Navajos stared at him wide-eyed from the fire.

The burros stepped nervously behind him as Everett waved hello. An old woman, a middle-aged man he assumed was her son, a younger woman holding an infant, and a young buck in his early teens all stared back at him.

The old woman painfully stood and walked to him. She seemed frail.

She welcomed him in Diné.

"*Yá'át'ééh ałní'íní.*" Good evening.

Everett slid off his burro and stiffly walked to the fire.

He replied, "*Yá'át'ééh.*" Hello.

She motioned for him to sit, and then went about preparing food for him. The younger woman moved to help, but the grandmother indicated that she stay put with a flick of her wrist.

Everett felt a bit uncomfortable watching her. It seemed like a lot of exertion for someone so old, and she kept mumbling something in Diné that he couldn't understand.

She served him black coffee and burnt fry bread, but he was starving, and he told her through gestures how much he enjoyed it.

"*Ahéhee'*" Thank you, he said.

Her son, a man with a short, stocky body, appeared to be in his forties. He poured himself a cup of coffee, and his round face held a placid expression as he watched Everett.

After he had eaten, the grandmother crouched beside Everett and said, "You help me on my journey."

Everett smiled at her, surprised that she knew any English. A lock of thin white hair blew across her face as she stared at him.

She motioned for him to lay down by the fire, and he nodded.

"*Iłhosh.*" Sleep, she said.

He nodded. He retrieved his bedroll and set it down by the fire. Then he returned to the burros, took off the saddle and kyacks, and rubbed them down before hobbling them for the evening.

The family watched everything he did unblinkingly.

Everett returned to the fire and lay down on his Navajo blanket. The older man leaned forward and examined it and then nodded and sat back.

When he closed his eyes, the old woman began to chant an ancient song.

He wanted to listen to the ancient chant, but he was exhausted, and within minutes he was asleep.

When he woke in the morning, he was alone.

Everett rode Cockleburs, who also carried most of the supplies in his kyacks. Leopard followed behind, looking a little stronger every day. Everett put a light load on him and tried to let him recover some more.

They had ascended from the plain, gaining altitude one clip-clopped step at a time, up the flank of Navajo Mountain.

The ten thousand-foot-high dome was visible from many parts of Navajo land, and Everett had yearned to explore it since he'd come west. Its Navajo name was *Naatsis'aan* which meant 'Head of the Earth Woman.'

He glanced south, in the direction of the high mesas and deep canyons of Monument Valley, and guessed he had come about four hundred miles since leaving Chilchinbeto. Then he turned back to face the mountain, which the Navajo considered to be sacred. It was almost as if he'd come to the completion of a pilgrimage.

The sky above was clear, and sunlight filtered through the boughs of the trees, but he could see a dark storm coming down from the north, and the distant lightning flashes already made the burros jumpy.

There was no wind. It was the calm before the storm that had sucked away all sound.

The sky darkened, and they took shelter under a large pine as the rain came down. The burros stood there with their heads down and water dripping off their ears. Thunder rumbled loudly around them.

Everett walked out into the rain and held his arms up to the sky. He spun in a slow circle, with eyes closed, relishing the wetness on his dry skin.

He opened his eyes and was looking at Notah.

The Medicine Man began to chant at the rain, and Everett followed his lead and sang with him.

When the downpour let up, Notah turned to Everett and said, "It is time for you to come with me."

Oddly enough, the old man had with him four bags of sand.

He nodded and gave Everett a rare smile when he set the bags in Cockleburs' kyacks, two to a side.

The rain stopped, and they continued northward, traveling in the wake of the sunset that seemed to burn below and on the left. The mountaintop was nearly level, and under a gleaming silver moon, they passed three peaceful ponds surrounded by glades of meadow grass and aspen. It was a stark contrast to the desert, and the recent rains, Everett thought, must have made this oasis even lusher.

Notah made camp by the third pond, under a cluster of low, sprawling oaks. It was late. He lay down in the soft grass, and within minutes the old man was snoring.

Under the remaining moonlight Everett took off the burros' tack and the kyacks. He hobbled only Cockleburs who tried to kick off the rope. "Stop complaining," Everett said and slapped the burro's side. "I know you'd be the one to get in trouble if I let you free range — you can still eat and get a drink. Get out of here!"

Reluctantly, the burro small-stepped out into the grass and began to graze. Leopard limped the twenty feet to the pond and drank.

Everett yelled after him, "Don't flaunt your freedom, or I'll hobble you too!"

He watched them. They were his family. At times, on the trail, he had to be short with them, but it was only because he didn't want them injured. When they stared at him with their lustrous brown eyes, he could never remain angry.

One evening they had run off after being spooked by coyotes. He'd searched for hours, making larger and larger circles around his camp until he finally came upon their tracks. He'd then followed the prints for an hour — to an abandoned hogan.

Everett had stood outside, listening, and then heard a snort from inside. He'd called, "You have the entire desert to find a bed and you choose a hogan?"

Cockleburs had stuck his head out, a guilty look about him, and Everett had laughed uproariously.

Now he looked at them, the moon backlighting their furry ears as they stood knee-deep in meadow grass with wildflower blossoms in their lips, and he couldn't help loving them.

He watched them silently swish their tails until the moon had dropped and the night was dark.

Everett had decided not to make a fire. The wood was wet, and Notah wanted to head out at first light. He wrapped himself in the Navajo blanket and lay on his back, watching the stars.

Sleep came to take over, but as always, he fought it. The rustling aspens around him sounded like people walking through the forest.

In the silence before dawn, he woke to see two horses in the pond, belly-deep. Everett wondered if they were wild.

The burros watched them from the shore.

The horses chewed swamp grass and swished their tails.

A gentle breeze picked up, and with the first glow on the horizon, a flock of ducks arrowed in and landed on the far side of the pond.

Everett turned to Notah. He watched the old man sleeping for a while and changed his mind and decided to build a small fire so that he could make coffee. In one of the kyacks he carried a package of dry tinder. When Notah sat up, Everett handed him a cup of coffee and then started to get the burros ready.

By the time they were loaded, the horses and ducks had disappeared from the pond. Notah nodded and began walking, and Everett followed with the burros in tow.

He looked over the peaceful clearing and the pond and thought about returning someday. Notah had not explained why he wanted him to come with him, and Everett didn't ask; he would follow the old man anywhere.

Wildflowers dotted the meadow, and they nodded at him as he passed.

On Navajo Mountain, Everett rested near War God Spring, lying in the shade of an ancient juniper with his head on the Navajo blanket. Notah had informed him that they were just a little way south of the summit.

The spring trickled beneath a glade of aspens filled with butterflies; tiger and zebra swallowtails were dancing through the trees. A gentle breeze had been whispering all day and the air smelled of sage.

The silent, empty desert extended all around them. They were high in the clouds, and from their perch, vertical yellow sandstone cliffs dropped away into vast canyons.

In the distance he could see Shiprock, another towering volcanic plug. It stood like a sentinel, shimmering on the horizon.

A cloudless turquoise sky did nothing to shade the hot scorching sun that beat down on the desert below, and Everett was glad when Notah had led him to a cool place to rest.

"How did you know about this place?" asked Everett.

The old man grunted. "My people have been coming here for a long time."

Notah watched Everett for a moment.

"Why don't you live in cities like other white folks?" he asked.

Everett thought of his time in San Francisco. "Beauty has always been my god," he said. "It means more to me than people. And that's all cities are—lots of people living next to each other."

Notah nodded. "Now that you've seen this beauty, why don't you return and share it?"

Everett stared off at the dim, distant shape of Shiprock, which appeared to sail across the desert.

He sat up and sipped his water. He said, "You know, I have tried to convey this in letters and poems, but it seems that what I've experienced can't be shared with others."

Notah said, "That may be true."

Everett's expression sagged, and he suddenly looked depressed.

He asked, "So I'm supposed to contain all this within myself?"

"It is your decision what you hold in and what you share."

Everett peered into the old man's eyes, not sure of what he meant. "*Kintahgoo' bil i noolhtah?*" asked Everett. Why do you say that?

A sound drew their attention, and Everett looked up to see the family of Navajos he had camped with approaching.

"There is a way to help others," said Notah, "and share what's inside you at the same time."

The now full moon rose over the rim of the desert. A high wind roared through the pine tops above them but didn't descend to ground level. The aspens around their little camp flickered lightly.

The family had set up camp about forty feet away. A small fire burned in front of several rolled up-blankets. While they shared a meal of fry bread, Notah instructed Everett in preparing the ground.

They gathered the sand bags from Cockleburs' kyacks. Everett carried them to a flat area where Notah had swept away all sticks and rocks. He then traced the outline of a large square with a branch.

It was aligned with the sun. The east side remained open.

Notah twitched his lips at the open end and said, "Don't want to trap in any of the Holy People."

He opened the four bags, which contained sand of different colors. He selected one and began pouring it lightly into the square.

He gave the bag to Everett and indicated for him to continue with the task until the square was filled in. Everett crept closer and did as he was told.

The old Navajo chose another bag of sand and slowly poured handfuls of it around the square's perimeter. When he noticed Everett's knee moving close to the edge, he touched it lightly.

He said, "Be careful of the Encircling Guardian."

Over the next hour he taught Everett a simple chant which he repeated while they worked. Throughout, he watched the young man, who was trying hard to learn and be respectful. Too many of the old ways are fading, Notah thought.

The interior of the square was now almost completely covered. Everett was leaning over it, holding himself up with his left hand, which was placed in the middle of the square next to the bag. He lifted the sand bag and handed it to Notah, and then waited for the old man to slowly set it aside.

Notah sprinkled a pinch of corn pollen on Everett's shoulders and offered him a hand to stand up.

When Everett stood the old man completed the square with two fistfuls of sand, filling in the last spots where Everett's hand and the bag had been.

They sat back, and a few minutes later, the younger Navajo woman walked over and handed them each a piece of fry bread. Notah spoke to her, and she returned with a burning ember and some kindling.

Within a minute, she had made another fire closer to the square.

Pledge to the Wind

The grandmother lay in the middle of the square on her back. There was a pallor to her skin, and her chest barely moved when she breathed. Her family was gathered around the square.

A pot simmered over the nearby fire with a hot milky fluid. Notah used a painted gourd to scoop up a small amount of the potion and offer it to the old woman.

Her lips parted only slightly as she took a small sip.

Notah nodded and placed the gourd by the pot again.

"What's wrong with her?" Everett asked Notah.

He said, "She's dying. Her family brought her here so I could aid her."

The old woman looked at Everett, and he could see a faint twinkle in her eyes.

"Do you think you can save her?" asked Everett.

Notah looked at him. "That's not the aid she asked for."

The moon climbed higher in the sky and shone down on her. The old man faced the moon, wanting to make the ceremony perfect.

When Notah turned back to the old woman his face was set.

The younger woman holding the infant crouched nearby, waiting to assist if needed, but the man and the young buck both turned away.

Notah began the chant and Everett accompanied him. Then he motioned for Everett to hold two of the remaining bags of sand where he could easily reach in.

Everett smiled at the old woman and sang, and he felt a part of him reaching out to her. He didn't know many of the words he chanted, but he sensed their connection to the land — and to her.

Notah's fingers sifted through the sand, making a sprinkle here and a line there. He created symbols around the woman, and Everett watched it all come to life over the next few hours.

More and more, Everett's consciousness seemed to dissolve. All that existed was the chanting and the old woman's eyes.

By sunrise she had passed on.

Notah prepared to bury her properly. The men appeared skittish and fearful of the body.

After the body was buried, the family cooked a breakfast of hot goat's milk, gravy, mutton and *namskadi* bread and shared it with Everett and Notah. Everyone was relaxed. It was as if a burden had been released.

The family was heading back towards Kayenta, where he also was going, and he let the woman with the infant ride Cockleburs.

The man led Cockleburs around a bush so that she could mount. Charlie had told him that an Indian woman will never mount an animal in the presence of a white man.

Everett loaded his remaining supplies in his backpack and let Leopard follow without a load. But the tired burro wasn't destined to recover, and a few days later, he lay down and didn't get up.

On the open desert the smell of sage pulled Everett from the spell of the mountains. He glanced at the mesas and thought: What majestic country! How God has flaunted his work here! He glanced at the fading mountain behind him, blue in the distance, and felt glad to be alive and free.

The wind blew steadily. The image of the old Navajo woman serving him came back, her thin locks of white hair floating over her old face when she smiled at him with her eyes.

Chapter Twenty-Six

Dowozhiebito Canyon, Arizona
(July 1934)

*J*osé had heard a burro approach and stepped out onto the porch of the Chilchinbeto Trading Post just as Everett tied Cockleburs to the wooden rail. Everett leaned forward, and they shook hands.

José said, "You were gone longer than we expected."

Everett grinned triumphantly. He ducked under the railing and stood beside José. "I've been to so many beautiful places, and I didn't wish to taste but to drink deep, so I lingered."

José placed a hand on his shoulder. "I've missed your enthusiasm."

Everett smiled, "I've missed you too, José."

Then he laughed and added, "and maybe one or two others—but that's it. Even after traipsing all over for a few years, most people still don't get me."

José patted him on the shoulder. "Well, you're becoming a familiar face around here—maybe you'll come to be part of our little community."

Everett squinted at him. "I think it's the opposite—I'm becoming part of the land, not the people. The beauty of this country is embedded in me now. I feel more detached from life and somehow gentler."

José furrowed his brow and looked at Cockleburs.

"You seem to be missing a burro."

Everett nodded and frowned. "Yup, poor Leopard didn't make it. He took a fall coming out of Copper Canyon, and then halfway here from Navajo Mountain, he just lay down and died."

José walked over and checked Cockleburs for injuries and sore spots from the saddle or the kyacks.

Everett suddenly felt himself swaying. In his mind the last six weeks took shape again. His wanderings had become more reckless, and he'd blazed his own trails instead of sticking to existing ones — unless those led in the direction he wanted.

"Have any trouble finding water?" asked José. "It's getting pretty dry out there."

Everett sat heavily in one of the wooden chairs along the wall. "I got lucky and hit water as I went. Never spent more than two days without it."

José patted Cockleburs rump and said, "Well, you're gonna need another burro if you want to hook up with that archaeological dig."

"That's still happening?" asked Everett.

"Yes," replied José and sat down next to him. "Lyndon Hargrave has got a dig going on in about six months."

"That's great!" exclaimed Everett. "I met him at the Mesa Ranch School a few years ago. But six months is a long time off."

"Well, you could make your way to Dowozhiebito Canyon. They've got some interesting ruins there, and they're excavating right now. It's only twenty-odd miles away."

"Who's in charge there?"

Before José could reply, Tiba stepped onto the porch. Everett jumped up, suddenly invigorated, and held up a hand for her to remain where she was while he rushed off to get something buried deep in one of the kyacks.

"Hi!" he called over his shoulder. "Don't go anywhere."

José held back a smile and watched the young man scurry about. He also noticed that Tiba was trying not to look excited. But she was holding her breath, awkwardly standing there waiting.

Everett returned and handed her a twisted piece of wood that had been carved into the likeness of a young mule deer.

She smiled warmly, nodded, and disappeared into the Trading Post. Everett watched her with a slightly dazed expression.

"Ben Wetherill is coming by tomorrow on his way to the site," said José. "How 'bout I front you another burro and load you with supplies, and you can go with him?"

"Sounds good to me!" cheered Everett. Things were finally coming together for him.

He stepped off the porch again, unloaded a few bundles from Cockleburs, and then led him around back to the stables.

Ben Wetherill and Everett followed two heavily-loaded burros through Dowozhiebito Canyon. Tall sandstone cliffs stood on both sides of them, narrowing slightly as they penetrated deeper into the ravine.

The July heat was brutal, and many of the spring flowers were now gone. He saw no columbine or sego lilies, only a few sunflowers and scarlet buglers in damp, shaded spots.

Up in the cliffs, ruins were tucked away in high, seemingly inaccessible recesses, and Everett kept shading his eyes to scope out a scrambling route up to them.

Ahead they could see a camp with numerous tents and people scurrying about.

"Whoa!" exclaimed Everett. "I didn't think there'd be this many people."

Ben said, "Oh no, this is big. The Rainbow Bridge-Monument Valley Expedition is surveying all the sites in this entire area. The Indians aren't too happy, but it´s work for some of them."

As they got closer they could see young men setting up camp. Some were erecting tents or shelters, others clearing brush away, and a few shirtless boys dug a latrine. They were laughing, apparently unaware that the sun had colored their backs an urgently bright red.

"Looks like they have a bunch of college boys," said Everett.

Ben nodded. "They do. They're friendly, but they don't know a damn about the desert."

He chuckled and added, "Most of them signed up as volunteers, but what they weren't told was they would have to pay three or four hundred dollars for expenses—out of their own pockets—in addition to carrying out free scientific work."

Everett frowned. "I was hoping this was a professional dig."

Ben nodded. "Oh, it is. The college kids are just here to help out. There are plenty of archaeologists here, plus ornithologists, entomologists, botanists, zoologists and geologists."

They stopped under the shade of a juniper to rest for a moment before walking into camp. Everett pulled two metal buckets out of one of the kyacks and poured some water into them from his canteen. The burros went right to it, and once they drank, he had a sip.

He offered the canteen to Ben, who stared hard at Everett and said, "You know, I always thought of you as more of a free spirit that stayed away from people. You sure you want to get involved in all this?"

Everett looked back defiantly. "No, this is a great chance to understand the Ancient Ones."

Ben asked, "What about those Indians interests you? Frankly, I don't get them half the time—and that's the modern ones."

Everett glanced up at one of the ruins, far above them, just short of the rim. He said, "Sure, their way of life may seem an intricately tangled knot, but I find the way that knot unravels is wonderful."

"So you're here to untangle a knot?" asked Ben.

Everett picked up the buckets and placed them back in the kyacks. "Maybe," he said and looked at all the commotion. He scratched his head. "Listen, Ben, I think this might be a good place for me to earn some travelin' money. If there's any extra work, let me know."

Ben laughed. "What's in it for me?"

Everett gave him his best smile. "You can say you helped a friend?"

Ben spat in the dust. "Damn, so we're friends now?"

In the entrance to a large canvas tent ahead of them, a man of about thirty was looking at a clipboard. Ben jerked his chin and said, "There's Clay Lockett. He's the top dog—I'll introduce you."

They approached Lockett, and Everett's blood ran cold. Bad Jack, the angry Navajo, was standing by his side. That guy shows up like a bad penny, he thought.

Ben stepped around Bad Jack and extended his hand to Lockett.

He said, "Mr. Lockett, I want you to meet Everett Ruess. He's a packer, but he's also a good man to have about camp."

Lockett hardly glanced up from his board and said, "Bad timing, Ben—I just hired on this Indian as a camp hand."

Neither Ben nor Everett said anything, and the man finally raised his glance and looked over Everett, who was standing there holding his burros' leads. "Just keep him hauling in our supplies for now."

Everett caught Bad Jack´s gaze, who looked at him with triumphant condescension. He watched him for a moment and saw that there was also fear in Bad Jack's eyes. Fear of what? He wondered.

Ben said, "This kid's a real scrambler, and he'd be helpful in reaching some of the more remote ruins."

Everett turned to Ben, surprised.

Locket nodded. "Well that's something I could use. Send him with Mr. Barton, the biologist and plant guy. He's heading off to a cliff ruin called Bat Woman House."

Everett and Barton stood on the canyon floor, looking up at Bat Woman House. The ruin was perched halfway up the cliff and appeared to be in very good condition. Barton's eyes were almost squinted shut, and his pink skin glistened under a layer of sweat. Cockleburs stood behind them. His kyacks empty except for some rope and water.

"I can't see us getting up there without help," said Barton.

Everett chuckled. "No, this one is easy. We can follow that scree up to that rock shelf, and then there's a ladder."

"I don't see a ladder," replied Barton, taking off his hat and scratching his sweaty head.

Everett pointed out a series of divots that led up.

"That's a hand-and-toe trail that the ancient ones pounded into the cliff," said Everett. "The cowboys called them *Moqui steps*."

Barton looked skeptical. "I'll be damned if that's a ladder, son."

Everett grabbed a rope from the kyack and scurried up the scree.

"You'll see—just watch!" he shouted and quickly ascended.

Over the next twenty minutes, Everett made his way to the top of the scree. It was steep and loose, and he chose a path close to an adjacent cliff where he could use the solid rocks to prevent slipping.

He took a short break on the shelf and then moved up the hand-and-toe trail like he was half spider.

Mr. Barton closed his open mouth. "I can't look," he said and averted his eyes.

When Everett was inside the ruins, he tied the rope to a solid timber embedded in the back wall. Then he threw the other end down. "Come on up!" he shouted, but Mr. Barton looked nowhere near ready to try.

Up close to the shadowed cliff wall, Clay Locket held a meeting for the entire archaeological crew at camp. The bottom of the cliff had been worn away, and above a large ruin named Twin Caves Pueblo leaned over them.

A long panel covered with petroglyphs and pictographs ran along the base of the wall. The fifty-odd people that sat quietly listening to Clay speak all looked eager to begin excavation.

Clay said, "Team one will explore Twin Caves Pueblo. I'd wanted to put another team in the ruin above it, but we can't find a way to get there."

Ben didn't like speaking in front of crowds, and so his voice quivered slightly as he proposed: "We could use the old trail to get up onto Skeleton Mesa. 'Course the start is six miles away, and once you're up top, it's pretty squirrely to find the ruin since from up there you can't see below the rim."

Everett stepped back, away from the shadow of the wall, and eyed the ruin, which was at least three hundred feet up the wall.

Lockett said, "It would make things easier to haul the supplies to the mesa and have a base camp there, but I guess it would be pointless if we can't mark the ruin off."

"I can get there," said Everett, from about twenty feet away, where he stared up at the wall.

Everyone looked at him. Clay glanced at Ben Wetherill.

Ben nodded and said, "If the kid says he can do it, I'd let him try. From the ruin he could scramble up to the top of the mesa, and if he tied a flag to a tree there, it'd certainly make it easier to find when we get there with the burros."

"Good," said Locket, "that settles it."

The meeting ended, and everyone began to drift away. One of the young students by the rock panel noticed something odd—a sequence of musical notes laid out amongst the Indian pictographs.

The student said, "Look at this! The Indians painted music."

An archaeologist behind him shook his head. "That panel was created long before musical notation was brought to the Americas."

Another volunteer examined the notes, then reached into his backpack and pulled out a wooden flute. He paused for a moment while everyone quieted down, then he played the four notes.

Suddenly a Mourning Dove whistled back the same song in response.

"How do you explain that?" asked the student with the flute.

The archaeologist looked uncomfortable. "I can't."

As everyone drifted off, Ben Wetherill approached Everett. He stared at the notes on the mural.

He said, "You explored this area a few years ago, didn't you?"

Everett blushed slightly and nodded. Ben walked off chuckling.

Everett was high on the wall, following the barely visible trail, with a long rope dangling from his waist and two more coiled on his shoulder. From the ground the rock appeared vertical, and what he was doing looked impossible. Clay Lockett watched him, wringing his hands.

He said, "If that kid gets killed, I'll never forgive myself."

About halfway up, Everett stopped and tied two of the ropes together, then continued. The route he followed wasn't as bad as many he'd ascended in the last few months. After nearly an hour Everett reached the ruin and whooped.

He tied the rope to the trunk of a juniper that had taken root near one of the walls and dangled it down where he thought the scientist might make their most straightforward ascent.

"Great view from here!" he shouted to the crowd of onlookers. Since he'd started his climb, almost all activity in the camp had stopped.

There were several ruins tucked back into an alcove, and between two of them, Everett found a partially concealed path that led behind the ruin and then up the left side of the alcove and onto the mesa.

He scrambled up and tied a red bandana to a tree, about six feet off the ground. He then secured the final rope to the tree and trailed it back down to the ruin.

When Everett was at camp again, Lockett approached him with Ben and Bad Jack.

He said, "I want you three to take the mule trail to the top with supplies and set up camp.

Everett nodded. Ben thought for a moment, then said, "It's a twelve-mile trip, plus the ascent up the mesa, so don't expect us there before mid-afternoon tomorrow."

Lockett nodded and walked off. "Be careful."

Bad Jack shouldered a heavy pack, glared at Everett, and headed out of camp. Ben watched him go and said, "We're gonna take only your two burros. I think the two of us will manage fine without him."

The journey up to the mesa took all the skills Everett had developed over the last few years. The trail was precarious, and the burros balked at it. Cockleburs almost slid off the trail once, and after that became skittish; the burro José had loaned him had never ascended anything so steep and had to be constantly urged forward.

He was grateful to have Ben on his side.

About halfway up, they passed the bleached bones of a horse.

"Yup," said Everett, smirking, "looks like Skeleton Mesa to me."

Shortly before sunset, they made it onto the mesa top and decided to camp right on the edge.

Three hundred and fifty feet below the gray-yellow floor of the canyon glittered and shimmered in the heat.

When darkness had descended, Everett scanned the mesa, dreading to discover the flicker of Bad Jack's fire, but the wilderness around them looked deserted.

They built a fire, and Everett cooked a vegetable stew in a pot. After a few hours, they were both on the edge of sleep when they heard chanting coming from across the mesa.

Ben sat up and listened.

He asked, "Do you recognize that song?"

Everett took a guess. "It might be the Night Way. I was told it is used as protection against witches."

Ben stoked the glowing embers with a stick. "Superstitious, those Indians. Wonder what kind of witches they think are out here?"

Everett recalled bumping into Bad Jack his first year on Black Mesa after leaving the Hopi Lands. Bad Jack had fearfully eyed the dead snake that Everett was holding up and called him *Yenaldlooshi*.

He asked Ben, "What's a *Yenaldlooshi*?"

Ben instinctively looked over his shoulder, and in a quiet voice, he said, "That's a Skin Walker. All I know about them is they wear coyote skins, travel at night, and all Navajos fear them."

Everett laughed. "Are you afraid of them?"

Ben shook off his uneasiness. "No. But you don't want to say that word around the other Indians, or you'll get everyone spooked."

They lay back to sleep, but neither drifted off until about an hour later when the chanting stopped. Everett thought of the many miles he'd walked in the dead of night. Often, his dog Curly had been sitting up in the backpack, his paws on Everett's shoulders. He wondered if that could be considered a coyote pelt.

It took most of the next day for Ben and Everett to reach the rim above the ruin. From the top they could hardly see the bottom of the canyon, but the base camp was out of sight some eighty feet back under the cliff. It was only the bright red bandana that allowed them to close in on the archaeological site.

Once they spotted it, they found the rope and descended to the alcove where several archaeologists who had climbed up from below were already at work. Communication with the base camp was only possible by climbing halfway down and yelling messages back and forth.

Soon Everett discovered that it would be his job to scramble up and down whenever a tool was needed or a message had to be related.

Bad Jack watched from a dark corner of the ruin. He didn't offer to help in any way, and nobody asked him. His eyes smoldered as he watched the archaeologists paw through a row of graves along the back wall.

He kept his right hand tightly clasped to the medicine pouch he wore around his neck and smoked cigarettes with his left hand until he ran out.

There were three other men in the cave: an archaeologist, Todd, his assistant, and a photographer named Andrew.

Andrew was sweating heavily. When he saw Everett lean against the cool wall to relax, he set down his camera and approached him. Nervously, he asked, "What's the trail like? I'm dreading the climb out of this eagle's nest, and I'd rather walk the long way around. I barely made it up."

Everett shrugged. "Not bad, but it'll take you two days."

But it seemed that Andrew was bothered by something more than the scary descent.

"How's the dig going?" asked Everett. "What did you find in there?"

"We're just getting started. We're not all mountain goats like you," he said. "It took us most of yesterday just to get here—and it seems we didn't bring much food, so we're all pretty hungry."

Everett smiled. "I'll get right on some grub."

On Skeleton Mesa Everett sat under the shade of a lone juniper and peeled potatoes. Cockleburs stood by the supplies and watched the other burro trying to eat an empty tin can. Everett had a fire going with some sticks he'd collected and wondered how tough it would be to haul firewood up the cliff; there weren't many trees up on the mesa, and he hadn't found much that was burnable.

The archaeologist, Todd, came climbing up the steep trail and crouched down by the fire, panting. He nodded at Everett.

Everett paused the peeling. "How old are these ruins? I heard someone below saying they have been here over a thousand years."

Todd smiled, feeling rejuvenated by the fresh air.

"We call the earliest culture from this area the Basketmakers," said Todd, "and their society reaches back over three thousand years. But I don't think this is one of their ruins. I'd guess it's from a later society that we call the Pueblo People."

Everett stared at him expectantly until he added, "Maybe six hundred and fifty years. I'd guess this is Pueblo III.

"How long were they here?" asked Everett.

Todd scratched his head. "Well, that's part of what we're trying to determine."

Everett stood up and stretched his legs. "Are there any Pueblo IV ruins near here?"

Todd shook his head. "Not one in the whole Tsegi drainage — or at least we haven't found one yet."

"Why do you think that is?" asked Everett.

"We're not sure." He stared at the fire for a minute. "All the cliff dwellers in this area seemed to have left by the late 13th century, and we don't know why."

A gentle wind picked up and blew over the mesa, the first of the afternoon, with a hint of the evening cool. Everett gazed over the wilderness around them.

"What would make someone leave this place?" he asked.

"Could'a been a drought," said Todd. "There was a bad one about that time — or maybe another group of people competed for resources and drove them off."

Everett chuckled. "That sounds ominous."

He had hoped to get a laugh out of the archaeologist, but instead, Todd looked back seriously. "I think this ruin might hold some answers to that question."

Everett wanted to ask more questions, but again the pensive look in the man's eye made him feel something was bothering him.

"Hey, I'm going down the cliff now to get our mail and a few camp luxuries," said Everett. "Need anything?"

Todd took in a deep breath. "Well, we're about to start opening the gravesites—if I thought they had alcohol down there, I'd have you bring me a bottle. I could use a drink."

The next afternoon Everett scampered back into the ruin. Tied to his waist was a rope, and after he'd caught his breath, he slowly hauled up the load of wood that was connected to the other end.

When he had the wood safely in the ruin, he yelled down.

"All clear!" then shouldered the bundle and hauled it up onto the mesa.

With that accomplished, he returned to the ruin to see what was happening. Bad Jack napped where he'd last seen him. He looked around the site, noticing Todd at work over one of the burials. His assistant stood over him, holding a lantern and sweating profusely.

Andrew, the photographer, was crouched in the corner, watching with a nervous expression.

Everett walked over to Andrew and said, "They looked undisturbed when I first peeked in."

He nodded. "They were. We found twelve burials and fairly well-preserved mummies, and this..."

He held up a small box filled with bones. Bad Jack was suddenly there, awake and peering at the bones. He clutched his medicine pouch and backed away with fear in his eyes.

He said, "Those are not from an animal that lives here."

Andrew glanced at Bad Jack and said, "Mr. Barton thinks they belonged to a hedgehog. They might have lived in this area six hundred years ago."

Bad Jack shook his head and spoke with wide eyes: "No. That creature is from the spirit world."

He became agitated. "These rock hogans are home to the ghosts of the Old People—you shouldn't disturb them!"

The archaeologist stood and held out his hands, fingers splayed.

He walked up, looking worried, and said, "Listen, there's no need to get everyone worked up."

Andrew set the box of bones aside. He noticed that Todd was sweating heavily. Something *was* wrong.

"Well, what is it?" asked Andrew.

Todd said, "The burials look like they've been desecrated shortly after the bodies were first buried."

"But the burial sites were sealed when we found them," Andrew said.

Todd nodded, and despite trying not to, looked at Bad Jack.

"Yes. But the three burials we've opened so far all had skeletons that were missing their skulls."

Bad Jack turned pale and began backing away. He mumbled something in Diné and then turned to scramble up onto the mesa.

Everett didn't see him again, although he still listened for his song at night when he slept by his fire on the mesa.

That evening, having just finished washing the pot and dishes from the evening meal, Everett took out a pad and paper and began writing a letter.

Nobody felt at ease in the ruin anymore, and Andrew, Todd, and his assistant now joined Everett at night and slept close to his fire on the mesa.

Suddenly an owl swooped over Everett, screeching.

He jumped to his feet, feeling the hair on the back of his neck stand up straight.

He nervously watched the bird sail off, but moments later, it attacked him again. It was sure acting strangely.

Notah had explained to Everett once that sometimes ghosts returning to their graves would take the shape of an owl. Now Everett watched the darkness, no longer confident of what it contained.

He lifted his pencil again and started with the letter.

"Dear Waldo,
Please go into my boxes and mail me the leather bundle marked KEET
SEEL. Do it immediately."

The next few weeks were busy. At first, Everett stayed on the top of the mesa, cooking meals and occasionally helping to lower down artifacts or one of the archaeologists, and then they were on to the next ruin, and he helped cart the gear back down to base camp.

While cooking meals on Skeleton Mesa, he'd had time for painting several watercolors. He also read *Don Quixote*, and in some weird way, identified with the delusional man—who also rode a burro—and chased after dreams.

All counted, they had dug up eleven burials in the first ruin, and all of the skeletons they found had been headless. This had put a deep fear into the few Indians who worked on the dig, making everyone uneasy. It was taboo for the Navajos to touch or disturb the dead, and the digging up of graves with headless skeletons in them had to be handled by the archaeologists and the volunteers.

Everett helped the archeologists access one or two other ruins, and he had made a few trips back and forth to the Chilchinbeto Trading Post while they were starting to wrap up the dig. He had looked forward to seeing Tiba again, but she'd been away with Notah each time.

Everett led two burros to the porch of the Chilchinbeto Trading Post and called for José, but nobody came out. Everett had a wild look about him, with a face full of stubble and deeply tanned skin from living on the exposed flats of Skeleton Mesa, where there had been little shelter.

But then Tiba appeared. Her eyes were sad.

"What happened?" he asked, afraid of her answer.

She stared at him.

"José?"

She nodded. The Trading Post was quiet. He later found out that José had been riding the load on a truck when a wheel came off and the vehicle had rolled over him.

"I'm sorry about José. I liked him. Where has everyone gone?"

A strong breeze rattled the Trading Post, and she gestured that the others had blown off like the wind.

After a minute she disappeared inside and returned with a leather bundle. She handed it to him, and he opened it enough to see the aged jawbone he had found at Keet Seel two years ago.

"I have something I have to do," he said to her, "and I don't know if I'm coming back to the Trading Post after. It won't be the same without José."

She looked crestfallen.

"Would you like to meet me in a few months?"

She nodded.

"Do you know where the Escalante empties into the Colorado?"

She nodded again.

"The river is low this year but wait for me on the south side of the Colorado for the November full moon."

He grabbed the burros' leads, then turned back.

"Oh yeah, my name is Nemo now."

Everett walked up onto the Keet Seel ruins, which were shaded from the afternoon sun. He left the burros below. There wasn't another soul around, and a whistling wind moved through the forgotten pueblo.

He walked into one of the crumbling ruins, took off his backpack, reached inside, and took out the leather bundle. Tenderly, he unwrapped the jaw bone and gazed at it.

He looked over at the pile of debris in the corner where he had found the mandible. He walked over and dug down into it, making a hole.

He placed the bone inside and covered it.

"I'm sorry I disturbed you."

Chapter Twenty-Seven

The Hopi Mesas, Arizona
(August 1934)

With the monsoon rains approaching, Everett decided to travel south into the land of the Hopi. He had heard much about these "Callers of the Clouds" on his travels throughout the Southwest. Even the Navajos considered Hopi magic to be older and more potent than theirs, and Everett wanted to experience it.

He followed a dry, twisting track, watching the clouds slowly stack up, but they had yet to let loose their frail curtains of rain.

Before him, Black Mesa loomed off the Colorado Plateau, and in this roadless wilderness, the only paths followed the drainages. He trailed them, always moving southward and up in elevation.

He'd kept the burro José had advanced him; he had earned enough money at the dig to pay off the debt. José's passing still tugged at his heart.

"Get away from that edge, Chocolatero!" he yelled when the burro veered too close to a steep drop. Everett had named him for his rich, dark coat. The burro was young and strong, and Everett hoped that this would make up for his inexperience. Luckily, he seemed to get along with Cockleburs, too.

During his leisure time at the dig, he'd built a new kyack. The boxes were decorated with designs that he had copied from the pictographs on the rock art panel beneath the Twin Caves Pueblo. Chocolatero hadn't complained when he put them on, and Everett was glad they fit so snugly.

Now, he yearned for rain, but not until he was up on the mesa. He walked behind the burros and encouraged them to keep moving.

"Step it up, boys!" he shouted. "We don't want to be in a drainage when the skies open."

The kyacks held two jugs of water and their sloshing made him long for a drink. The smell of dust was in his nostrils, but he knew he had to conserve water. If he didn't have to find his way through this maze of arroyos, he would have traveled at night.

Besides snow, the summer thunderstorm season provided just about all the moisture this area had received over the last few years, which meant the waterholes would most likely be empty now. Ben Wetherill had described the land as waterless and bitter, but Charlie had claimed there were many springs to be found on the mesa if you knew where to look.

Everett didn't find any.

Severe dust storms were ravaging the mid-west. At the Chilchinbeto Trading Post, he'd glimpsed a month-old newspaper that claimed the entire area was turning into a dust bowl.

He wondered if there was a connection with the lack of rain in the southwest these last few years.

To make matters worse, Chocolatero stumbled on a root which made the water jugs smash against each other; they both broke and the precious liquid leaked onto the dusty ground. In the heat of the day all Everett could do was keep moving.

They continued through the late afternoon, climbing out of the washes and through pines and high sage under the sparse glow of a new crescent moon, and then later by starlight.

He wished desperately not to have lost all that water.

The evening's silence was broken only by the crickets chirping, but Everett knew the darkness was swarming with life. Little moved in the blistering heat of the day, but at night the desert thrived.

A nighthawk called from above, and when they rounded the next rise, he realized that they were finally on the mesa.

An hour before the horizon began to lighten, he unloaded the burros, hobbled them, and crawled under his blanket for a few hours' sleep.

The next day they passed by low cliffs with black seams of coal running through them, and Everett recalled that this was how the mesa got its name. The plateau was vast, and Everett felt tiny and insignificant as he rode along on Cockleburs with Chocolatero in tow.

Both the Navajo and the Hopi revered Black Mesa. It had little value as grazing land, but the holy men of both tribes found solace in its lonely crags. Among its towering cliffs, the Hopi collected eagle feathers for their ceremonies.

Everett's painter's eyes surveyed the colors as they plodded along: the blue-greens of the juniper and faded teal of the sage, the silver of the bunch grass, and dark green at the base of the pointy agaves. The rabbitbrush was in bloom with a vibrant yellow.

But since he wanted to reach the Hopi villages for the rain dances, he didn't linger to paint.

The country now sloped southward, which allowed him to follow the canyons as far as was practical. Unfortunately, there were no landmarks, and in some of the narrow gorges, it was easy to get lost, so he navigated by the sun. Only once did he have to resort to the compass the ranger had given him at the Grand Canyon a few years before.

He traveled slowly, camping in the open, and didn't see another human being until his third night when he passed a group of Navajos heading in the opposite direction.

He yelled a greeting towards them. "*Yá'át'ééh!*" Hello!

They laughed and waved back, and one of them replied, "*Yá'át'ééh,* Picture Man!"

Everett woke a few hours after dawn with a start when he heard the rattlesnake. He didn't move but instead listened, hoping to make out its location.

217

The previous day he had almost been bitten when a rattler had struck before he saw it. Only luck had saved him, or maybe the burros walking beside him had confused the snake, which had shot past his left leg with glistening fangs. It had been a close call, and he shivered thinking about it.

He figured this snake had crawled under his Navajo blanket in the night and was now somewhere under his right knee. He could feel it slither beneath him, and he lifted the leg ever so carefully.

He had made his camp under a large rock, and in front of him was his fire, which had died away. He didn't have anywhere to go.

He moved slowly, inching away from the snake and closer to the rock.

And then he glimpsed its head poking out from the edge of the blanket, next to one of the stones from the fire. It looked right at him, and then coiled more of its body free until the rattle appeared, vibrating.

The snake flicked its tongue and lifted its head slightly.

This time there was no escape. He was going to get bit.

Then another movement caught his eye and he saw someone traveling across the dried plain.

From the corner of his eye, he made out runners trotting across the plain with their eyes on the ground. They seemed otherworldly.

The snake inched closer, and he frantically looked for something to kill it with. He pressed tighter against the rock behind him, searching blindly for a stone.

And then his hand touched a rock about the size of his fist. He slowly closed his hand around it and gripped it tightly.

Everett looked up and saw an elderly Indian standing on the other side of the fire, watching him. When their eyes locked, the man raised his hand, gesturing for Everett to remain calm.

The man was painted with zig-zagging white lines across his chest. He was Hopi, Everett realized.

The man grabbed the snake from behind and quickly pulled it out into the opening. The snake headed for a cluster of brush; the Hopi produced a feather and began running it along the side of the snake.

, After a moment the snake stopped. The Hopi continued to stroke the snake, which relaxed and straightened out.

The man then grabbed the snake by the mid-section and trotted back to where he had come from. The snake appeared relaxed, and the man was unafraid of being bitten for some unknown reason.

Everett sat up and exhaled.

"Not even out of bed and I'm dodging snakes," he said to the burros who had watched the whole thing.

"Did you see that?" he asked, looking in the direction of the running man. Other Hopi runners were crossing the plain, and he realized that many of them were also holding snakes.

He hastily broke down his camp and started in the same direction that they were heading in. In the far distance he could barely make out the southern end of Black Mesa extending like three gnarled fingers. These were the Hopi Mesas, home to the oldest continuously inhabited settlements in America.

The deep blue sky was void of a single cloud over the open desert. Everett trudged along with his burros, his lips were cracked, and he felt about as dry as the land around him. He hadn't had a sip of water in forty-eight hours.

He had lost sight of the Hopi runners, but in the delirium brought on by the heat, it seemed to him that they were just ahead, leading him.

The air held not a drop of moisture, and the sun beat down on him as if he were an ant under the magnifying glass of a cruel kid.

And then, in the shimmering heat on the horizon, he made out what he hoped was Second Mesa. He put his head down and summoned the last of his reserves. The burros followed obediently. They, too, were parched but sensed shelter and water was near, and when they closed in on a village, they picked up their pace.

In the late afternoon Everett reached Mishongnovi Village on Second Mesa. On the outskirts, they had passed patchy cornfields along the drainages at the bottom of the mesa.

He found a path that led up onto the mesa and followed it.

Everett stumbled ahead of the burros, dehydrated and exhausted, and soon had a crowd of young children following him into the village.

Mutton jerky was hanging to dry in front of some of the houses, and his stomach growled.

One older boy of about sixteen addressed him.

"Hey! Picture Man!" he shouted. "Do you remember me?"

Everett barely heard his words. He still kept his eyes on the ground while he walked. Through the fog, the words slowly penetrated. He looked up at the boy. Must be Martin, he thought, the kid who had appeared with a glass of water when Everett had stumbled through Hopi land three years ago. He'd been out of water then, too.

"Yes," he said quietly, and then the image focused. He smiled and said, "Martin."

Martin beamed. His face was painted. He said, "The Antelope Dance is tomorrow. Everyone is preparing — come see."

Martin led them through the village slowly. He stopped before a small pen with a trough beside an abandoned stone shelter. "You can leave your things inside," said Martin.

While Everett led the burros into the pen, Martin disappeared and returned with a bucket of water. He poured most of it into the wooden trough and then handed the pail to Everett, who drank deeply.

Martin grinned when Everett poured the last cupful over his head, and he could see the life returning to the young man's eyes now that he refreshed himself in a shaded place.

Martin retrieved another bucket for the burros who had just about drained the trough.

Everett took their leads and lifted their heads when they were done.

"This is Cockleburs," he said, "and this is Chocolatero."

Martin greeted them, and Everett said to the animals, "Say thank you for the water."

The burros stared at Martin.

Martin then helped unload the burros, rub them down, and give them some feed. He disappeared for a moment and returned with some hard Hopi *piki* bread that tasted of ground corn and bacon fat.

Everett devoured it, nodding thanks.

Everett followed Martin to a large circle of stones with a log ladder rising from an underground room below. In the shade, a Hopi silversmith sat in front of a blanket with a display of turtle shells, parrot feathers, gourd rattles and other items used by the Hopi dancers.

Martin said, "He's trading that stuff for turquoise, which he will in turn barter with the traders or the Navajos."

Everett inspected the items, deciding to buy something for his mother as soon as he had a better idea of their value.

They climbed down the ladder into a large round chamber with about ten men practicing a dance in the flickering light of a fire.

They all stopped and watched him descend. And Martin feared for a moment he had done wrong by bringing Everett, who was the only non-Hopi, into the kiva.

But then one of the men called, "Hey, Picture Man! Welcome!"

The tension broke, and another man approached Everett with some white paint. He told him to take off his shirt, and then he painted several white lightning bolts on his chest.

The other men began to practice a dance, showing the steps to the younger men.

They both watched the man applying the paint.

When he was done, they sat down with their backs to the wall and watched the dancers.

Later the dancers took a break and shared a meal by the fire. The smoke rose and slowly spiraled out the door hole in the ceiling, which now revealed a beautiful sky, colored red and yellow in the sunset.

"The rains should have come by now," said Martin, "but we've had little so far."

Everett thought of the hot, arid passage he had made to get to the Hopi Mesas. He'd listened to a few Hopis complain about the dry conditions. One had claimed he had already thinned his corn three times.

"It felt pretty dry out there," said Everett.

Martin nodded and said, "The corn dies in the field, and there is no grass. We will find out soon if the clouds hear us when we call for them."

Back when Everett had stayed at Pat's cabin, they had been on the slopes of the San Francisco Peaks. When Martin mentioned that those very peaks were home to the *katsinas* for part of the year, he asked, "So what are these *katsinas*?"

Martin nodded. "We believe they are supernatural beings — and they visit us as rain clouds. It is the *katsinas* that oversee the natural world."

The dancers had begun to run through their moves again. One of them approached Everett and asked him to join in, and he rose to his feet and slowly began to follow their movements.

They sang when they danced. He had learned a fair amount of Navajo but didn't know much Hopi. Nevertheless, he stumbled through the chant, and over the next hour, the words and vocals began to sink in.

Darkness had settled above them, and Everett realized he would be spending the night in the kiva. Martin disappeared for a moment and returned with Everett's Navajo blanket.

"Your burros are fine," he said.

The dancers practiced again.

After Martin was seated again, he helped Everett memorize the songs, whispering their words softly by his side. Soon the others settled down for the evening. Some returned to their homes, but a half-dozen dancers lay down by the fire.

Everett lay awake for a while, and late at night, Bad Jack entered his thoughts. The last time he had seen him was at the dig. The headless bodies the archeologists excavated had given everyone the spooks, and once again, Everett wondered why Bad Jack seemed to have focused his agitation on him.

He asked Martin, who was also still awake, "Do the Hopis have issues with dead bodies, like the Navajo?"

Martin said, "No, we don't mind them—but we've got our own hang-ups."

"Like what? Do you believe in witches?"

"Once," Martin said soberly, "I saw a man turn into an owl and fly away."

Everett remained silent for a while. Martin finally asked, "Why do you ask about witches? We call them *powaqas*, and the Navajo have their own *powaqas*. Have you seen one?"

"No," said Everett. "But I was recently on an archaeological dig, and one of the Navajos seemed offended by what was going on. For some reason he kept glaring at me like he wanted to accuse me."

Martin nodded. "He probably thought you were a witch. But the first rule of dealing with a witch is to never talk about witchcraft with the person you fear might be a witch."

"Why would he think I was a witch?" asked Everett.

Martin was quiet for a moment, then said, "*Powaqas* are people with two souls—one of an animal and another of a human. We call them two-hearts. If he thinks you are one, then it is good for you."

"Why?" asked Everett.

The Hopi smiled. "Because he will stay away from you as much as he can."

Everett watched the coals burning in the fire. "I'm not too sure about that," he said. "This guy really doesn't like me, and I'm afraid that his hatred will one day trump his fear."

Martin laughed. "Just tell him you are the true *Pahana*."

"What's that?"

"The long-lost White Brother of the Hopi," said Martin gravely.

Everett thought he was making fun of him. "Seriously?"

Martin nodded. "When the Hopi began their migration to the Fourth World, the *Pahana* left for the east. It is said that he will return, and when he arrives, the wicked will be destroyed and a new age of peace will begin."

Everett chuckled. "Okay…"

Martin continued, "Or tell him you emerged from the *Sipapu*, in the Grand Canyon. Our ancestors first entered the present world from the *Sipapu*."

Everett stared at him, confused, and Martin continued. "The ancestors came from another place, in another time, and the *Sipapu* was the door. They say sometimes an elder finds one of these doors and disappears into it."

Everett lay back and closed his eyes. He would sleep in a little while, but first he had to think. He knew he wasn't a witch, and he doubted he was the *Pahana*, but he had to come to grips with Bad Jack someday. And the key to how best to do this was buried in these beliefs.

But how could a long, lost white brother or a time portal help?

Everett rose when other Hopis descended into the kiva the next morning. Martin helped to touch up his body paint and then draped some green vines over his neck and had him hold another in his mouth. He grabbed some vines for himself and tossed them over his shoulder.

"Now we're ready," he said with a smile.

Everett wanted to ask the significance of the vines but couldn't speak with the plants between his teeth. They climbed up the ladder and walked to a clearing in the center of the village. Other painted men joined them, and they danced together.

For the next few hours they danced, and in the late afternoon the skies began to cloud up.

Everett painted a panorama of Hotevilla village on Third Mesa and the plains that extended behind it. Children clustered around him, bumping his canvas in their attempts to watch him work.

He watched a woman make pottery containers and admired her progress as he painted. For some reason — most likely superstitious, he thought — she always made two at once.

Earlier, he had sketched some houses on the mesa rim, and an old man had shouted at him to go away. Several neighbors had intervened, and eventually, it became clear that the man was upset because he thought Everett was painting the kiva.

"Here," Everett said and gave the man the sketch. He took it reluctantly but appeared pacified.

Above, the skies were dark with clouds that had yet to release their moisture. The air was thick with rumbling thunder.

On the other side of the village, a group of dancers were in the final stages of a Snake Dance. Martin's younger brother Chusi, a kid of about twelve, grabbed Everett's hand and pulled him to watch. Chusi had volunteered to walk to Third Mesa with him. On the way he taught him some of the words for the songs of the Snake Dance.

They watched about twenty men stepping to the rhythm of their song. All were painted and carried snakes. Some held the snakes in their hands or over their shoulders. Others had the head clamped in their mouths. More dancers walked behind the men with the snakes and stroked them with a feather.

Everett said, "My enemy, the snake."

The boy shook his head.

He said, "No. Snake is good. He is our brother. He comes from the underworld like the Hopi."

Everett had no love for snakes. He had had numerous encounters with them in the southwest, and the Sierras, two had almost bit him while he was crossing Black Mesa. He shivered.

He watched the dancers and finally asked, "Why do they put them in their mouths?"

Chusi said, "So the snake will impart our prayers to the rain gods."

Every few minutes, a dancer carrying a snake ran off to the desert to release it into one of the four directions.

An old medicine man, draped in several snakes, walked across the plaza and stood before Everett. Another Hopi sauntered alongside him, tickling the snakes with a feather when they became agitated.

The old man leaned forward and placed his forehead against Everett's. Several of the snakes rattled, and Everett was terrified.

The old Hopi began to chant.

A crack of lightning cut through the chanting, and then the rain began to come down in curtains.

Chapter Twenty-Eight

Oak Creek Canyon, Arizona
(September 1934)

A low rumbling shook the ponderosa pine forest. High in one of the trees, a flicker lifted its head and paused in its pursuit of insects. The breeze shifted slightly and the disturbance faded. Below, Everett slept on a bed of pine needles. The evening had been cool, but between the thick carpet of needles and his Navajo blanket, he'd kept quite warm.

For once he'd slumbered past the gentle sunrise.

Now he lay there, gradually becoming aware of the muffled vibration.

A car, he thought.

No, probably a truck.

South of here. At least five miles away.

He got to his feet and brushed off the pine needles. His legs were stiff, but he felt rested. The wind changed, and he could no longer hear the vehicle, but now he knew which direction the road lay.

Several days earlier, he had stopped at the Grand Canyon to leave his burros with an artist friend at Desert View. He missed them. When they were with him, he could always locate nearby roads by following the direction of their ears when they pricked up.

At least that worked with Cockleburs.

Chocolatero still didn't know what was up most times.

He broke down his simple camp, shouldered his pack, and began heading south.

Clay Lockett's smile turned to a nervous frown when he opened the door of his cabin and saw Everett standing there. A pleasant light filtered down through the pines and lit Everett's frame and the grin on his face.

"Great place you got here," said Everett sincerely.

Lockett creased his brow. "Ruess? What are you doing here?"

Everett set down his pack. "You said to stop by if I was ever in the neighborhood." He gave his best smile and added, "So here I am!"

Lockett heard his wife shuffling inside and stammered, "Well, I only just returned home myself—I've barely unpacked."

Then he looked the young man over and saw that he was sunburnt, gaunt and half-starved. The last time they had met, he had been well-fed, but a little over a month later, Everett looked like he had just survived an ordeal.

"Now, where did you come from?" he asked.

Casually, Everett said, "I just walked from the Grand Canyon, and before that, I spent some time exploring the Hopi Mesas."

Lockett shook his head and invited him in.

At the dinner table Everett sat with Clay's wife, Florence, who looked aghast at the amount of food he was shoveling down.

"This is delicious!" said Everett. "I enjoyed my time with the Hopis, but I don't know how they survive their diet."

Over the next half hour, Clay and Florence asked him dozens of questions, and he answered them between bites. He devoured everything they placed in front of him.

"What you do sounds dangerous," said Florence.

"Sometimes," he said. "My last misadventure occurred when Chocolatero stirred up some wild bees."

"Did you get stung?" she asked.

"A couple of times, I guess, mostly around my eyes, and then on my hands when I swatted at them. A few more stings might have been too much for me. I was three or four days getting my eyes open again and recovering the use of my hands, and it made traveling difficult."

"That sounds horrible," she said, shocked.

He shrugged. "It wasn't that bad."

He lowered his eyes and creased his brow, then finally looked up and said, "What I find difficult is the fact that I can describe the ugly experiences I've had, and people get them right away, but when I try that with things that are beautiful, I seem to fail."

Now he had her attention. Florence said, "Well, tell us of the beauty that you have seen, please!"

His eyes took on a distant look as he began. "There have been so many—I've ridden over a thousand miles on a burro. You wouldn't believe the wild, untamed land that's out there. The white man sees desolation and calls it a desert, but the Navajo name for it means 'beautiful valley.'"

Florence looked at him expectantly to hear more about the mysterious lands of the Southwest. But instead, he kept on about his frustrations. "I write to my friends, and they complain that they can't think of what to write about, but I could write pages for every day of my life here."

"And what would you write about?" she asked.

"Everything!" The look on her face told him she still didn't quite get what he was saying. He figured they were just making small talk. And he had always found that frustrating.

He had learned that Navajo and Hopi didn't engage in conversation like whites. When they had something to say, they said it all in one rush and spoke until they were done, not pausing or inviting the comments of others, as whites did.

But Clay and Florence Lockett had invited him into their home and were feeding him. And he did enjoy their company, so he answered their questions politely until there was no more food on the table.

Later, he stepped outside to gaze at the stars while Clay helped his wife with the dishes.

Florence said quietly, "We barely have enough food for ourselves, let alone a freeloader."

Clay surprised himself by defending Everett. "He's more of a free spirit than a freeloader."

"Did you see how much he ate?" she asked.

He raised an eyebrow and asked, "Why did you keep filling his plate? You could have stopped after the second helping."

She gave him her most serious stare. "Your paycheck of thirty dollars a month won't last long with him around. I doubt our garden and those two chickens are going to keep up with him either."

"Don't worry, he doesn't sit still long," he said. "I just don't know how to say no to him. He seems so young and enthusiastic and full of love."

"Love?" she asked curiously. "What do you mean? Who does he love?"

Clay shook his head. "Heck, that kid loves everyone and everything. He loves the Navajos, the Hopis, his burros, dogs, kids, animals—you name it, he loves it."

She looked pensive for a moment, then asked, "What was he like on the dig?"

Clay laughed. "He scared the hell out of me. He climbed up those canyon walls to the ruins without a fear in the world. And yet he could have fallen and died any minute."

He rubbed his neck. "He would scurry up to a ruin in ten minutes, and it would take the rest of the day to coax the archaeologist up to the same spot—even with a secure line already top-roped."

She handed him the last dish and wiped her hands on a small towel.

She said, "Well, we're gonna be out of food in a day if he stays here longer."

Everett came back inside and settled into a rocker.

Clay took the seat next to him and said, "I've been thinking, have you ever seen Oak Creek Canyon? It's only a few miles away."

Everett sat on a sandstone ridge and painted a reddish-orange tower of rock with a backdrop of dark, inky clouds. He thought the color was close to persimmon. The landscape reminded him of Zion in many ways, and he wished he had more time to explore it, but he knew he had to head north soon.

He had descended Oak Creek Canyon slowly, leaving the tall ponderosa pines behind as they were replaced by smaller piñons. At first the rocks were a yellow ocher, but that was soon replaced with a bright crimson, and then a deep purple-red, near the canyon's mouth.

Oak Creek Canyon was considerably lower in elevation than Flagstaff, and the air was much warmer down here.

The creek itself was lined with old sycamores and cottonwoods whose leaves were just turning yellow.

The creek's trickling water and the tall, leafy trees were such a contrast to the barren, open desert of the last weeks that he spent the first half of the morning just laying along the creek, listening. He had brought some fishing line with him, and when he finally got up, he caught a trout for breakfast.

A large blue heron had been watching him from across a shallow pool.

He planned on staying only a few nights, camping lightly while painting, and maybe laying the prep work for a block print.

He skirted the town of Sedona, which sat at the mouth of the canyon and supported about a hundred residents, and continued, following the creek downstream until he caught sight of Cathedral Rock. There, he set up camp by a swaying patch of false palo verde.

Majestic red rock buttes surrounded him and inspired him to paint. He worked rapidly with watercolors, matching the colors of the rock where he could.

It was September, but the traces of fall he had felt on the Colorado Plateau hadn't reached Sedona yet. His mother would have called it 'Indian Summer.' Everett reveled in the warmth of the day.

Behind him a mule deer appeared and sniffed at him. He watched it, remembering that day long ago when he'd stared at a deer through the sights of his shotgun — and in the end hadn't pulled the trigger.

The clouds parted for a minute, and shafts of sunlight poured through. He raised his face to the sky and smiled, then painted again.

Clay and his wife sat at the table with Everett. His new painting of Cathedral Rock was on display over the mantle.

"You ought to get some good money for that in California," said Florence.

Everett laughed. "Oh, I'm not planning on returning to California. Besides, I made the painting for you."

Florence looked genuinely flattered. "That seems overly generous," she said. "Now I feel like we're rushing you out the door. Are you sure you can't stay longer?"

Clay looked at her, an amused expression on his face.

Then he turned to Everett and asked, "Whaddaya mean you're not going back?"

Everett looked out the window. "I've become a little too different from the rest of the world. Often when I'm alone in an endless open desert, I find it hard to believe the rest of the world exists anyway."

Clay marveled at this young man. Just like at the dig, he was going to throw all caution to the wind once again. "So, you're gonna just remain in the wilderness? What do I tell people if you disappear?"

Everett leaned back in his chair. "Say that I was tired and weary. That I'd been burned and blinded by the desert sun, but that I kept my dream."

Clay looked at his wife, exasperated.

Through an open window in the cabin Everett watched the San Francisco Peaks being lit up by the setting sun. A first frosting of snow was already covering their summits, and the mountain's flanks were golden with yellowing aspens.

Those were the sacred peaks. From August to February, the *katsina* spirits lived there before returning to the underground world.

A part of him yearned to rest. To settle down and let the winter pass, like the *katsinas* did. But then a breeze blew through the window and he knew it was time to move on.

Pat Jenks sat up in his bed late at night, unsure what had woken him. It was a windy night and the cabin creaked; outside the pines swayed in the coming fall weather.

A full moon fought to peek through the clouds, and during one bright moment, Pat looked out the window and saw a man standing about thirty feet away.

The man waved.

"Everett?"

He stood up quickly and grabbed his shoes. He returned to the window and looked out. The night was dark again and there was nobody in sight.

Pat ran outside and looked around, bewildered. "Everett!"

From behind the thick trunk of an aspen Everett watched Pat. He didn't know why he'd slipped away, but an inner voice told him to remain out of sight.

He felt the weather closing in on him. His brief stay in Sedona had made winter seem far away still, but back up here on the Colorado Plateau, its chill was already in the air.

Again, the wind whispered it was time to move on. He took a deep breath of it and then smelled the forest around him, sad to be leaving his friend but happy to be traveling again.

When Pat went back inside, he quietly stepped away.

He wasted no time getting to the Grand Canyon, traveling about twenty-five miles a day through a stately ponderosa pine forest for the first three days, and then through piñon pines and junipers.

The burros perked up when they saw him. They'd stayed in a cave below Desert View, away from the crowds of tourists. His friend had taken good care of them and they looked rested.

"You're getting fat," he told Cockleburs and patted his flank.

He examined their shoes and made sure they were seated well. They would be traipsing over a lot of hard ground and he didn't want their hooves to splinter.

As he gathered supplies from the surrounding stores, Everett suddenly felt hemmed in by the crowds. "We gotta get out of here soon, boys," he told the burros when he set down a large bag of oats he had just purchased. "All of these people are driving me crazy."

The only good thing about the hordes of tourists who gawked at the Grand Canyon was that some of them had money. So on his second day Everett stopped along the rim to paint a fiery sunset and sold three watercolors of Monument Valley before finishing the painting.

He carried only a few completed paintings, and before long, he had peddled everything he had. In total, he now had over twenty dollars, and he used the money to buy rice, a tarp, rope and a new pair of socks.

The trio stopped for two nights at the Indian Gardens campsite, sleeping under the Cottonwoods. The five-mile walk down from the rim was easy now that both burros were trained.

Cockleburs seemed to barely notice the steep switchbacks, and Chocolatero leaned away from the drop-offs, now mindful of the danger that lurked there.

"That's right, Choco," Everett encouraged, "just stay back and take it easy."

The last time he had descended to the Colorado in the heat of summer, and he remembered the grueling journey well. This time they left Indian Gardens well before dawn and reached the Colorado River just as the day began to warm up.

The temperatures were pleasant, and Everett was whistling when they reached the bridge that crossed the Colorado River on the way to the Phantom Ranch.

He had forded the river the last time, after failing to locate the suspension bridge. He found the bridge easily now, but Chocolatero balked at it. Everett was able to coax and pull him, but they weren't even halfway across when the burro finally refused to budge.

With hard-wrought patience, Everett made the crossing with Cockleburs, then returned with empty kyacks and filled them with Chocolatero's load. Finally, when he transported all of his supplies to the far side of the river and had Cockleburs tethered to a tree in the shade, he returned to Chocolatero.

"Move it!" he shouted while pushing his shoulder into the burro's rump. "You've gotta be the most stubborn burro I've ever owned!"

The water rushing thirty feet below them terrified the animal, and he set his feet forward, determined not to advance.

"What the heck are you tryin' to do there?" yelled a packer who was waiting to cross the bridge on the side Everett was heading. The man held the lead to a large mule, about twice the size of Chocolatero.

"He won't move!" shouted Everett over the rush of the water.

The man laughed. "Let me help!" he called.

The packer backed his mule onto the bridge and slowly approached the smaller burro. He shook hands with Everett.

Everett tied Chocolatero's lead to the mule's saddle, and together they slowly dragged the reluctant burro across the bridge. Chocolatero looked severely shaken when they stopped to rest in the shade on the north side of the Colorado, and Everett decided to wait a few days before making the fourteen-mile push to the north rim.

The following day Everett woke to Cockleburs braying loudly. He propped himself up on his elbows and realized a four-inch scorpion was crawling across his chest.

He shook it off and jumped to his feet.

"Double ration of oats for you today, buddy," he told the burro.

The warm temperatures lulled him, and he considered staying a few more days, but he wanted to get to the rugged lands of southeast Utah before winter set in, and on a cool, cloudy day, they made the long journey up and out of the canyon.

Over the coming days they traveled north over a desert plateau. When he came upon US 89, he followed it all the way to Kanab. The highway ascended onto the Kaibab Plateau, and he found himself back in cold temperatures again, shivering through the night and walking with the Navajo blanket wrapped around him.

Pledge to the Wind

It was mid-October and the wind often had a biting chill to it.
One evening he woke to see snow flurries coming down.
Chocolatero licked the snowflakes as they settled on his nose.

In Kanab he stopped only long enough to send off a batch of letters.

He was tempted to visit Zion again but instead veered northeast to Bryce Canyon, following his wanderlust through lands unknown.

Along the highway Everett saw many people, but at night he made camp just out of sight. Except for the postmaster in Kanab, he didn't speak to another soul for ten days after leaving Phantom Ranch.

"You got a new pal," said Everett to Cockleburs. A doe had walked into their camp and stepped right up to the burro and sniffed its face. A few feet away, Chocolatero watched, apparently afraid of the timid visitor. Everett was about to tell him to make a new friend but then thought of his own reclusive nature and decided against it.

The doe sniffed in Everett's direction. It seemed unafraid.

They were now camped in spectacular Bryce Canyon National Park. On their first day, he found a sheltered area inside the canyon that was mostly out of the wind. Various layers of orange, red and white ran through the rock, creating breathtaking formations.

Colorful, pointed spires of rock rose up all around them, many of their ends capped with snow. There were thousands of them, called *hoodoos*, and as the shadows thickened, many began to look like people.

They were at over seven thousand feet above sea level here, and it was the coldest place he'd been all year.

He huddled under his Navajo blanket, only a few inches from a low fire. The upper elevations around him were forested with pines and junipers, but there wasn't much fuel in the narrow canyons.

A relentless, cold wind seemed to blow through the park, and following a day hike to a natural arch called Tower Bridge, they moved on.

Everett met a ranger named Maurice, who invited him to stay at his place in Tropic, just a few miles away.

236

"Sounds warm," said Everett.

Maurice smiled. "Well, it is when the fire is burning, and we're all sitting around it—otherwise, keep your warm clothes on."

Maurice was a Mormon with nine children. He let Everett stable his burros in the barn and gave him a cot in the living room by the fire. A cold front had settled in, and Everett was happy to have a sheltered place to stay for a few days.

His first night there, all eyes had been on him when he approached the dinner table. He looked around at a bunch of curious eyes and sensed they didn't get company often.

Amongst Maurice's many children was a daughter named Rhea, who was a year younger than Everett, and a son named Gene, who was a year older. The two sat on each side of him at the table.

While the younger children besieged him with questions about his burros, Everett felt Rhea's eyes on him. She had soft blond hair with a light blue ribbon in it and wore a matching blue dress. She impressed Everett by telling him that she had made the dress herself.

"I wish I could sew better," he said. "It might help my clothes last longer."

She was of a pure, simple attractiveness, not enhanced through makeup and fancy clothes, like Frances in San Francisco.

Her green eyes followed him wherever he went.

When Maurice returned to work, Everett helped the children finish their chores.

"One of our cows has run off," said Gene. "Would you mind helping me find it?"

They pretended the cow was a rare animal and spent the next few hours tracking it. Eventually, they located it and brought the animal home.

There was a dance in town the next night, and Everett went with Rhea and Gene. He took a bath and combed his hair, but his clothes were worn and faded even though they had been cleaned.

Gene lent him a coat so that he wouldn't be cold. He had lost a lot of weight and felt like a scarecrow.

When the music began, Gene set off looking for a girl he had a crush on, leaving Everett and Rhea alone.

She smiled at him and said, "It must be exciting to travel all over and meet new people. All I see are the same ones, day after day — and most of them are related."

Everett offered her a chair and sat down beside her. "The honest truth is when I'm on the road, I generally avoid people — except Indians. I prefer their company."

Her eyes widened. "I've never talked with an Indian. We see them come into town to trade, but they're dirty."

He let the comment drop.

Rhea had put her hair up in ribbons, and he thought of asking if he could paint her. She seemed like a vision out of some Greek fable, and he wanted to tell her this.

"You know," she said, "you could find work in town here. Then you might stay around for a while." Her smile warmed his heart and he could feel himself falling for her.

"I'm not much of a town guy," he said. "I prefer the wilderness."

"Oh, that's not a problem. If you lived here, we could go off camping and hiking. I imagine it would be quite exciting exploring some remote canyon."

Everett gazed into her green eyes, captivated. He thought of Tropic as a base to explore Utah and wondered if she would go with him.

And then an image of Tiba took form in front of him, sitting across the fire, staring at him with a curious expression. Tiba, who was supposed to meet him soon, when the full moon rose above the confluence of the Escalante and Colorado Rivers.

He felt flushed and excused himself, stepping outside to get some air.

In the dark the wind caressed him, swirling through his hair with a cold chill. In his mind Tiba smiled at him, and then he looked to the horizon and saw a half-moon rising.

The next day he moved on.

He continued in the direction of Escalante, thirty-eight miles away, and passed through some of the most unforgettable canyon country in Utah. Then, while on the Paunsaqunt Plateau, a snow flurry overtook him and his burros, and they bedded down under a large pine.

The next morning, the sight of the pink cliffs covered in snow moved him so much that he attempted to paint it, but his paints were frozen, and after ten minutes of sketching, his feet became numb.

In the distance he could see the Escalante River drainage, and he hoped it would be warmer in one of the gulches down lower by the river.

He rode into the town of Escalante on a Sunday morning on one of his burros, leading the other. From a mile away, he heard the church bells ringing, and by the time he reached the main street, his feet just about touching the ground, everyone was in church.

The town felt ready for winter. The barns were crammed with hay, and the air was thick with the smell of burning leaves. Maurice had said that '34 had been a rough year. The area had suffered a severe drought, and cattle prices had plunged.

He glanced at the streets, which were thick with dust.

They passed a white sandstone meeting house and then a red brick schoolhouse but didn't see any sign of people until they reached the church.

The voices of the congregation rang out with a hymn. The soothing melody carried him along, and he approached slowly, as if in a dream.

When the song ended the only sound was the clip-clopping of Everett's burros. Through the windows of the church he could see a few dozen people watch him pass.

The Mormon bishop had his back to the window and continued with his sermon about the triumphant entry of Jesus into Jerusalem.

"On that day, Jesus rode into Jerusalem on the back of a borrowed donkey's colt, one that had never been ridden before. The disciples spread their cloaks on the donkey for Jesus to sit on, and the multitudes came out to welcome Him, laying before Him their cloaks and the branches of palm trees."

239

Everett stopped in the street and patted Cocklebur's neck, "They could be talking about one of your ancestors."

The priest sensed he was losing the attention of his congregation and addressed them in a louder voice. "This happened on the Sunday before his crucifixion. He had to know the end was near, but still, he went to Jerusalem!"

Politely, the congregation nodded, but their attention was still held by the skinny figure sitting on a donkey in the street. He appeared like a modern-day Jesus as he sat on his tiny burro.

The bishop continued, "But Jesus knew the road he was to travel. He'd had his time in the Judean wilderness, alone, fasting and praying for forty days. And there he had been tempted by Satan, but he persevered!"

His voice rose as he again quoted the Bible.

"Then the devil left him, and angels came and attended him."

Everett barely heard the words. But had he known their thoughts, he would have laughed and told them that God was to be found in nature and that to him, the only true church was the wilderness.

To some in Escalante, the world was a better place now that a Christ-like presence was out there, somewhere, drifting around the southwest. Over the next week he often found an apple pie, or some canned peaches, left by the simple camp he made under some cottonwoods by the Escalante River.

The town welcomed him, and he spent a week assembling the supplies he would need to winter over in one of the nearby canyons. He passed his days with the town's young people, acting like a young Mormon boy, getting in apple fights and exploring the surrounding canyons.

For a while, he wondered if he shouldn't have rushed away from Rhea so quickly. Town life didn't seem too bad when he was camped along the outskirts where he could slip in or out at will to catch a movie or go to a dance.

The weather held, and on most nights, he entertained one or two Escalante youths at his campsite. They showed up with chunks of venison which he grilled over his fire, and potatoes wrapped in tin foil that glowed in the coals while he told the young folks about his adventures. There had been a good piñon nut crop, and most of his visitors also arrived with a bag of pine nuts to roast.

The burros enjoyed the stop as well. They were happily resting and munching down on alfalfa.

He took off their shoes now that they wouldn't be crossing over hard terrain, and they jumped around like it was spring, light on their feet when he set them to graze. Their bells tinkled merrily to their movements and made him smile.

One night he took several of the boys to a picture show. They saw *Death Takes a Holiday*. In the film, Death wants to experience life so much that he suspends his usual activities for three days, and in the end, discovers love.

The movie left him feeling restless, and when he returned to his camp, the growing moon compelled him to motion. He saddled Cockleburs and rode off into the desert, leaving Chocolatero and most of his gear behind.

He had only ridden a short way when he heard a Navajo chanting.

He followed it until he came to a fire with several young men sitting around it. Everett held up a jar of peaches he had been gifted, and the men nodded eagerly.

Over the next few hours they sang songs and talked. Everett shared his peaches, and they, in turn, offered him roast mutton with black coffee. Now that he had a grasp of their language, the songs took on a deeper meaning, and he felt a great sadness when the horizon began to lighten, and they prepared to move on.

He left the sandy desert and returned to Escalante, which now seemed even tamer and cultivated. The songs of the Navajos still echoed in his head.

He packed up his things that day, said a few goodbyes, and set out into the wild country that descended toward the river, following the Hole-in-the-Wall Trail.

He felt prepared and ready for the lands he was about to explore.

That evening he drifted off to sleep confidently. But deep in the night he was awakened by the sharp report of a gunshot.

Robert Louis DeMayo

Chapter Twenty-Nine

The Hole-in-the-Rock Trail, Utah
(October 1934)

*E*verett led Cockleburs and Chocolatero over a rocky mesa of sage and snakeweed. They were on an open plain cut by deep ravines, following the Hole-in-the-Wall Trail as it ran south by southeast out of Escalante.

A cold breeze greeted him, and he had his head down.

The Mormon trailblazers who had created this trail had eventually stopped at the town of Bluff, one hundred and eighty miles from Escalante. Everett´s destination as he entered this remote wilderness was the Colorado River, about sixty miles away. To his right lay the Kaiparowits Plateau, whose steep canyons drained into the Escalante, and directly south was Glen Canyon.

Late in the afternoon he came upon a gentle stream that flowed by the base of a sandstone cliff, and he prepared camp. "This place looks like it was made for us," he told the burros as he unloaded the saddle and kyacks.

Above them, a towering wall of rock lit up orange and yellow in the afternoon sun. Tall pines grew by the stream and sprouted on the cliff face wherever a small shelf had collected soil. Far up on the top of the wall he could see stunted, twisted pines that were now highlighted in gold as the sun set.

He made a small fire, boiled water for rice, and tethered the burros with enough lead to move but not get into trouble. He hadn't seen another human since setting foot on the trail, only squirrels, lizards and birds, and he relaxed by the fire, enjoying his solitude.

Later, the fire had died down to glowing embers, and he decided to write in his journal. He sat with it on his lap, watching the night, listening to it breathe around him.

He was about to jot down an entry when he heard Navajo chanting.

It was far off, barely discernable over the chirping of the crickets that lived along the stream. He thought of the young Navajos he had encountered a few nights before.

He leaned forward, opening his ears more. Cockleburs shifted by his side and he shushed him.

Then it came again. There was only one singer. The song seemed muffled and he couldn't make it out, but the hair on the back of his neck stood up. He felt sure it was one used against witches.

He was up before the first shade of pale lit the horizon. He saddled Cockleburs and loaded the kyacks on both of them, then tethered them to a robust stand of bushes.

He left his camp and walked to a rise to survey the plain, looking for smoke from a fire or puffs of dust that might indicate a man walking through the arid country.

He walked about a half-mile away and then began an extended circle around his camp. The sun was almost high enough to use the slanting light to read tracks.

If there had been someone out there, he should see signs of it.

He jumped at a sudden movement ahead of him and exhaled when a jackrabbit scurried off.

And then he came across a low clearing where the tall sage had been flattened. Whoever had camped here may not have seen Everett's camp, but he would have been close enough to occasionally hear him converse with the burros.

He rose slowly and surveyed the land all around him but saw nobody.

244

The trail was becoming rough, lined with stubborn scrub oak and steep canyon slopes. Several times he had to drive the burros forward and down at precarious angles, and he was glad they hadn't fallen.

They continued along the trail, wandering through the cold. In the middle of the day the sun shone brightly, and he shed a layer or two, but soon as a cloud obscured it, a heavy chill set in again.

The song from the night before had him on edge, and throughout the day, he glanced over his shoulder repeatedly.

Whenever they rounded a point with elevation, he would descend to the other side, then creep back and survey the horizon: first the far hills, then the middle distance, and finally the bush before him.

He saw no signs of anyone following, but he was still jumpy.

The country was wild and untamed, and as he trailed his burros, he felt himself drifting into a dream-like state. His senses were on fire and he yearned to paint the landscape, or at least write about it, but the chanting from last night that echoed in his head urged him to put some distance between himself and whoever might be out there.

His pulse quickened when he saw a nearly full moon appear on the horizon, low on the skyline, about an hour after sunset.

An hour later he passed a cowboy in the middle of butchering a cow. Everett jumped when he first saw him.

The man looked up with a guilty expression.

"Howdy!" shouted Everett, but one look at the guy and he knew he was up to no good. The cow had a bullet hole in its forehead.

Everett waved non-committedly and continued.

The Rustler was about thirty-five, but years of hard living made him look more like fifty-five. He stood and watched Everett disappear, and when he was satisfied that the young man wasn't doubling back, he spat and sat back down to work.

That night Everett camped in a dry wash, hidden away from the mesa he had traveled on. He kept his fire small and stayed quiet while writing about the day's events in his journal.

Again, several hours after the sun had set, he heard the chanting. This time it sounded closer.

He put his journal away. He lay there for an hour, listening and thinking. The chanting didn't last long, but now he had heard it twice and knew it hadn't been his imagination.

He watched the moon continue to arc, and when its light no longer illuminated the desert so brightly, he shook off his blanket and silently crept up onto the mesa behind him.

The burros watched him curiously.

The singing had come from the west, and he scanned that direction first, but then just north of him, a lone fire caught his eyes.

He returned to his camp and pulled the fuel from his fire so it would burn out. He also changed his boots for softer moccasins before returning to the mesa.

Over the next hour he slowly snuck closer to the other fire.

Later, the moon a memory, the Rustler sat by a small fire and swigged on a bottle.

Everett spied on him from underneath a creosote bush, about twenty-five feet away. He kept his head down and waited for a chance to back away, now that he had identified the stranger.

He had retreated maybe a dozen feet when he heard someone else approach. In the darkness this other man walked less than ten feet from him, but his attention was fixed on the fire and the man sitting by it, not the scrub around him where Everett was ducking.

The Rustler stood up and pulled his gun.

Bad Jack stepped out of the darkness and held up his hands in a peaceful gesture. He crouched by the fire, but the Rustler kept the gun leveled at his chest.

Bad Jack asked, "You seen a young guy with two burros?"

The Rustler slowly nodded.

Bad Jack stared at him for a minute, then said, "I've heard he's been telling the authorities about cattle poachers."

"What's that to me?" said the Rustler, cussing all informants under his breath. From the bushes Everett cursed the Navajo for stirring things up.

"Don't know," said Bad Jack, "but ranchers been complaining about some missing cattle."

The Rustler laughed. "Cattle go missing in this country all the time. Don't mean nothin' to me."

Bad Jack said, "People go missing too."

The Rustler took a swig off his bottle. "That's a fact."

Everett felt a chill go down his spine. He moved backward, silently.

Bad Jack slowly straightened up and stretched his legs. "I hear he's heading for the Colorado—gonna follow this trail 'till he hits the water."

The Rustler laughed. "He isn't going anywhere. He'll never get his burros down the chute without help and a lot of rope."

"I don't think he has enough," said Bad Jack.

The Rustler grinned. "Hey, it's a dangerous place. Maybe he'll fall to his death."

Bad Jack said, "It would be a shame if he didn't make it to the river."

The Rustler held up his hands, pleading innocent. "He's your problem, not mine." Bad Jack watched him for a moment, silently, then backed away into the darkness to the north.

"Sure, as long as he doesn't rat you out?"

About five minutes after Bad Jack disappeared, Everett slowly retreated. When he finally returned to his camp, he lay down to think. He doubted he would sleep, and he worried about that chute.

Was he moving into a trap? He lay there wondering.

Several hours later, dawn was still a ways off. A coyote called out, and Everett thought back to a conversation with Notah on Navajo Mountain.

War God Spring had been flowing pleasantly under a sky filled with twinkling stars. There was no moon, and the heavens seemed to breathe above Everett and Notah as they sat on either side of a low fire.

The night was warm.

Down below them, in one of the many sandstone canyons, a coyote yipped three times, then in a long, full-throated bay that seemed to empty its soul.

Notah said, "He's telling you to watch out."

Everett laughed. "I would guess he's telling me he's gonna steal my jerky when I go to sleep."

The old man shook his head. "The Coyote People may cause a lot of trouble, but they are good about warning people. Don't dismiss them so readily."

Everett nodded respectfully and Notah added, "The Coyote People only steal the excess. When you have little, you guard it better."

Now Everett sat up, laughing. He said, "You know, you're right. This has been a full, rich year for me. I've left nothing undone that I wanted to do — but I never had much excess. Maybe that's why I didn't see too many coyotes around my camp."

"It's the same with the Diné," said Notah. "Our way avoids all excess. We call the Navajo Way, the Middle Way."

They sat listening to the night. Everett thought about the coyote's call and what he might be telling him to watch out for. He added a few small logs to the fire and sat back.

"How do the Diné deal with someone who is out of control?" he asked Notah when he had collected his thoughts.

The old Navajo peered at him over the fire, watching him, thinking slowly with the crackle of the fire. Everett waited, knowing that eventually, Notah would say what he had to say.

"The white man punishes people who break the law. They lock them up and turn them into hardened criminals. That is not our way."

He adjusted his blanket underneath him and continued. "We Diné believe your judgment is only destroyed when the dark wind has entered you — then you forget the rules of behavior and harm others. When this happens, you are out of control."

Everett nodded but said nothing.

Notah continued, "These people are best avoided. You can worry about them and feel joy when they are cured of this insanity, but you should stay away from them until they return to *hózró*."

Everett knew *hózró* meant being in peace and harmony with one's environment; being empty of anger and free from worry. It was a concept he had embraced.

He let Notah's words sink in and didn't speak for some time.

Finally, he asked, "But what if you can't avoid someone who the dark wind has overcome?"

Notah thought for a long while and then said with smiling eyes, "In that case, you could always scare them away."

He lifted a small rattle and shook it, and Everett envisioned the rattle that Tiba had shaken at Bad Jack.

Back on the Hole-in-the-Rock trail, Everett was up the next morning before the sun. He pushed the burros hard all day, and by noon they had gone nearly fifteen miles.

The terrain had little cover, and he didn't see anywhere that he might hide. Then, in the distance, he noticed several ruins built into a cliff on the right. There was no vegetation leading to them, and anyone looking for him would see his tracks.

But he inspected them anyway, knowing he needed a place to hide and there was nowhere else to go.

There were two rooms. One still supported a roof and four walls. The interior was thick with shadows, and it took a few minutes for his eyes to adjust.

He sat quietly and waited, listening to the wind whistle through cracks in the wall with his eyes closed.

He opened them slowly and looked around. The room was empty, except for a large owl perched in a corner. Everett was surprised his entry hadn't scared the bird.

He slowly backed out of the ruin and returned to the burros.

He continued on the trail until it led out onto a peninsula with an odd, notched rock at the end. When he peered through the gap, he sucked in his breath.

"It's like we're on the rim of the world," he said out loud. He was standing on the lip of a vast chasm. The long, steep cliff that extended down to the river wasn't vertical, but it was too steep to walk, or even slide, down.

Cockleburs stepped up behind him and glanced down the chute to the Colorado River, far below, and immediately began backing up.

"Easy, boy," said Everett. He led both burros about thirty feet away and tied their leads to the base of a scrub oak.

Everett returned and reexamined the steep slope, hoping to find a way down. He could see now that the notch in the rock had been created so the Mormon pioneers could lower their wagons over the edge, and if he'd had help — and a lot more rope — he could see how he might pull off lowering his burros. But Bad Jack had been right in his assessment: Everett had no hope of getting down by himself with his burros and current supplies.

About a thousand feet below him, the Colorado River snaked through the Plateau. To the east and west, he could see to the far blue horizon, and countless canyons and desert plateaus extended toward it. Sunset was a few hours off, but the warm colors were already lighting up the rocks around him. To the north, the sheer face of the Kaiparowits Plateau was already in shadow.

He untied the burros and began backtracking. It would be dark soon, and he scanned the horizon for signs of Bad Jack.

The Navajo approached the chute just as large the moon rose over the horizon. It would be full the next night.

When he crawled up into the notch and looked down, he was surprised not to see Everett and the burros desperately trying to descend. He had hoped just to cut the rope and be done.

He sat back and smoked a cigarette. He looked around.

And then he was surprised again to see the burros tethered to a small juniper tree by a ruin on the right.

"This is too easy," he thought and walked toward the ruin.

The structure was small; its two rooms were dark. If Picture Man was inside, he had no fire going.

He slowed, now that his prey was in reach. He didn't make a sound.

Suddenly, chanting came from inside the ruin.

You are mine now, witch, he thought.

He stepped into the first room, a large knife in his hand, and then his heart stopped as the blood-curdling screech of an owl filled the

250

darkness. He snatched his medicine pouch and held it before him just as something came at him from the darkness.

Bad Jack dropped his knife and stumbled out of the ruin with a large owl screeching and flapping around him. The bird had gotten its talons tangled with the thong that held the pouch around Bad Jack's neck, and it struggled to get free. Again and again, the owl's sharp claws struck the Indian's face.

He fell backward, and the thong broke. The owl ascended away with Bad Jack's medicine pouch dangling from its feet.

The Navajo scrambled back to his feet. Blood poured from the gouges on his face and blurred his vision.

He kept grabbing for the missing pouch, unable to accept that it was gone.

Finally, he turned and fled back up the trail in the direction of Escalante. Everett peeked out of the ruin and, in the moonlight, saw the man scrambling and glancing at the night sky, afraid the evil owl could return.

Chapter Thirty

Davis Gulch, Utah
(November 1934)

*H*igh on the wall of one side of Davis Canyon, Everett sat on a shelf by an Anasazi ruin. He surveyed the land. There was an eagle feather in his hair.

The gulch served as a tributary to the Escalante River. Water often rushed through it in the stormy summer monsoons, but it was dry with plenty of grass for the burros during the winter.

He had stumbled upon it the day after scaring Bad Jack away.

Everett was in a pickle. He knew he couldn't make it down the chute, and he didn't want to take the Hole-in-the-Rock trail back to Escalante for fear of stumbling into Bad Jack once again. Even though the Navajo had been stunned, Everett thought it best to avoid him entirely.

And the Rustler was still somewhere out here, probably ready to put a bullet into anyone he suspected of wanting to snitch him out. If he was determined to come after him, Everett figured it would be on the Colorado or the river's far side where the trail continued to Bluff.

So he had veered north, and after about five miles had come upon this paradise with high sandstone walls, pockets of water, and plenty of shade. At first it appeared as a deep crack in the earth, maybe twenty feet deep and only ten across, but he scrambled into it for the prospect of shelter, pushing the burros down a drainage, until the rim was a hundred feet above or more.

The burros seemed at ease here, most likely because they were out of the wind. The yellow rock of the cliffs was smooth to the touch, worn by wind and water.

Between patches of rough grass, cactus and juniper trees dotted the sandy canyon floor, and the way was easy as they followed the dry course where water would have rippled in the summer as it wended downstream through the cliffs.

A large buzzard nest crowned one prominent pinnacle and Everett hoped to paint it.

After securing the burros at the bottom of the narrow canyon, Everett crept back to wipe out their tracks with a juniper branch. It took a few hours to erase all signs of them.

By evening he had reunited with the burros and descended several miles further down the canyon to a bend where box elders and willows surrounded a natural alcove.

He made camp and blocked off both ends of the canyon with some logs, leaving the burros corralled. He used a few juniper branches to hide his gear in the alcove.

He felt reasonably safe there, so he unloaded their kyacks and took the saddle off Cockleburs, but he kept on the bridle and halters in case he had to move quickly.

He barely slept that night. He didn't think he was being observed, and he heard no chanting, but still, his mind fidgeted.

The chatter of birds woke him early the next day, and he set off to explore some of the ruins.

By late afternoon he was on his way back to check on his camp. He had stopped to climb to a ruin and found the spot so pleasant that he had lingered. He could see the burros, about five hundred yards away. Cockleburs was resting in the shade, but Chocolatero was sniffing around the supplies. Everett watched as the burro pulled down one of the dead juniper branches that blocked access to the gear.

From his perch, about eighty feet off the ground, he could see up and down the canyon for about a mile in each direction. The sides of the canyon sloped down, creating slick rock domes that he thought would make it difficult to peer down from above.

Around him lay a small village of Indian ruins. Many had panels decorated with pictographs and petroglyphs near them.

On the wall by one of the ruins he carved: NEMO 1934.

He shouldered his pack and began to descend the old hand-and-toe trail. Some of the divots had worn away, and his foot slipped out of one, and he had to catch himself with his hands.

The wind swirled around him as he dangled from the cliff. He shouted, "You almost got me there!"

There was a rock art panel at the cliff base and Everett stopped to paint another sequence of notes amongst the pictographs, right next to images of dancing men and lizards.

Afterward, he rinsed his paintbrush and placed it in his backpack, then continued to his camp.

The two burros watched Everett return. Chocolatero had a face full of flour and was licking his lips. "What have you gotten into?" asked Everett with a grin. What's a little flour worth? he thought. Not enough to spoil my *hózró*.

Everett diligently created a more substantial brushwork fence to prevent the burro from getting into his gear again. The two bad men were slowly fading from his mind, so he took the tack off the burros and hung the bridle and two halters over his makeshift fence.

"That better?"

He walked into the alcove and grabbed some oats to feed the burros. He noticed the flour sack on its side and shook his head, then stood it up.

Only a little was missing. He said, "Guess he don't like flour."

The afternoon sun was waning, but it was still hot, so he grabbed his backpack and walked about thirty feet, across the narrow canyon, to an ancient cypress. There he crawled under the thick lower branches and spread out his Navajo blanket.

He lay back against the pack with a pencil and his journal in hand, and jotted down a few ideas that he hoped to include in a letter.

"As to when I shall visit civilization, it will not be soon, I think. I have not tired of the wilderness; rather, I enjoy its beauty and the vagrant life I lead, more keenly all the time."

He stopped and took in the land around him. Beyond the blanket the ground was strewn with light blue berries and fragments of bark, and he lifted a handful and breathed in their scent. He listened to the birds fluttering deep in the shaded parts of the cypress and looked beyond the tree at the marvelous yellow sandstone walls, now turning amber with the first traces of sunset.

He continued writing.

"I prefer the saddle to the streetcar and star-sprinkled sky to a roof, the obscure and difficult trail, leading into the unknown, to any paved highway, and the deep peace of the world to the discontent bred by cities. Do you blame me for staying here, where I feel that I belong and am one with the world around me?"

He looked over his few possessions: The burros, the saddle and kyacks, worn gear, the painting supplies, a Navajo blanket and a silver bracelet.

His gaze drifted over the bracelet, enchanted as always by the way the light gleamed on the three embedded pieces of turquoise.

He stowed his journal in his backpack, shifted the pack under his head, and soon fell asleep.

Everett woke around sunset when he heard a twig snap. He didn't remember hearing it. It was more of a memory that had worked into his dreams. But it had jolted him, and now he lay there, without moving for several moments, while he decided where it had come from and what might have made it.

Too loud for a squirrel or ground animal, he thought, and I haven't seen any deer in this canyon at all. Most likely a man.

Cautiously, he lifted his head and looked around.

He sucked in his breath when he saw the Rustler walking past the burros. He entered the alcove and pawed through the kyacks, which were draped over a log.

Then he got up and slowly surveyed the camp. Everett lay flat against the ground, still deep in shadow under the tree. He didn't think the Rustler could see him from where he stood, but any closer inspection would find him out.

He was glad his backpack was with him. If he had to run, at least he would have some bare necessities.

While the Rustler rummaged through his art supplies, Everett slowly crawled out from under the tree. For a minute he considered taking the Navajo blanket but then thought it too bulky; he could double back and get it later.

He would have to come back for the burros anyway.

Everett quietly shouldered the pack and readied to slip out down the canyon. The Escalante River wasn't far, just a few more miles down the gulch. If he could reach it, he thought he could get away.

There wasn't much cover in that direction, but thankfully the Rustler was distracted. Everett moved slowly from bush to bush, and when he was finally around the bend, he scrambled down the canyon in the direction of the river.

The Rustler might eventually find his tracks and follow, but he didn't have time to cover them.

Everett paused at the edge of a seventy-foot drop off. The closer he got to the river, the more the land seemed to fall away. It was getting dark.

He tightened the straps of his pack and looked around. Near the base of the cliff, a large pine had taken root on a shelf. The upper branches were twenty feet below him, and for one fraction of a second, he considered jumping to it.

A gust of wind pushed him forward, slightly, as if encouraging him. "Are you crazy?" he said out loud.

He looked to the right and spotted a narrow, water-carved channel, almost a tunnel, which descended to a shelf about halfway down. He figured from there he could clamber the rest of the way.

He looked down at the tree below again. The wind pushed him forward another time and he laughed. "No way, I can do this alone."

A sound from up the canyon caught his ear, and he flopped on his stomach and quickly began lowering himself backward into the steep channel. His legs were dangling, and his chest close to the ground, when suddenly a rattlesnake shot out and struck his right shoulder.

He never saw it or heard the rattle.

He reeled in shock and dropped into the chimney-shaped channel. The walls were too steep to cling to, and he spastically kicked his legs and grasped with his hands for a root or outcrop to arrest his fall.

He came to a stop by the base of a large rock after sliding thirty feet. Water had eroded a deep hole underneath it, and he was half-tucked into it.

The snake had fallen with him and now rattled angrily in front of him, blocking the exit from the hole. They faced off, only two feet apart. The snake coiled up and looked ready to strike again.

"Easy there."

Everett picked up a stone and was about to smash the snake when he had an idea. Slowly, he reached into his hair and grabbed the eagle feather.

The snake rattled quicker when he first moved, but he continued, slowly and patiently. Then he began stroking it with the feather. Soon the serpent lost some of its fury, and after a minute, it straightened out.

He took a breath, grabbed the snake by the middle, and lifted it and set it a few feet away on the trail. He slid out of his backpack and sank deeper into the hole.

He examined his arm. A pair of puncture wounds glared at him, red and angry, from his right shoulder.

He said, "I sure hope that's a dry bite."

Then he heard footsteps crunching above. He pressed his back to the wall and pulled his legs close to his chest, out of sight.

A moment later the Rustler appeared at the top of the chimney. He paused for only a moment before descending the channel with his legs in front of him. His eyes were further down the scree, and he didn't see the snake until he was about to slide into it.

"Jesus!" he screamed and somehow got his feet under him. Then, he leaped over the snake and continued down the canyon.

Everett thanked the snake for the distraction and lay back to rest.

A full moon had risen and now lit up the mouth of the canyon. Everett stumbled toward the Escalante River, feeling feverish. He had nothing in his pack to alleviate the snake bite, which was throbbing now.

The cottonwood leaves flickered silver in the moonlight, and the gurgle of the water was soothing. He sat on a rounded gray rock with his head in his hands and paused just long enough to catch his breath.

He looked at the full moon again, then rose and walked to the river's edge.

Suddenly, a shot rang out and he spun and fell.

He grabbed his left shoulder and looked around, bewildered.

Another shot hit a rock by his feet and shattered it.

"Thought you could rat me out?" shouted the Rustler. "Take that, boy!"

Everett stumbled into the water as a bullet splashed by his side.

When he was up to his knees, a fourth shot slammed into his back and he fell face forward into the water.

The weight of his pack took him under and he floated off, half-submerged.

Everett lay on the shore, thoroughly drenched. He looked around and realized he was on the other side of the river from the moon's position. His backpack was missing.

He was tucked behind a boulder. His left shoulder felt warm, and when he touched it, he realized he was bleeding.

His body ached. He seemed to be burning up.

A low whistle caught his attention, and he turned to see Tiba by another rock. From her stance, he could tell she had been searching for whoever shot him.

She nodded that all was clear and crept to his side.

His right wrist hurt hellishly. His arm had swollen and his bracelet was now preventing circulation.

Tiba held up two fingers like the fangs of a snake. He nodded, and in a coarse voice, he said, "Yup, one finally got me."

He twisted the bracelet but was too weak to remove it. Tiba scanned the far shore of the river again, then tried. His arm hurt when she moved it, but he was relieved when the bracelet finally came off.

She offered it to him, but Everett weakly shook his head, saying, "No. For you."

She nodded with a smile and put it on. Then she helped him out of his shirt and examined the gunshot wound. Her probing fingers told him what he already suspected. The first shot had nicked his arm, and his backpack had deflected the last one.

Tiba took his torn, bloodstained shirt and hid it under a large river rock.

He wondered if the bullet had hit his journal. Could my writing have saved me, he thought, almost smiling. And then he realized both the backpack and journal were lost in the river.

He rose on shaky legs, peering across the dark water.

A small canyon cut into the plateau behind them, and Tiba helped him limp, now shirtless, into it. The full moon lit their way as they disappeared into the canyon. Everett felt they were back in Zion, entering the Narrows with the great White Throne looming above them.

But this canyon was bone dry, and the wind whistled through it at full volume. Within a few minutes his hair was dry, and his mouth parched.

He stumbled and would have fallen had it not been for Tiba.

He knew now that the snake had indeed envenomed him. His arm was bloated. The effects of the venom clouded his mind, confusing him. His arm and shoulder were stiffening too.

Again, he looked around and thought he was in the Narrows.

And then the wind circled him, growing stronger.

He closed his eyes and his mind flooded with memories of the wind embracing him in the Narrows. He had felt himself spinning and twisting with his arms outstretched — and he had never felt more loved.

And then that next year—his second in the southwest—he had felt the wind by his side, guiding him, helping him.

"I always stayed true to my pledge," he said.

The area around the bite mark throbbed painfully.

He thought of the tree below the ledge and how the wind had encouraged him to jump. Had it known about the snake?

"I should have gone for the tree," he said.

He closed his eyes again and the wind picked up once more. He enjoyed its embrace, letting the pain and the dry, dusty heat that surrounded them fade away. All he knew now was the love he felt in the embrace of the wind.

Then he opened his eyes.

In the silver glow of the moon he glimpsed a form coming at him, but his eyes had become sensitive, and he had a hard time focusing.

He felt no fear.

The form came closer and he gasped when he recognized himself.

He looked younger... happy.

The other smiled back, and he reached out, through a glow, to touch his hand.

When their fingers connected, Everett suddenly found himself alone, standing in freezing, ankle-deep water. The moon was gone, as was any trace of the wind.

Pericles stood about twenty feet away, watching him. The burro lowered its head and came sloshing through the shallow water. There was a glow from above, and in amazement, Everett realized that the sun had risen.

"Let's make camp somewhere dry and have breakfast."

They turned around and trudged downstream, and soon the great White Throne came into view, greeting them with the new day reflecting off its flanks.

Pledge to the Wind

262

Robert Louis DeMayo

Three Years Earlier

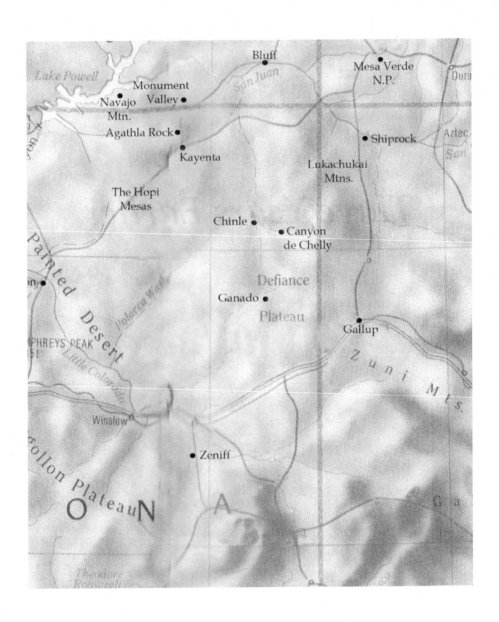

Chapter Thirty-One

Zion Canyon, Utah
(September 1931)

Like in a dream, Everett and Pericles were walking through the Narrows, heading downstream, following the gentle bends in the canyon. A glow surrounded him, and he listened to the sweet music of water rippling intermingling with bird song. He was happy to just be in the energy that encircled him now, embracing the speckled light, the warm sun on his skin, and the wind in his hair.

His mood must have been contagious because Curly poked his head out of the top of the backpack and began licking Everett's ear.

Curly barked, and the echo sounded off repeatedly as it moved through the narrow canyon. Curly began to howl and Everett said, "Settle down, Curly. It's just your echo."

It wasn't until midday that they encountered people at the Temple of Sinawava. Usually, the many tourists would have unnerved Everett, but today he smiled at them and passed and kept walking.

The wind was on his back while they continued down Zion Canyon, and he felt supported by it now, urged forward. He knew it was time to leave Zion. Winter was close at hand and the breeze carried swirling leaves, crimson maples and yellow aspens. It had been warm in the Narrows, but he knew he had to move south, or the cold would be upon him.

He felt overcome with a deep love of life while they followed Highway 9, traveling east out of the park, and the burro trailed along complacently.

"If I didn't know better, I'd say you were smiling," Everett said to Pericles.

And he knew Pericles was in a rare mood. When they reached the mile-long tunnel that led out of Zion, the burro walked through it without a complaint.

Before long they were on US Route 89. The road led southeast, in the direction of Kanab, and a row of poplars lined one side. A cattle trail ran along the trees and they followed it.

"Looks like smooth sailing from here on," said Everett.

Almost in response, a robust gust of wind blew through the treetops and the leaves shivered. Everett peered through the tree trunks at a dark storm that filled the eastern sky. Soon the cloudburst was upon them, and then hail beat down, pelting the grass.

They moved to the shelter of one of the trees and watched. Across the field, two young boys were riding a horse, hurrying for the protection of the trees. When their horse saw Pericles, it bucked, tossing both boys into a mud puddle.

They sat there laughing, small hailstones bouncing off them, until a thunderclap. Then one of them jumped up and went after the horse, grabbed the reins, and they moved quickly back the way they had come.

The hail continued to pound down. Everett waited, and Pericles ate as many hailstones as he could. Curly stayed low in the pack, even after Everett had set it on the ground.

A break in the clouds appeared. The sun came out, the wind picked up, and soon the land was dry.

Over the next few days, they continued to follow US Route 89, walking along the road by day and camping out of sight at night. The road passed through Kanab, and Everett stopped to check for mail and pick up more oats and rice.

The next day they crossed back into Arizona, and the following morning they climbed up into the pine forests of the Kaibab Plateau.

They had ascended to about eight thousand feet when the wind began blowing furiously. Everett flipped his coat collar up, jammed his hat down tight and walked bent forward.

The air was so thick with dust that it was almost impossible to see. Everett fought against it, determined to knock out a few more miles. He knew a place near here where he had camped before and wanted to reach it today.

They stopped at noon in a deep gully where the wind didn't reach. The burro's eyes were crusted with sand, and Everett wiped them.

"That was a hard push," he said. "You did well."

After an hour they struggled on, the gale blowing just as hard.

They came upon the old campsite about an hour before sunset.

The wind finally died down and he got a fire going on a hill near a grassy slope.

In the silence that followed in the wake of the storm, not an insect chirped nor a bird sang. The night was strangely devoid of even the slightest breeze, and Everett could hear his fire crackling from fifty feet away when he walked off searching for more wood.

In the coals he had several yams cooking in tin foil, and he toasted some bread sprinkled with cheese on a forked stick.

Curly had finally surfaced and was rolling around in the dirt by his feet. Small sticks and leaves were sticking to his white fur.

Everett left one of the yams for breakfast, banked the fire, and crawled under his blanket. Curly joined him, snuggling close for warmth.

He had almost drifted into sleep when he heard the twig snap.

Instantly he was wide awake, listening.

Soon he heard dry leaves crunching. His hand snuck out from under the blankets and found a fist-sized rock.

He waited until the intruder was about ten feet away, then jumped to his feet with his arm cocked back. He had stoked his courage and was ready for a fight, but what stood before him turned out to be far from a threat.

A boy crouched on the other side of the fire. His right arm was extended, and he was reaching for the last yam that lay in the coals.

He jumped back.

"I'm sorry," he said. "I'm just so hungry."

Everett motioned for him to sit by the fire, and he sat opposite him.

"What're you doing out here?" he asked.

The boy shrugged. "Dad lost his job, and Ma's been outa work for a while, so I left not to handicap them."

Everett nodded. "You want that yam?"

The boy stared at it like it was a Christmas turkey.

"It's yours," said Everett. "I'll make you some cheese toast, too."

Halfway to grabbing the yam, the boy stopped. He stood and stepped around the fire and extended his hand.

"My name's David," he said.

Everett shook his hand and gave him his name. Up close he could see that David was a few years younger, maybe sixteen.

Everett watched the skinny young man with the gaunt face pick up the yam and thought, I've been broke and hungry many times, but I wonder if I've ever looked that bad.

"You seem like you're having a rough time," said Everett. "How are you faring?"

David looked at the fire. "I don't know what I'm doing. When I left home I just wanted to spare my parents, but now I'm starving, and I feel lost."

He still held the yam, and Everett nodded at it. "Eat that while it's warm."

Everett threw a few sticks on the fire, then unpacked the bread and cheese. He found the forked stick and began toasting a piece of bread while watching David devour the yam, including the burnt skin.

"You get pretty worn down living out here," said Everett, and David nodded, "but only once was I ever too tired to eat when I was hungry."

268

He handed him a piece of cheese toast and then a jug of water.

"It's not just the lack of food," David said, chewing. "I'm always cold, and I'm dirty. The thing I miss most would be a nice warm bath."

"I haven't seen a bathtub since I left Hollywood eight months ago," said Everett with a grin. "But I don't find it difficult to stay clean. Heck, you can swim in a stream, a river, or shower under a waterfall. The only trouble is if you're in the desert."

"The water I've come across was freezin'," said David.

Everett smiled, knowing how cold it could be. "Sure it is, but it lifts my spirits—you should try it."

David nodded and stared at the fire again. "I should have paid more attention in school—then I wouldn't be so bad off."

Another piece of cheese toast was ready and Everett handed it over.

"School hasn't helped me out here. I suppose you could argue that I use math when figuring distances, but the Latin and French have never been of practical use."

They sat in silence for a while, then Everett asked, "Where do your folks live?"

David paused for a moment. Eventually, he said, "They're in Kanab."

"But you don't want to go back there?"

David shook his head. "I've got an uncle who works at the Grand Canyon. He's stationed at the North Rim."

Everett pursed his lips. "Well, you're in luck. That's where I'm heading. You're welcome to travel with me."

The boy's face flooded with relief. He walked off into the woods and retrieved a ratty backpack and an old horse blanket riddled with holes. He lay down by the fire and pulled the tattered blanket over him. Everett dug out one of his extra blankets.

"Put yours underneath and cover yourself with this one."

Within minutes David was sleeping, but Everett stayed up a bit longer, watching him as the moon rolled through the clouds, unsure of the task of being in charge of another human.

Six days later they reached the North Rim of the Grand Canyon, and they sat on a cliff with their feet dangling over the void. To the south and east purple mesas stretched, and above them puffy, swirling cloudbanks arched overhead, broken up here and there by shafts of sunlight.

"You found your uncle then?" asked Everett.

"Yup, thanks to you."

The trees behind them were bare of leaves, which lay scattered on the ground, yellowed and blackened. They crunched underneath Everett and David when they moved.

Everett looked around. "The snows will be here soon, but I won't. Tomorrow I start down the hole."

"How long will it take you to cross?" asked David.

Everett thought for a moment. "In a week I should be at the South Rim—I think we will rest a few days at the Indian Gardens campsite. After that, God knows where. I think I'll be heading south toward the cactus country."

A cold wind shrieked up the cliff face and they leaned back. The seasons were changing.

The mesas below them, caught in the late afternoon sun, were golden brown and cardinal red. The western hills were rimmed with orange that faded to green and then deep blue.

"It's like a painting," said David.

Everett smiled. "I've painted this very scene."

"Why don't you sell your paintings?" asked David. "I'm grateful for the meals you've shared with me, but it seems you're close to broke too."

Everett nodded. "I've often only got a dollar to my name. And I would love to sell my painting, but not for God's sake, or yet for Hell's sake, can I sell any. The world does not want art—only artists do."

David stared at him curiously.

Everett continued. "Oh, I have sold something over six dollars' worth of prints, and I traded one sketch for a sheepskin and another for some grub. I made a calculation recently: This year I've spent 136 dollars all together. Considerably more than a third went to equipment—all the rest to food."

"That's not encouraging," said David. "I don't have any money at all."

Everett shook his head. "You don't need money as much as food. And if you are willing to work, you can always find food."

"Really?"

"Sure," said Everett with a wide smile. "I've earned dozens and dozens of meals that way."

David extended his hand and they shook. "It was sure nice meeting you, Everett. I wish you luck."

He shook the young man's hand, then stood up and walked a few steps to where Pericles was tethered to a tree. As soon as darkness set in, they would descend into the canyon.

Pledge to the Wind

Chapter Thirty-Two

Zeniff, Arizona
(June 1932)

Halfway up the lower side of Roosevelt Dam, Everett stood on a platform with both hands on the cement, feeling the turbines humming deep inside. Behind him the powerhouse was roaring like a bull, and the water that shot out of it was whipped to a froth before hitting the river below.

Everett had been exploring central Arizona since March, after returning from a three-month visit back home. But Hollywood had seemed like a bad dream that he couldn't wake from, and Christmas was especially difficult. Part of his soul was still in the Southwest, and he would be incomplete until he was reunited with it. He would have left sooner if he could have scraped up money faster.

In the end he left with barely enough to return to the Southwest and get outfitted. Winter still had a grip on Utah, so he headed south to the Salt River Valley.

The wind shrieked through the wires above the dam like it was cursing the man-made structure. He climbed to the top of the dam and looked out over Roosevelt Lake, which was flecked with whitecaps. A storm was building in the distance and the clouds were scudding by above.

He whistled loudly, and his horse, Nuflo, looked up.

Nuflo was tethered below, to a willow that bent down in the wind. Everett's possessions were in tied burlap bags that hung on either side of the horse's rump. Piled on top of that were his blankets and a rolled-up cowhide he hoped to use to make some new kyacks.

"I'm coming!" he shouted, and instantly barking echoed off the cement walls. Everett smiled when he saw the bouncing white ball of fur tugging on its leash beside the horse.

"Calm down, Curly. I'm on my way."

Everett had purchased Nuflo for seven dollars when he arrived back out here in the four corner region. The horse was so old that the cowboy who sold him looked at Everett like he was a fool, but he didn't waste a second when the money was offered to him and grabbed it quickly.

"What are you planning on doing with him?" asked the Cowboy.

"I hope to travel north, to either Utah or Colorado."

The Cowboy turned away so his hat would shield his smile, but Everett could hear it in his voice. "Damn, son, it's one hundred miles to Zeniff, and that's not even halfway to the Colorado border."

"I aim to travel slowly," said Everett.

"Oh, you will!" he had shouted. "And watch out for the Holy Rollers if you make it to Ganado. I guarantee they'll try to get their hooks in you."

Everett was ready to travel again. He had explored in all four directions from the dam, lingering only because he was looking for work.

He'd found none. Most people looked at his skinny frame and laughed, refusing even to consider him. This put him into a low mood which prevented him from painting or even writing home. Physically, I'm not very strong, he thought. But I know my capabilities, and if they gave me a chance, I would work hard.

He stuck Curly in his backpack, which he shouldered, then climbed up on Nuflo.

"Time to move on, boys!" he said and clicked his tongue and gently nudged Nuflo with his heels.

Everett prided himself on being independent, but in his last letter home, he had broken down and flat-out begged for money. In the four months since he had been back in the southwest, he hadn't earned any money at all, and his supplies were just about gone.

"If you are going to send any money, right now is the time to send it. Put money first on the list."

He felt bad about the request, knowing his parents were struggling financially as well. When he entered the Tonto National Forest, his spirits picked up again, and he tried to describe it in a letter to his mother, hoping to convey a different mood.

"The hills are covered with flowers: lupines, poppies, paintbrush and daisies. A crow is clacking his beak in the cottonwood overhead. Quail are calling. A cardinal has been here."

They struck out into the mountains, following a steep trail that climbed high in the pines. Many branches lay broken on the ground, and it was clear that the winter had been long with lots of snow.

Three times boulders had skipped down at them when they attempted to cross a long scree, and now Nuflo was spooked. The horse became jumpy and side-stepped while Everett searched above them to figure what had dislodged the rocks.

He couldn't see anything, but he had the distinct feeling of being watched. They made it across the scree and continued upward, deeper into the mountains.

Later, he noticed one of the saddle blankets had slipped out, and when he backtracked to find it, he discovered an Indian ruin. The blanket lay in the middle of the trail, near what he now referred to as Rockslide Canyon, and when he dismounted, two dwellings were visible, tucked up into a high alcove, one above the other.

He tied Nuflo's lead to a tree and put Curly on the ground. After giving the horse some oats and water, he set off with the dog.

"Come on, boy, let's go exploring."

The lower ruin extended back into the cliff about fifty feet, and the one above it went back even further. Everett was surprised when he reached the end to find the last room opened out onto a balcony on the other side of the mountain.

Nuflo was reluctant to enter the ruins, and Everett had to leave him behind outside initially. Eventually, he persuaded him to be led to the chamber with the balcony where he had built a fire.

When the old horse had been supplied with grain and water, Everett tied a piece of cloth around his head, covering his nose and mouth. He had learned of explorers who got sick from inhaling the dust, and now he always wore a mask if he was digging in a ruin.

He grabbed a burning log from the fire.

In one of the interior rooms, he pawed through a pile of debris. He set the burning log by the pile. It illuminated dozens of soapweed cords and two head straps, all coated with piñon pitch. Alongside them, he found desiccated mini corn cobs, pumpkin shells and countless chips of pottery.

He picked up an arrowhead that looked like it was made from petrified wood and pocketed it.

There wasn't a sound to be heard and the silence spooked him. He returned to the balcony when his log began to burn out, and spent the next few hours scanning the land below for movement.

He woke in the morning when the sun peaked over the horizon and shone on him, slumped over on the balcony.

Several days later he left the cool mountains and entered hot, flat Arizona cattle country. He was passing a ranch gate when a gust of wind swiped his hat off his head and into the air.

He watched it land on its edge and roll right through the tall gate marked with the words "Rocking Chair Ranch."

"Well, if that wasn't a sign."

He rode Nuflo through the gate, hopped off, grabbed his hat, and continued until he neared the ranch house.

A weathered man of about fifty walked out onto the porch and eyed him. "Can I help you?" he asked a little suspiciously.

"I'm looking for work," said Everett.

"Well, we've got plenty of work here," said the man, whose name Everett would learn was Albert.

"How much do you pay?"

Albert rubbed the stubble on his chin. "I can't pay much—if anything."

Albert paused and looked over Everett's horse and his skinny frame in the saddle. "And before you get too excited, what can you do? You ever brand a cow?"

Everett shook his head. "Nope, but I pride myself on sincerity and steadiness, and I don't have much trouble getting along with people."

The rancher laughed so hard he almost fell down.

Finally, he wiped his eyes and stared hard at Everett. "Listen, you look pretty starved. If you work hard, I'll feed you and your horse 'til you're back on your feet."

Everett said, "For the last few days, all I've eaten is parched corn and jerky. And I'm just about out of oats."

"That's not good," he said, "get off that horse, and I'll show you where we can put you up."

The next morning, he was introduced to Manuel, the ranch foreman. He was Hispanic, in his forties, and had a serious air about him. He glanced at Everett's hands and gave him some leather gloves.

"You do what I say, and we no have problems," he said.

Everett nodded and followed Manuel behind the ranch house to a large corral containing several hundred cows.

"We work hard here," said Manuel. "But they feed us good. Is plenty of meat, milk and butter, cornbread, honey, even applesauce. Everything nice."

Everett's face showed his relief. "I was afraid I'd be working for Mexican strawberries."

Manuel laughed. "Beans? No, we eat better than that here—just work hard."

And over the next week he did work hard—harder than he ever had in his life. He was driving cattle from one pen to another, separating the cows from their calves, wrestling the calves off their feet once their legs were tied, stoking the fire and keeping the branding iron hot, and finally, pressing the red-hot brand on their flanks while they bellowed in pain.

In just a few days they branded over two hundred calves. And when that was done, they repaired fences and cleaned the stalls in the barn.

At night he lay down exhausted, but he felt his body responding to the hard work and good food. Nuflo looked better, too. Manuel found some wooden boxes, and together they created a new set of kyacks for Nuflo. He was tempted to stay. He liked both Albert and Manuel.

Then one evening Nuflo broke loose and Everett spent several hours chasing him in the moonlight until he cornered him in a steep arroyo. The desert seemed magical under the moon's soft glow, and if Nuflo had been loaded with his gear—and Everett had had Curly with him—he would have headed north right then.

Instead, he waited until morning to thank Albert for the food.

"You worked hard for it," said Albert.

Albert looked over Nuflo and said, "That horse has just about had it. Why don't you get another to carry your gear, so he's not so hard-pressed?"

Everett stood, restless. "Well, I don't have any cash for another horse—or even a burro."

Albert held up a finger. "Come with me."

Everett followed him to the barn, where a tired old black horse stood in a stall, munching hay.

"This guy is even older than your horse, but he makes a fine pack animal."

"I told you I don't have any money."

"I heard you. I'm giving him to you. His name is Jonathan."

Everett nodded thanks and stepped forward, and felt the horse's soft muzzle. "Hello, Jonathan."

The skies above Zeniff were filled with dark racing clouds when Everett left town. Jonathan bucked when Everett tried to put the new kyacks on him, so for now, he didn't carry a load.

Albert's remark about Nuflo worried Everett, so instead of riding him on top of the load, he walked in front of him, hoping he could train Jonathan soon. After about five miles they passed several hogans, and by one of them, he saw an old Navajo with wispy white hair. Everett stopped and nodded at him.

Thunder rumbled in the distance.

"Storm coming," said the Navajo.

Everett glanced at the sky, where the clouds had crammed into an ominous mass, and they were indeed moving toward him.

"If you help me hoe my corn, you can stay here. I will feed you too."

"Okay," said Everett. He had enjoyed working on Albert's ranch and felt more confident about his abilities. He still didn't have more than a dollar on him, but he quite liked working for food.

Over the next few days he lived in the man's hogan, watching the old man and trying to learn some of his ways. Everett taught him some English words, and the old man in turn shared a few Diné phrases.

During the days they hoed corn.

At night Everett trained Jonathan, first with a blanket, then with the empty kyacks on the horse's back. He walked him around like that, and eventually, he began adding weight.

Three days later they had finished harvesting the man's field. That evening the old man explained that he had to go to an Indian council for a few days.

"You can stay with my son-in-law while I'm gone."

The son-in-law lived seven miles away, on the banks of a nearly dry river. He couldn't speak a word of English, and it took considerable effort even to get his name, which was Sam. The morning that the old man had departed, Sam showed up and gestured for Everett to come with him. There was no indication of how far away he lived.

Everett saddled Nuflo and piled most of the gear on him. Jonathan followed with the empty kyacks, and Everett walked behind them both. He didn't feel Jonathan was ready for the road yet. They followed Sam all morning. They were going south, in the opposite direction he wanted to go, and several times he considered leaving.

Sam's hogan was in rough shape with several holes and a layer of dust covering everything, and it was clear he lived there alone. He did have plenty of feed for the horses, but his own fare was basic and barely palatable. For two days they had only black coffee and cold squaw bread, *namskadi*.

They hoed Sam's cornfields from first light until dark, and Everett crawled under his blankets each night, dead tired. Again, he wondered if he should just leave. Sam refuted Everett's attempts to communicate with him in Diné—instead, he explained what work needed to be done with gestures.

The morning Everett decided to go, another Navajo showed up. He spoke some English and seemed friendly. He also knew a lot about horses and gave Everett some pointers on how to care for them.

While they were talking Sam left without a word.

The Navajo watched him walk off and said, "My name is Lefty. You can stay with me."

Lefty also had fields that needed tending. The first morning they hoed a cornfield and a bean patch, and that afternoon they plowed an area where they sowed oats. The next day they hayed a field using scythes.

At Lefty's, Everett ate better, and some nights they even feasted on mutton.

Jonathan had become accustomed to the kyacks, and by Everett's second night with Lefty, the packhorse even let Curly ride in one of the boxes while they walked in circles in the field.

On his third morning in Lefty's hogan, Everett told him he was moving on. Lefty thanked him for the help and gave him some jerky.

When the horses were saddled and the kyacks loaded, they turned north and set out with the rising sun on their right.

Robert Louis DeMayo

Chapter Thirty-Three

Ganado, Arizona
(July 1932)

A blinding sandstorm swept over the barren land, and Everett stumbled through it, correcting their course only when he got a rare glimpse of the sun, continuing north by northeast. He had a thin fabric tied over his eyes, but he could still just barely see. He doubted Nuflo could see anything. Jonathan trailed along behind them, oblivious with his eyes covered but following obediently with his kyacks loaded.

They had traveled close to one hundred miles since leaving Zeniff. In the beginning he let the horses walk ten miles a day, then found a sheltered location to rest. But they were now just about out of water. If they didn't find some soon, or reach Ganado, it would be the end of the line. So for the last few days, he had pushed the horses harder.

The July heat was unforgiving. The monsoon season had yet to begin and the skies were cloudless. Everett's lips were parched, and Nuflo was limping slightly.

When he first saw the storm his hopes soared, but soon he realized it brought no rain, only wind and sand.

He pulled back Nuflo's reins and stopped the horse, then jumped down.

Curly had retreated deep into the backpack, but now he stuck his head out and looked around.

"Not a good time to get out," said Everett.

He hung the backpack on the saddle horn and Curly sank back into it, then he searched through the kyacks until he found a burlap sack that he placed over Nuflo's head. The horse would be blind like that, but at least his eyes would be protected from the blowing sand.

He grabbed the lead and walked ahead, trying to keep them moving in the direction of the town, which he hoped was only a short way ahead.

In the hottest part of the afternoon, Everett led Nuflo down the small main street of Ganado; Jonathan stumbled behind them. He would have stopped hours ago if he had found even a small sheltered area, but the low bushes and snakeweed had offered none.

He was just about as worn out as Nuflo. All three of them were taking small steps, dragging their feet through the fine red dust.

On the porch of one of the stores a well-dressed man watched Everett approach. The man sported a three-piece suit and a recent haircut, and he held a clipboard.

The man waved Everett over, and before he reached the porch, the guy had ducked inside and returned with a glass of water.

He handed Everett the water, and Everett drank it down without a word.

"What the heck are you doing, son? This is no weather to be traveling in."

Everett nodded. "I came from Zeniff."

The man whistled. "That's a haul for this time of the year."

The man's clothes were immaculate, and Everett wondered how he kept them so clean in this dry, windy environment.

Again, Everett nodded. His tongue was still thick with dust and he had a hard time speaking — or making his mind work.

"I'm Mr. Cosby," said the man. "You look like you could use a few days out of the wind and sun. Would you like to stay at my place and rest up?"

Everett tried to smile, and his lips cracked. "Sure."

Curly poked his head out of the backpack and Mr. Cosby looked at him amusedly. "Your dog can stay too. I've got a bunch of daughters who would love to have a puppy around."

Mr. Cosby locked the front door to his shop, slid the key into the little pocket in his vest, and walked Everett down the street to his house, about a block away.

Through a window, Mrs. Cosby glimpsed them, walking and came out to greet them. She was a plump woman with several layers of dresses and an apron wrapped around her front.

"My goodness," she said. "What have we here?"

Mr. Cosby grinned. "Company. Why don't you take him inside and show him where he can sleep, and I'll bring his horses into the barn."

Everett wanted to help, but Mr. Cosby declined.

"That's okay, son. I'll give them water and oats and bed them down on some straw."

Before Everett could protest, Mrs. Cosby said, "You look like you could use a nice bath."

As Everett followed the woman through the house, he thought of David, the young man who he had met on his way to the North Rim almost a year ago.

He wondered how he had managed with his uncle and if he had been lucky enough to get a warm bath every so often.

Mrs. Cosby showed him to a deep tub filled with warm water. After she had left him, he dropped his clothes and sank into it, overwhelmed by how his skin tingled. He stayed in the tub until the water turned cold and his flesh was wrinkled.

That night he sat at the table with Mr. and Mrs. Cosby and three of their daughters. The older two girls had gone to a rodeo in the next town over and wouldn't be back for two days. Mr. Cosby seemed quite upset about this. "You're telling me they won't be here for church in the morning?" he had asked with a note of disbelief.

Mrs. Cosby didn't meet his eyes when she replied.

"They're staying with my sister. They'll be fine."

He glared at her and she mumbled, "I'm sure Lucinda will take them to church in the morning."

He grunted and checked his temper when Everett sat down at the table. Mr. Cosby looked him over and said a little mysteriously, "We come from Mormon stock, and church is important to us."

In Zeniff, a cowboy had warned him about the "church folk" in Ganado. Everett asked, "Are you a Holy Roller?"

Mrs. Cosby blushed, but her husband laughed. "No, I'm not. I may be religious, but I've never rolled on the floor while reciting scripture."

When it came time for grace, one of the younger daughters asked God not to send her sisters to hell for going to the rodeo instead of church.

Mr. Cosby got Everett up early the next day. From the hallway he could smell breakfast cooking in the kitchen, and he was a bit let down when Mr. Cosby steered him into the bathroom instead.

"I'd like to bring you into town today," he said, "but I think we need to clean you up first."

Before Everett was fully awake, Mr. Cosby had shaved him, given him a haircut, and then handed him a bucket of water to wash with.

"You've had your Saturday night bath, so this should do."

Everett rolled up his sleeves, and Mr. Cosby glanced at his silver bracelet. The embedded turquoise stones glimmered, and Everett smiled.

"My lucky charm," he said.

Mr. Cosby frowned at the Indian jewelry like it was a rotting piece of meat. "I'd get rid of it," he said flatly, "you'll not gain luck from heathen trinkets." Then he forced a smile and added, "Besides, you can't take things like that with you when you pass on to the next world."

Everett rolled up his other sleeve and splashed water on his face.

When he finished he discovered that Mrs. Cosby had washed his spare shirt and pants the night before, and they were just now drying in the sun. He barely recognized the shirt, which had also been mended.

He dressed and came out to the table, which was set with hotcakes, eggs, cereal, and bacon.

He had barely taken a bite of the sugarless cereal when Mr. Cosby began asking about his religious upbringing and beliefs.

"What Bible do you read?" he asked.

"I believe we have the King James version."

Mr. Cosby narrowed his eyes. "You mean at home, with your parents?"

Everett nodded, and the man asked, "You don't have one with you?"

Everett shook his head.

"Before you leave, I'll have to find you a *Book of Mormon*."

Everett didn't know what to say. There was a reason he didn't travel with a Bible. He enjoyed reading it from time to time, but he had his church — the wilderness — and its words were written in the wind.

Mr. Cosby perched his fingers on his temple. "And your parents, do they not mind you drifting around the southwest like this?"

"Well, I am an artist, and I'm trying to develop my painting skills. This is a great opportunity for fieldwork," said Everett, feeling a pang of guilt over the fact that he had barely painted on this trip.

Mr. Cosby´s brow suddenly furrowed.

"I have to say I don't approve of what you're doing."

In the heavy silence that followed, Everett wondered if he should eat as much as he could before they threw him out. Instead, Mr. Cosby folded his hands, closed his eyes, and prayed while Everett finished breakfast.

When he was done, Mr. Cosby said, "I think we need to talk with Mr. Brown, the bishop. Your immortal soul is in danger, and I don't feel comfortable having it in jeopardy."

An hour later Everett was walking down the streets of Ganado with Mr. and Mrs. Cosby and their three daughters. He could see others that he figured were also on their way to church. They were all in their Sunday best, and they swaggered like mannequins.

There was something in the way they stared at those not going to church that made Everett uncomfortable, and he thought, in this town, people probably go to church just because they fear being ostracized. Still, the Crosbys were kind; they had fed him and cleaned him up. Took care of the horses, too, he thought, as he continued down the street.

On the steps of the church he was introduced to Mr. Brown, the bishop. "This is our new friend, Everett," said Mr. Cosby. "We're hoping he might stick around for a little while."

Mr. Brown grasped Everett's hand in both of his and shook it warmly. "Nice to have you with us," he said.

He had three daughters of his own with him, the eldest rather pretty, and Everett was introduced to them. The Brown girls went inside with the women and Mr. Cosby's daughters, and Everett would have liked to have gone with them, but the men remained outside and so did he.

Mr. Brown rubbed his eyes and Mr. Cosby asked, "Late night?"

Mr. Brown nodded. "A bunch of cowboys came back from the rodeo late last night. A few were pretty drunk and about a dozen ended up in the tank. One fell off his horse and thought he was going to die and wanted to make a confession."

Mr. Cosby shook his head. "What's this world coming to when the jail contains as many people on a Sunday morning as the church?"

"It's just a sign of the times," said Mr. Brown. "It all coincides with the prophecies in the *Book of Revelations*. The end of things is near."

Everett leaned forward and asked, "You think the end is coming?"

Mr. Brown smiled. "Just yesterday, I heard that the Bank of America has failed. If that's not a sign!"

Everett felt a smile come over him when he realized that was the exact same words he had used when his hat had blown off and rolled through the gate of the Rocking Chair Ranch.

"Just because a bank fails doesn't mean the world is gonna end," said Everett.

The two men stared at him. Mr. Brown cleared his throat and said, "It's one of many signs, and if you look for them, they are out there."

When Mr. Brown took the pulpit, the twenty-odd people in the congregation became quiet. He remembered Mr. Cosby had said he came from "Mormon stock," but he couldn't quite figure out what church Mr. Brown preached for.

Everyone was expected to read from the Bible, and when it was Everett's turn, he chose a passage from the *Book of Ruth*.

The room was silent when he, a stranger, began.

"Entreat me not to leave thee,
or to return from following after thee,
for wither thou goest, I will go."

After, they sang songs about Judgment Day and dining with Jesus. Everett had been missing music, and he sang loudly, trying to fill the void inside him.

There was also a song called *The Royal Telephone*.

"Telephone to Glory,
Oh what Joy Divine!
I can feel the current
coming down the line,
sent by God the Father
to his blessed own,
I can talk to Jesus
on the royal telephone."

Before the congregation broke into smaller groups for Bible study, Mr. Brown warned everyone against Christian Science, Universalism, Unitarianism, and the evils found in big cities.

Everett didn't consider himself a religious person, but he had hoped the morning in church would help him connect with the spirituality of the people he now stayed with. But now, listening to the bishop warning about other faiths and the evils of modern society, he realized how much more he preferred his simpler love of nature.

He felt the overpowering presence of religion even stronger in the little group he was assigned to, where they all seemed to be afraid of everything. And whatever they feared, they prayed for deliverance from.

They began praying for rain and then an easy winter. But then moved on to praying for the sick, the old, and then for one little boy with a broken arm. His mother was in hysterics for fear it would be stiff, and several women cried with her. They also prayed for the drunk husband of another woman.

Everett listened to one woman talking to Mr. Brown when he stopped by the group. She wept uncontrollably because her son wouldn't come to church.

"Will he be condemned to hell?" she asked.

Mr. Brown consoled her with a comforting hand on her elbow. He said, "Maybe with time, he'll change his mind and come to his senses."

By the time church was over Everett was ready to hit the road again, but the sky was black, and it looked like rain. While they walked back to Mr. Cosby's house a lightning bolt hit the edge of town, and they all ducked and hurried before the rain began.

At Mr. Cosby's house, they saw the barn door open and discovered that both horses had panicked when they heard the thunder and had taken off.

When the storm had passed, Everett followed the horse tracks out of town. He was heading north, in the direction of Chinle, about forty miles away. He carried with him a rope and some tack.

About an hour from Ganado, he came upon an old Navajo who indicated with his lips the direction the horses had gone.

"*Ahéhee'*" said Everett. Thank you.

Everett walked another twenty minutes and found Nuflo and Jonathan grazing with some Navajo horses by an abandoned hogan. Jonathan was skittish and wouldn't let him get close.

He slowly approached Nuflo and spoke quietly to him until the horse relaxed. He slipped a bridle over his head and rode him bareback to town. He planned on returning for Jonathan shortly.

Mr. Cosby's expression dropped when Everett told him he was moving on. It was clear he had other hopes for Everett.

"You can't leave now — we were making progress."

"Thanks for all your hospitality," said Everett, "but I have to be moving north."

Mr. Cosby's eyes widened. "North? That's crazy. You'll never make it. The hills are full of heathens that will probably rob you, and before you reach Chinle, you have to pass through some scrub that's thick with snakes. You're going to die out there!"

He held up a finger, warning, "Beware the Serpent!"

Everett extended his hand and Mr. Cosby reluctantly shook it. Then he walked to the barn and saddled Nuflo. When he returned to his belongings in the house, he found a Mormon bible on the top of the pile.

He grabbed his belongings but left the Bible on the bed. He wished they had given him some food so he wouldn't be leaving without supplies, but he could see Mr. Cosby talking to his wife in the other room, his face a mask of frustration, and he sensed it was time to go.

In the barn, he put the kyacks with all his gear on Nuflo, figuring the horse could handle the load over the short distance to where Jonathan waited. Curly rode along in one of the kyacks.

He wondered about the Mormon's claim that the end was coming, and then laughed and pointed Nuflo north, out into the desert plain.

The wild, erratic wind comforted Everett, and he liked the fact that he was traveling with his back to the church, moving away from it. He had his own Altar of Beauty and didn't need another.

"I'm through with whites for a while," he said out loud. Then he looked over his shoulder at the little white dog and added, "No offense, I wasn't talking about you."

Jonathan held his head down when he approached, and Everett put a halter on him and trailed him by a lead behind Nuflo.

They crept into the hills, passing a few hogans before crossing a bridge over a deep arroyo. It began to rain.

Everett put on an old poncho Manuel had given him. It covered his whole saddle but leaked slightly on the right shoulder.

The rain beat down steadily, but Everett didn't mind. The smell of the wet desert and the exquisite panoramas of the misty land lifted his spirit.

"How much better to be here with rain dripping off my poncho than in a schoolroom watching it on the windows?" he asked Nuflo.

Rain trickled off the rim of his hat and he felt like a hero. He found a trail that continued north, circling a magnificently layered terra cotta butte.

Later that day, they came to a pleasant spring, and he decided to stop. Two abandoned hogans and an old corral stood a short way away.

The larger of the two hogans was in reasonable shape, and Everett unloaded his kyacks and brought his gear inside. He remembered Mr. Cosby warning about thieving heathens in the hills, but it looked like nobody had been around the hogans for a while. The corral had good grass growing in it.

He turned the horses loose in the corral and climbed a hill behind the hogans. The rain had stopped, and a deeply colored rainbow arched over the cedar-capped hills. A long flat plain of low scrub stretched to the north, and he figured a few miles beyond it lay Chinle.

He took things easy the next morning. He repaired a strap on one of the kyacks, and they didn't set out until midday, moving north through the plain. They had only gone a short distance when Nuflo whinnied and rose on his hind legs.

Everett heard the rattle and jumped.

Nuflo was trying to stomp the snake, which repeatedly struck at him. Everett had difficulty getting to the snake, trying not to be bitten or stepped on by his horse at the same time.

Finally, Nuflo managed to kill it with a well-placed hoof.

Everett calmed Nuflo down and inspected the horse's legs nervously.

"Let's hope he missed you," he said and climbed onto Nuflo's back.

Just minutes later another snake struck out, but this time Everett was ready and pulled back hard on the reins, forcing Nuflo to back up.

Everett killed the snake with a rock. He patted Nuflo and looked out over the plain, Mr. Cosby´s warning ringing in his head.

He probably fears the Indians because he never befriended them, thought Everett, but he might be right about dreading the snakes. The brush on the plain was just high enough that he couldn't see them, and a rattlesnake bite could be deadly.

So, he turned around and led the horses back to the abandoned hogan. There he pawed through the kyacks until he found a large piece of rawhide.

He had initially hoped to line his kyacks with the thick leather, but now he cut it into two long pieces and punched holes along the sides with an awl.

An hour later he stood with a rough pair of chaps that covered his legs from his boots up to his hips.

"Not bad, eh?" he asked Curly while he paraded around.

Then they left the Hogan for a second time to cross the plain. Everett walked ahead of the two horses, holding Nuflo's reins. He passed the two dead snakes and continued.

The sun was now directly overhead, and he watched the grass before them carefully. But the snakeweed and rabbitbrush that covered the ground was so dense that he didn't see the next snake until he was upon it.

"Whoa!" he shouted as the snake launched out of the brush right at him. It sailed through the air and then glanced off his right leg.

Everett grabbed a stick and threw the snake into the far grass.

He fought to regain his breath, then whooped.

"I will not 'Beware the Serpent!'" he shouted.

They pushed on, and over the next two miles, he stepped on another snake and stirred up two more, but the chaps protected his legs from their fangs.

He knew that snakes could feel vibrations through the ground, so as he continued, he stomped his feet. He also sang loudly. *The Royal*

Telephone was still in his head, but he shook it off and instead shouted Beethoven over the quiet plain.

On the outskirts of Chinle he saw a young Navajo woman leading a burro, coming his way. When they were closer, he realized she was the same shy woman who helped Notah, the elder.

He stopped when they got closer and said, "Hi!"

She stepped back slightly and stared at him.

"I remember you," said Everett. "Do you remember me?"

The woman, whose name he didn't know, tried to go around him.

"No, wait!" he said. "I have something for Notah. Will you see him again soon?"

The woman tried to skirt him again, and he stopped her once more by holding out his arms. She glared at him. "Notah," said Everett. "You know Notah, don't you?"

She nodded only slightly. Everett quickly slipped around to Jonathan's side and retrieved a rolled-up canvas from one of the kyacks. "Would you please give this to him?" he asked.

He thought she probably didn't know much English. "Here," he said and gave it to her.

She reluctantly accepted it.

"Tell him Everett wanted him to have this."

When she didn't reply he asked, "You understand?"

He couldn't understand why her eyes were now filled with anger.

He tried speaking slower and louder.

"EV... VER... ETT... You try it!"

She only scowled at him and then forced her way past him.

He hoped she would give the picture to Notah.

Now that he had delivered it, he felt relieved. The road ahead looked easy, and he knew the way through Canyon del Muerto and figured it wouldn't be that difficult.

But the skies overhead were dark and rumbled ominously with thunder.

Robert Louis DeMayo

Chapter Thirty-Four

Mesa Verde, Colorado
(August 1932)

Nuflo trudged up the steep trail, his head down, his legs shaky. In the saddle rode Everett, hat tilted forward. Dark circles lined his eyes and his pale, tired face bobbed over his shoulders as he barely clung to the saddle horn. The lower half of his poncho had been torn, and a tattered remnant dragged in the mud.

The horse now carried both Everett and the kyacks, but most of his gear was missing.

Jonathan was nowhere in sight.

Neither was Curly.

The murky sky above was webbed with lightning, and the sharp echo of the thunderclaps rolled overhead and then boomed off the walls of the canyon.

Everett pulled his hat down tighter.

The trail up and out of Canyon del Muerto passed through a narrow section, and they were in the middle of it when the skies opened up and the cloudburst came down.

Everett slid out of the saddle, flipped the reins over the horse's head, and led him up the trail. They had only taken a few steps when floodwater began to cascade down at them, plunging from a thousand sources.

Instantly the track turned into a stream. The only safety lay up the trail—upstream now—and Everett leaned forward and sloshed upward through the muddy waters.

When the trail widened he could finally see the edge of the canyon walls were lower, and he hoped he might see a break where he could ascend, but as he stared at them, a vivid arrow of flame pierced the darkness and struck the wall with such intensity that the ground shook.

Both Nuflo and Everett stopped instantly and then watched a mass of rock silently slide down the cliff face. The ground shook again, but the rain muffled the deep rumble.

They forced their way upward for a solid hour.

The rain lessened when they approached the rim of the canyon, but Everett could not see a way out. His legs were rubbery, and he stumbled a few times. The left wall offered a few sheltered areas, and under one, he found sheep tracks overlapped by prints of bare feet.

He left Nuflo there, tied to a gnarled juniper root, and followed the footprints to a nearby dry cave about fifteen feet deep. There was a fire pit by the wall, and next to it, a few logs that the last visitor had collected.

He returned for the horse and led him to the shelter, where he sunk to the ground with relief. The rain came down hard again, and outside waterfalls were forming. But they stayed dry. After taking off the kyacks and saddle, he fed Nuflo some grain and said, "I don't think I'll ride you anymore."

The horse looked at him with dark, soulful eyes.

Everett searched the kyacks and found a small, plastic-wrapped bundle of tinder and matches. His hands were shaking as he prepared the fire.

He looked up at Nuflo again.

He said, "I don't think I'll buy another horse, either. I haven't the money, and I can get by without one if I walk."

He thought about Jonathan's passing.

Nuflo watched silently as the match took, and then the fire grew.

Everett lay on his side in the sand, leaving his soaked bedroll in the kyacks. He stared off into the rain as he recalled the long day's events.

He tried not to think about Curly.

Sleep was trying to claim him, but he fought it off and looked at Nuflo again. He said, "I can take care of you better now that I have only you." The slightest of smiles touched his face, and he added, "You'll have more oats, and there'll be no more hobblers—you're free to go whenever you want."

And then, just before his head dropped into the sand and he slept like the dead, he said, "You've got nothing to prove to me."

Everett woke to the sound of a Navajo whistling a herd of sheep along. His fire was down to smoldering embers, and Nuflo stood by the cave entrance, drinking water from a puddle.

The morning sparkled from the sunshine jumping off a million raindrops. He heard the whistle again and hiked in that direction for about ten minutes until he saw a few sheep, and then the trail out of the canyon.

Now that he knew the way out, things didn't feel so desperate. He had not eaten since the morning before, so he rekindled the fire and heated some mutton and sweetbread.

Later that day, he led Nuflo onto a plateau bordered by a range of purple mountains and buttes in the distance. Everett said, "That's got to be the Lukachukai Mountains."

Deep in the Lukachukais, Everett stopped at a quiet canyon lined with pines and firs and made camp by a clump of aspens. They were shivering in the wind and sounded deceptively like running water, and their shade lulled him while he read a collection of Robert Browning's poems.

A few feet away Nuflo munched on a patch of grass that the Navajo sheep had somehow missed.

Everett called over to the horse.

"What do you think of this one?"

> *"If you get simple beauty and naught else,*
> *you get about the best thing God invents."*

Nuflo didn't even look his way. Everett found another one he liked. "I bet old Pericles would have liked this one."

"A lion may die of an ass's kick."

The morning had lifted his spirits, and now Browning's poetry helped whisk away the sorrows of the last few days. He flipped through the collection, silently thanking his mother for mailing it to him.

In his last letter from her, he had also received a ten-dollar money order, and he looked forward to purchasing more supplies.

He gazed at the mountains in the distance. That was the far northeast corner of Arizona, and he knew once he reached them, he would soon be leaving the plateau country and entering Colorado and its mountain ranges.

He read another quote.

"Take away love and our earth is a tomb."

Behind him a quail called out and he scanned the brush trying to spot it. The bird cooed again and ran out from under a bush, followed by four young chicks.

Everett laughed at their sight, then froze.

In the bushes from which they had emerged a bear was watching him.

For a minute Everett was concerned it might be stalking Nuflo, but there were plenty of berries about.

He felt no fear. He'd been around bears in the Sierras and knew they were only trouble if you provoked them.

This one just looked curious, and the way it stared back at him, unafraid also but intent, amused him.

In the timeless moment that followed, the Navajo story of the Changing Bear Maiden sprang up in Everett's mind. According to the legend, a girl had accepted a bear as her husband. Her younger sisters told this to her father, who killed the bear with the help of his seven sons. The girl then changed herself into a bear and killed all seven brothers.

Many nights Everett had stared at the Big Dipper and Seven Sisters sparkling in the sky. To the Navajo, these stars represented the Great Bear and the seven slain brothers.

The bear stayed where he was, watching him. Everett picked up the book, but then he put it back down and pulled out his journal instead. Folded inside was a letter he had written to his brother, Waldo.

He opened the letter and read from a paragraph on the bottom, raising his voice so the bear could hear it.

"I have been thinking more and more that I shall always be a lone wanderer in the wilderness."

The bear watched him. Sniffing the air from time to time, but eyes locked on him. Everett continued reading.

"God, how the trail lures me. You cannot comprehend its resistless fascination for me. I'll never stop wandering."

When Everett finished reading, he addressed the bear.

"I bet you never stop either!" he shouted.

The bear watched him a moment longer, then slinked back behind the bush and Everett didn't see him again.

About a week later they reached the Mesa Verde ruins. In 1888 John Wetherill had been with a group that rediscovered the Anasazi site while exploring the area. It turned out to be one of the largest and best-preserved collections of cliff-dwellings in the world. The entire mesa — an area of eighty square miles with more than six hundred intricately constructed cliff dwellings — had been proclaimed a National Park in 1906 by President Theodore Roosevelt.

Having met John Wetherill, Everett felt a pang of jealousy in his discovery. He would have given almost anything to find an undiscovered ruin. Sometimes he wished he could have been an explorer fifty or a hundred years ago.

He became a regular at the Mesa Verde ruins and befriended quite a few of the rangers. Soon he was staying at the rangers' quarters, where they had a few extra beds. The nights were chilly, and the fall days brisk, and he was glad to have a warm, clean bed. In addition, his gear was stored in a dry place, and he could take a shower whenever he wanted.

A hot shower, he thought. What a luxury.

The Government Mess Hall offered meals for thirty cents each, and since he had cashed the money order from his parents, he ate there every day.

Nuflo's limp had gotten worse, so Everett led him to see the horse wrangler, a guy named Jim English.

Jim shook his head when he had finished examining the horse.

"I think old Nuflo has just about had it," he said. "Look at his teeth—they're so worn down he can hardly eat. That leg he limps on isn't going to get any better, and his back is developing sores from the kyacks."

Everett nodded. He had suspected this might be a one-way trip for the old horse.

The next day Jim led Everett and Nuflo to a peaceful glade about two miles away. Several horses were grazing on the other side of the clearing, and Nuflo raised his head and whinnied softly in their direction.

"He'll do fine here," said Jim. "I can come by from time to time and check on him, but those fellas over there are also retired, and I think it's a good place for him to spend his final days."

Everett took off the lead and halter and then put his face close to the horse's soft muzzle.

"We've had our time in the sun, haven't we? Thank you."

He was happy to leave the horse here, but still, his eyes teared up on the way back to the Ranger Station.

He soon grew restless. One of the rangers, a guy his age named Fritz, had some time off, and they decided to set off together and explore. Early one morning they left for Wetherill Mesa, which was only about four miles, but Everett planned on making a large circle that veered southwest and eventually went down Ute Canyon to the Mancos River and then up Navajo Canyon to the Ranger Station again. Probably a thirty-mile loop, he guessed.

It had rained for the last few days, and both young men took the bright, rising sun as a good omen for their adventure as they headed out on foot. The sun drove away the remaining clouds, and the mist that hovered over the damp foliage spiraled into the air and vanished.

Fritz was a tireless hiker and also a fan of exploring ruins. He had been born in Connecticut but had moved out west with his family when he was ten.

"From Wetherill, we can get to Wild Horse Mesa quite easily," he said. "There are good ruins there, and I'm hoping you can help me figure out how to access a couple that I couldn't get to last time."

Everett liked having a friend with a similar disposition. They slept in the open, by their fire, and ate from the one pot they carried, sparingly, of whatever soup they could put together from their meager supplies.

Fritz had also contributed some elk jerky he bought from one of the packers.

Without pack animals, Everett had severely diminished carrying capacities and had to leave a lot behind, but he didn't think he had it in him to watch another horse die and gladly went without. Jonathan's dying face came back to him, staring up from the patch of prickly pear cactus he'd fallen into.

For the first few days Everett and Fritz methodically climbed through every ruin they passed. Most were easy to reach and didn't pose much of a challenge. Then, on their third day, they passed a ruin near Horse Springs that left them both standing in the sun staring.

Fritz rubbed his chin. "I don't know about this one. We might be able to worm up that vertical crevice," he said, pointing, "but we would still have to traverse that whole section of the cliff face."

Everett squinted up at the approach. "Let's give it a shot."

"After you," said Fritz with a smile.

The narrow aperture was just big enough to stick in a hand and make a fist. Once Everett had gotten this handhold set, he placed a foot in the lower part of the crevice and slowly began climbing, pulling himself up by fist over fist. It was slow progress, and when they finally reached a shelf, both of them had little strength remaining in their arms.

Next, they had to crawl under a truck-sized boulder that perched precariously on the edge of the cliff with water flowing under it.

"That thing looks about ready to tumble off," said Everett.

"Just don't bump it."

A two-foot-wide stream of rainwater was rushing through a narrow channel underneath the boulder, and they had to lay flat in the stream and shuffle on their back to get under the rock, and then cling to the other side while moving around it onto a narrow ledge.

The ruin sat on the ledge and had two rooms and a third structure that was still sealed.

"That's a storehouse," said Fritz. "Let's leave it intact."

"You don't think there'd be anything inside?"

Fritz shook his head. "Just rotted grain or corn."

They searched the other structures but didn't dig. Fritz worked with several archaeologists and didn't want to be known as a looter.

But Everett found a bone awl in one of the ruins and pocketed it.

Two days later they were hiking down Ute Canyon, moving toward the river. The sky was overcast, and throughout the morning, the clouds had darkened.

Suddenly they heard a low boom of thunder.

Everett looked back up the canyon in the direction they had descended. Dark, ominous clouds had gathered there, and far off, he thought he could make out long ribbons of rain.

He looked at Fritz and scanned the canyon around him.

"This place is a death trap in a rainstorm," said Everett. "We should get out of here."

And then they both heard a faint rumbling.

Everett looked at the closest side of the gulch, where a steep scree climbed the canyon wall. "Run!" he shouted.

They fled to the scree as the rumbling rose to a roar, and they had barely begun to scramble up the scree when a wall of water rounded the corner and swept down the canyon. Then, as quickly as they could, they climbed higher.

They reached a shelf, panting heavily, and crawled up on it. Then, wide-eyed, they watched the rolling mass of water with sticks and logs and boulders rush past. For one panicked moment, it seemed that the water might rise high enough to sweep over their ledge, but then it began to retreat.

"That was lucky," said Fritz.

Everett sat down and began unpacking his pack. Fritz gave him a questioning look and he said, "Get a fire going and we'll make some coffee—we're not going anywhere soon."

The next afternoon they ascended a grassy way to the north brink of Mesa Verde at 8,300 feet. Everett felt short of breath.

The terrain was a drab olive. A lurid glow shot off the sun as it peeked through the one smoky cloud on the horizon. The sky was otherwise cloudless. The storm had passed. Small lakes gleamed below them.

In the morning they planned on descending to several ruins that Fritz thought might interest Everett. But, for now, they had made a simple camp on the rim, and on a low fire, Everett had a pot of rice cooking.

The sun was nearing the horizon, now almost totally obscured by the clouds, and in the soft orange light, two dark birds of prey were spiraling over the canyon below them.

"I came here last month with a group of rangers," said Fritz. He nodded at the birds. "Those black vultures have been nesting in the ruins below, and it's been decided that they have to go."

Everett smiled. "Need someone to chase them away?"

Fritz pursed his lips. "No, we've tried that. So few people visit these ruins, so they just come back. The last I heard, they were going to poison them."

The birds flew out of sight for a moment and then returned, angling higher and behind them. Eventually, one coasted by and Everett got a look at it.

"That's a big bird," he said. "Probably has a five-foot wingspan."

He looked at Fritz. "It seems a shame to kill them. Couldn't they just relocate them?"

Fritz shrugged. "They might if they could catch them."

"The Navajo and Hopi both catch eagles. Just do what they do."

Fritz shook his head and smiled. "Currently, we've got no rangers who are also Indians with eagle-catching experience."

"I could do it," said Everett.

It got darker and Everett could just barely make out the dim lights of Cortez in the distance.

Several hours before dawn, Everett made his way down off the mesa to the ruin below. Before he had turned into the ruin, he passed a waterhole with cattails growing in it. Fritz had explained where the buzzards roosted during the day, and Everett navigated through the ancient buildings until he found the location. It was dark, and he moved slowly, feeling his way.

The ruin had some twenty dwellings, some with two stories, and the birds seemed to prefer the roof of the ones near the front of the cave. The bird droppings along the front edge of one of the buildings pointed Everett to where they perched.

There was a low wall on the roof, and Everett figured he could hide behind it and not be seen until the birds landed. The horizon was just beginning to lighten when he settled down to wait.

He lay on his back, listening to other birds twittering and fluttering around in the cool air. From the other side of the ruin, a large raven clicked his beak, and a couple of doves cooed from a tree below the shelf where the ruin lay.

Water trickled somewhere behind him. It was lovely to be in a place with so much water. The recent rains had left pools in the flat rocks that stretched in front of the buildings, and water was still flowing down the narrow canyon below them.

The rising sun lit up the back of the ruin. Soon it would rise higher, leaving the old building in the shade for the hot part of the day, but the morning sunshine looked pleasing, and Everett yearned to escape the cold shelter of the wall he hid behind and stretch out in its warmth.

He thought of Fritz, sitting by their fire on the mesa while he waited.

And then he heard a heavy swoop of wings and faintly made out a shadow on the back wall.

The bird flew directly for the wall, intending to land and then turn around. Its feet had just touched the old stone wall when Everett's hands shot out and grabbed them.

The vulture's talons wrapped around his hand, and he saw the sharp beak about to hack at him, but he dodged it and yanked the bird's feet up and spun it upside down.

The bird screeched in anger and flapped its wings, trying to raise its head high enough to peck at him, but Everett nimbly moved out of the way, spinning in a circle until the bird got tired and lowered its head.

He whooped with joy, and a few minutes later when Fritz appeared on the edge of the ruin, he held the bird up high.

"I told you I could do it!" shouted Everett.

Pledge to the Wind

304

Chapter Thirty-Five

Gallup, New Mexico
(August 1932)

*T*he battered old pickup drove off in a cloud of dust, leaving Everett standing by a pile of gear. It had been a good ride, all the way from Mesa Verde, but the driver was turning east now that they merged onto Route 66, and Everett wanted to go west, to California.

A few buildings stood in the lonely landscape. His gear was stacked in the shade of a large water tower behind him, and a string of telephone poles ran up and down the highway.

A tumbleweed rolled across the road, passing a dusty gas station with a small one-car garage.

A diner faced the road fifty feet away, and two cars sat in front of it. Everett walked there and entered. Bells on the door announced his arrival, and he thought of the tinkling of water.

The waitress and the one customer sized him up.

"You sure have a lot of stuff," said the waitress. "We watched you unload."

Everett nodded. He had hoped to make it to Flagstaff, so he could ship it all home, but he still had over a hundred miles to go to get there and worried that it would be hard to hitch a ride with all this equipment in tow.

He needed to sell a few things, both to lighten his load and also to get some money. The cash from his mom´s money order was long gone. He was hungry like a wolf, and the smell of coffee and fried eggs that wafted out of the kitchen were making him lightheaded.

"Know anybody that might want to buy a saddle?" he asked.

The waitress looked at the one customer, an old cowboy who wore his hat even in the restaurant.

The man said, "If old Clifton is around, he might."

The waitress pointed to a sandy hill visible through a window, about a hundred feet away.

"If you go over that rise, you might find an old Indian sleeping in the shade of a telephone pole. He waits there for his nephew to pick him up. He might buy something."

Everett thanked them and left.

He stopped and looked over his belongings before searching for the Indian.

I don't feel in the mood for a big change now, he thought. But I know it's bound to come. He sighed. Lack of money, he reluctantly thought, does seem to be sometimes paralyzing — it closes all roads.

He sensed the end of something great.

If only I had found work that paid, he thought. He knew that he would experience poverty more acutely in the city than he did in the desert. In the wilderness, having no money only meant you went hungry from time to time.

The wind swirled around him.

He thought of the things he missed. I shall look forward to concerts and symphonies and having a library at my disposal.

Most of his paints had been used or dried up, and he planned on purchasing a complete set of oils. Then, if I can find a way to make money, he thought, I would like to buy a camera.

He walked to the pile and grabbed his saddle, then started walking toward the sandy rise.

The wind picked up. It came from the direction of the sandhill and blew straight at him, like it was trying to stop him.

He dreaded returning home. He knew his father would pressure him to go to college, and he figured he would probably get talked into giving it a try.

He didn't think it would be a good fit.

He questioned whether he could make it as an artist. If only a few more tourists had bought my paintings, he thought.

And if not art, then what? I could never endure a life of routine, regular hours, and monotonous work. It just doesn't seem worth living without new experiences, broadening horizons, and some sense of adventure.

Most people's lives do not appeal to me, he thought. I would not want to trade places with any of them, regardless of the shortcomings of my position.

There isn't anyone I've met whose life I would aspire to, except maybe the painter Edward Weston. With a sudden rise in spirit, he thought of taking a trip up the coast of California to visit him.

Memories of California swam through his mind. Maybe I'll finally traverse the Sierras, he thought. Or go to San Francisco and immerse myself in the art scene there.

Maybe I could try my hand at writing my adventures, he thought as he approached the top of the sandhill. He could see the Indian sitting beyond it; he was a Navajo, old, with long white hair.

Reluctantly he took the first step down the hill, and the wind stopped completely. Again he felt he was leaving something behind.

Ending something.

But he continued. He needed to sell a few things and return to his parents and get organized. But he knew he would be back. He would always come back.

He looked out over the plain and felt in his heart that a part of him would always be out there, exploring the canyons and mountains.

He just had to go home for now. The little money he might get from selling some gear would be enough to ship his other belongings home and buy some food. With a little luck, he might even have bus fare. He had no intention of getting stuck in Needles again.

With another sigh, he hefted the saddle a little higher and walked down to the old Navajo who watched him with his back to the pole.

1935

Robert Louis DeMayo

Chapter Thirty-Six

Kayenta Trading Post, Arizona
(March 1935)

Notah stood on the porch of the Kayenta Trading Post, facing a line of reporters. He tried to look right through them like they weren't there, but there were too many. They had come back repeatedly, drawn by bigger headlines as the search widened.

A reporter asked, "Mr. Notah, why do you think nobody can find Everett Ruess? No one has seen him since November. Are the Navajo hiding him?"

Notah remained quiet and watched a large raven land on the roof of an automobile belonging to one of the reporters.

The reporter looked frustrated. "If you know something, tell us. This manhunt is spread over an area almost the size of New England. Where did he go?"

Another man cleared his throat and asked, "Mr. Notah, is there any truth to the rumor that he had an Indian bride?"

The old Navajo had had enough. He turned to leave, but a journalist right in front of him asked politely, "Please, sir, we are told you knew Everett well. Can you tell us what happened to him?"

The old man paused and collected his words. The raven flew off.

He said, "Everett Ruess is dead."

"Dead?" questioned the man. "How did he die? Where's the body?"

Notah looked beyond the heads of the reporters, out over the plains surrounding Kayenta. In the distance he could see a giant stone tower soaring up into the sky. The setting sun had left its black form silhouetted in gold.

He gave a rare smile, and half the crowd turned to see where he was looking. Suddenly a warm breeze stumbled through, snatching papers from the hands of one of the reporters and scattering them.

It circled Notah, who turned and went inside. He slammed the door behind him.

Notah's room had only a bed and a chair, but a canvas had been tacked on the wall. The old Navajo stood before it, peering into the image.

Agathla Rock lay sketched in heavy black lines. They seemed to flow with a powerful energy, and at times Notah could see them moving.

Near the top of the peak was a break in one of the lines. It could have been a simple mistake, but when Notah stared at it long enough, he saw the Picture Man.

He touched the bottom of the canvas, smiled, and turned and slowly shuffled to his chair.

*

Deep in the twisting labyrinth of the Narrows, Tiba followed a shallow stream while the rapids echoed musically off the high sandstone walls. This was her first time to Zion, and when she'd had her initial glimpse of the Great White Throne, she understood why Everett had talked about it so much.

Everett had called a magical spot, several miles into the Narrows, his *Sipapu* — his place of emergence — and as she made her way through the slender canyon, she watched to see if she might find it.

At one bend, the light from above reflected off the ripples in the water, casting diamonds of light on the rocks all around her. She felt at peace there, and oddly, sensed Everett wasn't far away.

A gentle breeze caressed her face.

She reached into a pocket and pulled out the silver bracelet Everett had given her when his wrist had swollen from the snakebite. It had taken her two weeks to walk from the Escalante drainage, but now that she stood in what she believed to be the very spot he had talked about, she knew it was worth it.

She stepped into the river, letting the cool fluid flow over her bare feet, and then tossed the bracelet in the water.

It twisted as it sank, catching the light and reflecting it as it fell deeper.

"I will see you again," she thought with a smile before turning and walking back the way she'd come.

*

A hawk spiraled over a clifftop, searching for a meal. Soon it landed at its nest, which sat above a ruin high on the cliff wall. The land below was wild and untamed.

A few feet away, an inscription had been carved into the wall: NEMO 1935.

A light breeze swept over the words, blowing a scattering of sand and whispering...

"Onward from vast uncharted spaces, forward through timeless voids, into all of us surges and races the measureless might of the wind."

Wilderness Song
by Everett Ruess

I have been one who loved the wilderness:
Swaggered and softly crept between the mountain peaks;
I listened long to the seas brave music;
I sang my songs above the shriek of desert winds.

On canyon trails when warm night winds were blowing,
Blowing, and sighing gently through the star-tipped pines,
Musing, I walked behind my placid burro,
While water rushed and broke on pointed rocks below.

I have known a green sea's heaving; I have loved
Red rocks and twisted trees and cloudless turquoise skies,
Slow sunny clouds and red sand blowing.
I have felt the rain and slept behind the waterfall.

In cool sweet grasses I have lain and heard
The ghostly murmur of regretful winds
In aspen glades, where rustling silver leaves
Whisper wild sorrows to the green-gold solitudes.

I have watched the shadowed clouds pile high;
Singing, I rode to meet the splendid, shouting storm
And fought its fury till the hidden sun
Foundered in darkness, and the lightning heard my song.

Say that I starved; that I was lost and weary;
That I was burned and blinded by the desert sun;
Footsore, thirsty, sick with strange diseases;
Lonely and wet and cold, but that I kept my dream!

Always I shall be one who loves the wilderness:
Swaggers and softly creeps between the mountain peaks;
I shall listen long to the sea's brave music;
I shall sing my song above the shriek of desert winds.

Robert Louis DeMayo

Author's Note

Waldo Ruess

In 1935, when much of America was searching for Everett Ruess, there was one notable exception—his brother, Waldo. Late in 1934, Waldo went abroad to China, and there he developed an unquenchable desire to see the world. He lived overseas almost exclusively from 1935 until 1958, in such diverse areas as China, Japan, Algiers, El Salvador, Mexico, Iceland, the Soviet Union, and Spain. He soon spoke English, Spanish, French, Russian, and Mandarin Chinese fluently, as well as commanding a working knowledge of Japanese. He was friends with Madame Chiang Kai-shek, Eleanor Roosevelt, Jawaharlal Nehru, Mahatma Gandhi, and the prior Dali Lama (with whom he lived in Nepal for a period). He kept extensive journals and took thousands of photographs, and later became a member of The Explorers Club.

A photo he took of the Japanese bombing of Chung Ching, China, was published in 1939, unattributed, on a two-page spread in *Life Magazine* and later in *Life Goes to War*. He was a conscientious objector in World War II, but he did believe war was evil and that, while he had no intent to kill anyone, he did have an obligation to work to end the conflict. To that end, he joined the State Department, where he served from 1939-1946.

In the end, he didn't follow in Everett's footsteps but instead blazed his own trail.

Robert Louis DeMayo is a native of Hollis, N.H., but has lived in many corners of the planet. He took up writing at the age of twenty when he left his job as a biomedical engineer to explore the world. His extensive journaling during his travels inspired four of his novels and far-reaching work for the travel section of *The Telegraph*, out of Nashua, NH, as well as the *Hollis Times*. He is a member of The Explorers Club and chair of its Southwest Chapter.

His undying hunger for exploration led to a job marketing for Eos Study Tours, a company that served as a travel office for six non-profit organizations and offered dives to the *Titanic* and the *Bismarck*, Antarctic voyages, African safaris and archaeological tours throughout the world.

For several years after that, Robert worked as a tour guide in Alaska and the Yukon during the summers and as a jeep guide in Arizona during the winter. He was made general manager of the jeep tour company but eventually left the guiding world to write full time.

DeMayo is the author of seven novels: *The Making of Theodore Roosevelt*, a fictionalized account of Roosevelt´s first acquaintance with wilderness living; *The Light Behind Blue Circles*, a mystery thriller set in Africa; *The Wayward Traveler*, a semi-autobiographical story following a young traveler on his adventures abroad; *The Legend of Everett Ruess*, a fictionalized account of the life and times of the young solo traveler of the American West; *The Road to Sedona*, the story of a young family that heads up to Alaska to find work in the wake of 9/11; and recently, *The Sirens of Oak Creek*, a historical mystery of Oak Creek Canyon, Arizona spanning twelve centuries. And *Pithecophilia* which follows DeMayo's life-long quest for primate encounters, and how they filled him with hope. Collectively, his books have won ten national awards.

His next novel, *The King of the Coral Sea*, follows Michael Fomenko's 1957 journey from Australia to Dutch New Guinea.

Currently, he resides in Sedona, AZ, with his wife Diana and three daughters: Tavish Lee, Saydrin Scout, and Martika Louise.

A Few of my Sources

Everett Ruess, A Vagabond for Beauty by W.L. Rusho
Peregrine Smith Books – 1983

Finding Everett Ruess by David Roberts
Broadway Paperbacks – 2011

Into The Wild by Jon Krakauer
Anchor Books – 1996

The Pink Nectar Cafe by James Bishop, Jr.
Wildcat Publishing – 2011

Secret Native American Pathways by Thomas E. Mails
Council Oak Books – 1988

Navajo Trader by Gladwell Richardson
University of Arizona Press – 1991

The Dark Wind by Tony Hillerman
Harper Paperbacks – 1982

Robert Louis DeMayo

Books by Robert Louis DeMayo

The Making of Theodore Roosevelt
(Historical Fiction)

The Wayward Traveler
(Memoir-based Non-fiction)

The Light Behind Blue Circles
(Travel Fiction)

The Legend of Everett Ruess
(Historical Fiction)

The Road to Sedona
(Non-fiction Travel)

The Sirens of Oak Creek
(Historical Mystery)

Pithecophilia
(Non-fiction Scientific Memoir)

The King of the Coral Sea
(Historical Fiction)

Also by Robert Louis DeMayo

"This book explores an aspect of Theodore Roosevelt's life that is not usually addressed when it comes to information regarding this president. Although this is a fictionalized story, DeMayo perfectly presents the essence of a young Roosevelt. The story is based on local recollections of Roosevelt's visits to the wilds of Maine, where he learned the ways of the woods. DeMayo seamlessly captures the local vernacular and paints an accurate picture of the time in which the story is set. The story is an enjoyable read that is appropriate for young adults as well as adults."

–Kathleen Kallfelz

THE MAKING OF THEODORE ROOSEVELT

The true tale of how two rough Maine woodsmen took a young Theodore Roosevelt under their wing and introduced him to the beautiful but unforgiving woodlands of the Northeast. Under their guidance, the frail but strong-willed New Yorker becomes a worthy outdoorsman. This experience significantly shaped the world view of the man poised to become the 26th President of the United States thirteen years later. This is a fictionalized account of a true story. Historical Fiction. 1878.

Historical Fiction

Wayward Publishing
Available in print, eBook
& audiobook

Also by **Robert Louis DeMayo**

"I enjoyed this book immensely. It is a way to see the world from the safety of your home and yet feel like you are experiencing the thrills, adventures, fears and exhilaration along with the main character, Louis. This book is so well-written that I didn't want to put it down as I followed Louis's adventures around the world. He met every type of person...from the dangerous to the glorious and everything in between. His descriptions of animal encounters left me breathless and envious for the same experiences. If you have any interest in traveling and a general guideline for that and for life, you should read this book! I was so inspired, I applied for my passport...although I doubt I would ever be as willing to jump into adventure as Louis did."

–Heidi Benson

THE WAYWARD TRAVELER

This memoir-based novel follows the adventures of Louis, a young American who, in 1985, is determined to travel the world. The story takes place in forty countries and spans ten years: from the deck of a felucca on the Nile to the scorched dunes of India's Thar Desert to the mighty Beni River in the Amazon Basin. Louis feels disenchantment with his former life, and a yearning to understand the foreign lands he encounters on his travels. He's broke most of the time and spends considerable effort trying to get by. Along the way, he develops a list of Rules to help him get by, and yet, there's a restlessness to his travels. He continues to wander into new countries, and through it all, his Rules save him.

Travel Fiction

Wayward Publishing
Available in print or eBook

Also by **Robert Louis DeMayo**

Pithecophilia

The powerful true story of one man's quest to unravel the mysteries of the world's primates.

From the steep slopes of the Virunga Volcanoes to the steamy jungles of Sumatra, *Pithecophilia* explores author, Robert Louis DeMayo's life-changing search for ape encounters, as he discovers the secrets of their history, biology, and what they can tell us about ourselves.

Touching on the efforts of the world's leading conservationists and scientific institutions, you'll also discover how the early exploration of Africa and Asia's untamed wilderness shaped our knowledge of apes and how their efforts to document our planet's wild animals eventually led to efforts to save them.

Imbued with touching memories, humorous anecdotes, and over fifty years of wondrous, magical, and sometimes terrifying experiences, *Pithecophilia* paints a beautiful picture of how primates are, in many ways, windows into our own souls.

Non-fiction Scientific Memoir

Wayward Publishing
Available in print & eBook

Made in the USA
Monee, IL
06 November 2023

45887532R00177